THE TWELVE
Dogs of Christmas

ALSO BY SUSAN WIGGS

The
Twelve Dogs
of
Christmas

A Novel

SUSAN
WIGGS

wm

WILLIAM MORROW

An Imprint of HarperCollins*Publishers*

THE TWELVE DOGS OF CHRISTMAS. Copyright © 2023 by Laugh, Cry, Dream, Read, LLC. All rights reserved. Printed in the United States of America. No part of this book may be used or reproduced in any manner whatsoever without written permission except in the case of brief quotations embodied in critical articles and reviews. For information, address HarperCollins Publishers, 195 Broadway, New York, NY 10007.

Designed by Bonni Leon-Berman
Title page art © rvika/Shutterstock

ISBN 978-0-06-325351-3

For Barkis, Lenny, Fisher, Goose, Dug, Daisy,

Enzo, and all the good good *very* good dogs who

warm our days and nights . . . and our hearts

PROLOGUE

Tiny Tim

Emergencies never happened during normal business hours. It was always the weekend, or late at night, or on a holiday.

Sometimes, it was all of the above. Sometimes, disaster happened on Christmas Eve.

That was how Brenda Dickens found herself careening into the parking lot of the emergency clinic at nine o'clock on Christmas Eve, with her husband, Grant, in the back seat, exhorting Tim to hang on.

"Just hang on," Grant pleaded in an anguished voice. "Almost there, honey. Please hang on. Stay with me. For god's sake, *don't die on me.*"

Brenda glanced in the rearview mirror and caught a glimpse of Tim's darting eyes. "You're scaring him."

"Because it's damned scary," Grant shot at her. "I don't even know if he's still breathing. Oh god, his stomach feels like a balloon."

She stopped directly in front of the ER entryway and slammed the car into park. The parking lot was virtually deserted. She jumped out and opened the door to the back seat and reached for Tim.

"Be careful," she said, her voice breaking. "Oh, Tim. Oh, honey. He seems to be in so much pain."

Grant eased Tim into her arms and then got out and held the door. A swag of Christmas lights greeted them with a sad twinkle. There was a med tech in pink scrubs at the reception desk.

"This is Tim. I called you about him, and we got here as fast as we could," Brenda said. "Oh, my lord, I can't lose him. He's only two years old."

"I'll take him back to Dr. Penn," said the tech, reaching for the little guy. "Come on, buddy. We'll take care of you."

Brenda settled him into the tech's arms. Then she cradled Tim's face between her hands. "I love you, baby boy. I love you with every bit of my heart." She pressed a swift kiss on his head, and he gave a quiet whimper.

And then he was gone. Whisked away through the surgery doors, his fate uncertain.

Brenda's knees felt weak, and she turned to Grant, but he didn't seem to notice. He was pacing back and forth, slightly unsteady, thanks to the champagne he'd been drinking at the Christmas party. Brenda didn't care for champagne, and since the party was at their house, she had been too busy looking after people to indulge in a drink.

Now she was drowning in guilt, because she didn't know how long Tim had been suffering before she noticed. Tim was her best friend. When she'd first met him, he was a shy, quivering ball of undifferentiated fur, punctuated with button-bright eyes and a shiny little nose. She had bathed the little puppy in warm soap bubbles and love, winning his trust and training him with the skills she'd learned as a puppy raiser for Guide Dogs. Tim had grown into a handsome, silken-haired mongrel with ears like ponytails and a heart of gold. He kept her company each day, and he kept her warm on the nights when Grant had to work late.

"I can't lose him," she whispered. "I just can't."

Grant scanned the dim, vacant waiting room. "How the hell did this happen?" he asked. "He was fine at dinner. Chased his tennis ball all over the house—down the hall, under the bed. . . . Damn, we still have a house full of people."

Brenda's shoulders tensed. It was their turn to host this year. Grant's family was obsessed with Christmas. They started celebrating on Christmas Eve and didn't stop until Boxing Day. In preparation for tonight, she had prepared a lavish dinner and wrapped all the gifts, doing most of the work herself, because Grant had a last-minute meeting in town to finalize a deal, and he'd showed up just as she was lighting the candles at the table.

Brenda didn't even like Christmas, but she'd slaved all day, wanting to make everything perfect for Grant's parents and siblings. There was even a flaming Christmas pudding and Christmas crackers for the little ones. Brenda and Grant didn't have kids yet, but they had four adorable, mischievous nieces.

She snapped her fingers. "The Christmas crackers."

"What?" Grant frowned.

"You know, those damn decorated tubes that you crack open and the toys fall out. I got them for the nieces. Maybe Tim swallowed one of those little plastic toys."

"Right, let's blame it on my family. You've always had an attitude about them."

"What? Are we really going to do this now?"

He dismissed the question with a wave of his hand. "How long is this going to take?" he asked, though he had to know Brenda couldn't answer that question. "Can Dr. Penn save him?"

She batted away tears. "He sounded confident on the phone. Said it presents like a classic case of twisted gut. I saw it happen to a service dog I was training in college. Emergency surgery fixed him. And it'll fix Tim."

"You don't know that."

She didn't. She wished she felt more confident. Twisted gut—gastric volvulus—was serious. It could be deadly. When there was an obstruction, the chest cavity filled up with gas and displaced the lungs so the animal couldn't breathe. Their only hope was that they'd noticed in time that Tim was in distress.

Grant paced some more and swore. Carols played endlessly in the waiting room, spreading twinkly cheer like a virus. Brenda couldn't stand Christmas carols. They were all earworms, impossible to forget once they took hold, songs of joy and merriment about matters she had stopped believing in long ago.

To distract herself, she studied the display on the reception counter. There was a collection bank for Underdogs, the rescue organization that had brought them Tim.

"Do you have any cash?" she asked Grant.

"What? Why? We can pay the vet with a card."

"I want to make a donation." She gestured at the bank on the counter.

He pulled out his wallet and handed it to her. She took out a bill and stuffed it in the bank.

"Hey, that was a hundred," Grant objected.

"It's Christmas."

"I was going to use that to buy you a gift," he said.

Thus confirming her suspicion that he hadn't bothered to buy her anything yet. "You just made a donation in my honor," she said. "Thank you."

She grabbed a handful of stale candy from the dish on the reception desk and munched on it, garnering a look of silent reproach from Grant. Although he hadn't dared to say anything, she knew he thought she should lose a few pounds. He wasn't wrong, but tonight was not the night to focus on herself. She chewed a piece of taffy while eyeing a drooping curl of tinsel that had been there far too long. Why did people think tinsel was pretty, anyway? It was an environmental hazard. It had a lousy carbon footprint.

Brenda turned away and studied a display on the wall—things swallowed by dogs and recovered by the vet. Stuffed animals, car keys, an old-school iPod, a misshapen ball of expanding glue that had swelled in a Lab's stomach. There was even a partial string of Christmas lights. Further proof that Christmas was toxic.

"Look at all this stuff they pulled out of dogs' stomachs," she said to Grant.

He scowled at the display. "Tim probably ate something bad. You should have kept an eye on him."

"Me? I was busy wrapping ten thousand gifts for your family, because god forbid you would pick up a roll of wrapping paper yourself."

"Oh, excuse me for being busy at work, so we can *afford* the ten thousand gifts," he snapped back. "Maybe you can write about this in one of those books of yours." He made air quotes around *books*.

Brenda glared at him. It was just like him to boost himself up with a dig about her failed writing dreams.

She ducked into the ladies' room. There was nothing to be accomplished by bickering with Grant. All married couples bickered from time to time, but lately they'd been going at it. Work stress, no doubt. Grant's real estate firm was sometimes a runaway train. He made a lot of money, but it took a lot of strategy. A lot of meetings. A lot of Brenda's time publishing his firm's glossy magazine that highlighted the listings.

She dabbed at her face with a damp towel, cleaning up the mascara streaks. Studying her face in the mirror, she vowed to take better care of herself. Get to the salon for a more flattering hairstyle. Join a gym, maybe the one that Grant had signed up for last year. He managed to get in an hour a day there. She could do the same. Maybe it was something they could do together.

There was a brochure on the wall about Underdogs, and another about the clinic, featuring Dr. Penn's smiling face. He seemed like the perfect guy—so handsome, so compassionate. He'd held her hand last year when the cat died. Now Tim was in trouble and she shouldn't be thinking about the attractiveness of the vet. Her even more attractive too-tipsy-to-drive husband was in the waiting room, agonizing over their dog's fate.

Chastened, she returned to the waiting room and offered a weak, conciliatory smile. "Grant, I'm sorry. Bickering isn't going to help Tim, is it?"

He offered a weary nod. "Yeah. You're right. Damn. *Tim.*"

They hugged and then sat together in the waiting room watching the minutes tick by on their phones. Grant's mother and sisters sent text messages, offering reassurances and letting them know they'd locked up the house.

Merry Christmas to us, Brenda thought.

After what seemed like an interminable wait, Dr. Penn came through the door, his scrubs smeared with dark fluid, a mask obscuring the lower half his face. "Mr. and Mrs. Dickens?" he said, his voice soft with compassion.

Her heart dropped as she surged to her feet. Tim. Oh, Tim.

The mask came off, revealing a weary grin. "He's okay. Your good boy is going to be fine."

Brenda's knees gave out and she sank into a chair. "Can we see him?"

"Well, I guess since it's Christmas Eve and you're the only ones here, I can take you back. He's waking up, but still groggy."

She jumped up and followed him through the surgery doors, Grant close at her heels.

Lying on a covered pad, Tim struggled to lift his head. His silvery-brown coat was matted, and one leg was bare where it had been shaved for an IV. He blinked and whimpered softly. Brenda's eyes burned with a hot flood of tears. "Oh thank heavens."

The friendly little tail quivered, then thumped. Tim cocked his head as if listening to the Christmas carols playing softly through a speaker. *Bring a torch, Jeannette, Isabella . . .*

"Hey, buddy boy," Grant said.

"He's a lucky dog," said the vet. "Good thing you brought him in. He's looking really good. I think he can go home with you tonight."

Flooded with relief, Brenda sank back against Grant, still regretting the harsh, stress-induced words they'd exchanged. She'd make it up to him at home later. Home—where his family had probably left a post-party mess behind.

Dr. Penn and his assistant tackled a different sort of mess on a surgical tray. "It was an obstruction," the vet said. "I thought you'd like to know. Here's the culprit." He whipped out a limp reddish wisp of fabric and held it up in his gloved hands.

Brenda frowned and leaned forward. On closer inspection, she saw that the object was a woman's thong, edged in discolored lace with a little satin bow at the bikini line, a sheer triangular patch, and not much else.

The vet chuckled and shook his head, giving Grant the old conspiratorial wink wink nudge nudge.

Brenda didn't wink. She didn't nudge. She stared at the damp undies, and then at her husband. Grant looked as if he'd soiled himself.

No one spoke. The Christmas carols played on. Brenda took a step back. She drilled her husband with a lethal glare.

"That's not mine," she said.

PART ONE

I hate, loathe, and despise Christmas. It's a time when single people have to take cover or get out of town.

—KRISTIN HUNTER

1

One Year Later

Three Invitations

Brenda ran early, taking advantage of the relative chill in the morning air. Even in December, Houston had a habit of heating up to a steamy temperature, so she liked to get her seven miles done while the sun was still rubbing its eyes, trying to make up its mind about how much to torment the residents of the city's inner loop with untimely heat.

Tim skimmed along beside her, familiar with every blade of grass along the route that followed Buffalo Bayou through a lush, green trail. Her dog was the perfect running partner, keeping pace with her, never complaining, never leaving her side.

Which was more than she could say for any man.

A year after the divorce, Brenda had kept the dog and reclaimed her maiden name. She'd always preferred Malloy to Dickens anyway. Grant took the business, the big suburban house, and presumably the woman whose underpants had nearly killed the dog.

The other thing Brenda had kept was a feeling of loneliness and failure, along with a firm belief that Christmas was an evil to be avoided at all costs.

In the aftermath of the breakup, she'd found support from friends and family, but at the end of the day—at the end of every single damn day—she went home alone. One of her first tasks was to scrub her social media clean of photos and posts of the seven-year marriage. She spent her evenings removing all traces of Grant and his family, deleting pictures of happier times. She didn't want to erase the past. But she didn't have to show the world what she had lost. Back then. Back when she thought she knew what love was.

Now Brenda wondered when the deception had begun, what had triggered it, and how she'd missed the telltale signs. And she saw the photos through new eyes. She hadn't noticed how dumpy she looked, how careless she'd been about her appearance. So many of the photos showed her hovering in the background, stepping aside while Grant took the spotlight.

Divorce was a wound. It could be every bit as painful as a physical injury, but it was invisible. No one could see the pain she was in—the loneliness, the humiliation, the sense of failure. Maybe she would garner more sympathy if she had a cast on her leg, or a line of stitches or a series of livid bruises. Instead, she held the damage in a hidden place, struggling to power through the dark times.

Dr. Penn, likely out of guilt at being the instrument of destruction, had encouraged her to get involved with Underdogs, helping herself by helping homeless dogs.

It turned out to be the distraction she needed to keep from ruminating constantly about her failed marriage. Last Christmas was the dividing line. The *before*. Since then Brenda had changed everything about herself. Fitness first—that had always been her mother's mantra. A thirty-year career in the army had convinced Margaret Harkness that change didn't always have to happen from the inside out. Sometimes it happened from the outside in.

Maybe, Brenda reflected, her mom was on to something. In one short year, Brenda had changed everything about herself, outwardly. It had been a year of profound changes. Some were a breath of fresh air. Others were as pleasant as passing a kidney stone.

She had a new job, because there was no way she could keep working for Grant, although he'd had the audacity to ask her to stay on with the firm, publishing the glossy, high-end magazine that supported his real estate business. *I'd rather be waterboarded*, she'd told him. Her days of laying out pristine, aspirational photos of flawless homes and gardens and writing cheesy articles about luxury real estate were over.

These days she had gone freelance, writing and editing newsletters and website content for clients she wasn't married to. Clients who didn't cheat. Clients who didn't treat her like an old piece of furniture. She wasn't getting rich with her new enterprise, but it kept the lights on.

She had moved to a tiny sweet bungalow in the vintage Montrose district. The brick-red frame house had just enough yard behind a picket fence for Tim. It was a far cry from the rambling suburban tract mansion of her marriage. The new place suited her. She liked her eclectic neighbors who came in all sizes, shapes, and proclivities, liked the old-fashioned sidewalks that sadly ran out after a few blocks, liked the park where children played from dawn to dusk no matter what the weather.

Okay, so she didn't love the muggy heat of summer, the mosquitoes, the fire ant mounds, the drone-size roaches in the pecan trees, the traffic, the hurricanes. But thanks to her mom's career, Brenda was used to living in all kinds of places, from the sand dunes of Fort Hadley to the bitter cold of South Korea to the breezy shores of the Hampton Roads.

Houston was as good a place as any to settle into the single life and, like Tim, to make her forever home. She'd had her fill of moving around during her mom's career. Now that Margaret was about to retire, she and Lyle had bought a nice house in the Heights, a shady neighborhood not far from Brenda and her sister. Cissy and her husband, Dilip, were expecting their first child.

In addition to adopting a strict new fitness routine, Brenda had changed her hair—standard in any divorce, according to Cissy, who had never been divorced but knew everything anyway. Brenda's married hair had been a mane of neglected brunette waves, usually caught up in a messy bun. The new style featured a sleek bob with golden highlights that required a monthly visit to the salon—something that had been unthinkable during her marriage. Her wardrobe had gone through an upgrade, too, because the unavoidable stress of the divorce process had caused her to shrink like a ghost fading into the woodwork. She remembered coming home from yet another failed settlement conference and catching a glimpse of herself in the mirror and breaking down in tears. She had looked as pitiful as one of the pups from Underdogs—poorly groomed and pathetic.

The next day, she hired a personal trainer and embarked upon a course of self-improvement. The trainer had turned out to be the architect of Brenda's life. Every other day for the past six months, Carla Wynn had encouraged, coaxed, exhorted, and prodded Brenda to put herself first. As an added bonus, Carla's wife, Nancy, was a personal stylist. The two of them had founded a lifestyle brand, and Brenda was one of their first projects. She couldn't afford their services, so she traded her own. Carla and Nancy turned out to be her second-favorite clients, after Underdogs. She created a digital newsletter for promoting their lifestyle brand. It was easy to create content for a process Brenda believed in.

Back when she was married, her mornings had started with coffee and donuts and a barrage of email, scheduling issues, meetings, and printer deadlines. Now she began each day with a rotating schedule of swim, bike, run, like an athlete in training. When she'd confessed to

Carla that she had no interest in training for a competition, Carla had said, *You're training for life*.

According to her therapist, all of Brenda's outside-in changes were commendable. The real change would take hold when she tackled the hidden corners of herself.

"I have no hidden corners," Brenda objected. Both she and the therapist knew this wasn't true. Her hidden corners came in handy, actually. She swept things there, not wanting to deal with them. In the later years of her marriage, she had known something was not right between her and Grant, but she'd avoided the issue—until the proof, in the form of intimate apparel, had waved itself in her face.

Sometimes Brenda wondered if she had failed at her marriage to Grant, or if she'd simply quit. He had done the cheating, but of course in the aftermath of the Christmas Eve incident, he had tried to find every excuse to make it her fault. She was distant. She didn't understand him. She didn't need him the way he wanted her to need him.

Although the infidelity had been her husband's doing, Brenda realized that she might have been the one to create the distance in her marriage. When she'd first met Grant, they'd seemed like a perfect match. Their marriage fit her image of what a happy life should be—except at its core, that life was empty, the relationship transactional, more like a business arrangement. Looking back at recent years, she realized with a sense of guilt that she had neglected herself and put herself last in the marriage. She'd set aside her dream of writing children's books in order to support Grant's business. She'd lived in a big, suburban house that never felt like a home to her. She'd endured holiday celebrations that made her feel like an event planner.

Just to distract herself from thinking of the past, Brenda had recently begun to experiment with dating, though her heart wasn't in it. At the moment, she had a sort-of boyfriend, but she didn't trust her feelings because she didn't feel her feelings. And sometimes, she felt seized by a terrible fear that there was no person out there for her.

But her therapist approved of casual dating, saying the process would help her gain confidence through vulnerability. Which sounded to Brenda like a complete and total non sequitur, but she discovered that scrolling through dating apps was weirdly diverting.

She and Tim ended their run with a sprint to the house. She paused at the front gate to grab her mail, and then they headed inside. "Come on, boy," she said. "Let's go see what the day has in store for us."

The dog went straight for his water bowl while Brenda opened the fridge and downed a glass of blissfully cold water. Then she sat at the kitchen bar and sorted through the mail. Separation of living and work-space was supposed to be an essential principle of mental health, but in her tiny house, it was impossible. She worked and ate at the counter. These days, instead of coffee and donuts, it was green tea and a quinoa patty, which tasted a bit like Styrofoam but filled the void.

Today's mail consisted of the usual assortment of bills, statements, and straight-to-recycling ads and solicitations. She was startled to come across a Christmas card from Dolly Prentice, a family friend and one of the key people at Underdogs. Did people still do that? Send Christmas cards in the mail? Why?

The glitter from the bucolic snow scene stuck to Brenda's fingers. Annoyed, she wiped them on her jogging shorts. Now the glitter stuck to her shorts. Lovely.

Elsewhere in the stack of mail she came across a surprise. Three surprises. "Check it out, Tim," she said, showing him a brochure. "I'm invited to a writing seminar. They're going to make all my writing dreams come true." She sighed. "I wish." She made a face and added the brochure to the recycle pile.

Brenda did have a writing dream. For as long as she could remember, she had dreamed of writing novels for kids like the one she used to be, stories that took them away from themselves. She yearned to create the kind of books that felt like friends to a lonely child. Brenda had always been a voracious reader, finding refuge and comfort in books.

Thanks to her mother's career, she had changed schools every year or two, and books had been her most constant companions. In school, she had never learned to deepen and trust friendships, knowing they were destined to come to an end.

The stories she read gave her something to focus on when the unthinkable happened. At the age of nine, she had lost her father in the worst possible way, a loss that reverberated through her life even now. After her father was gone, she'd lost all confidence and turned to books, hiding inside other people's stories. Books offered different worlds for her to retreat to; they gave her solace and refuge from a painful reality.

When her mother remarried, Brenda never warmed up to Lyle. But all the books she read about blended families and lost parents brought her a sense of comfort.

Even now, Brenda's best friends were still with her, neatly lined up on the bookcase wall. Harriet the Spy. Ramona Quimby, Ralph S. Mouse, Harry Potter, and Despereaux. The Boxcar Children and the entire cast of the Baby-Sitters Club. Margaret, awaiting the onset of her period. The Twilight vampires, scary but mesmerizing.

Brenda's books had always been the sort of friends she could count on. They never called her *new girl* or failed to make room for her at the lunch table. They never forgot to invite her to their birthday parties. They never picked her last for teams.

She had set aside her writing plans in order to work for Grant. Now that she was free of that commitment, she still hadn't made much progress. She hadn't managed to write anything a kid would want to read, according to the publishers and literary agents she sent her work to. Most of the rejection letters declared her work exceptionally well-written but lacking in sentiment. Or poorly written and overly sentimental. Or not compelling enough. Or too strong for this audience.

She was forced to consider that maybe something else was holding her back. She knew she would need more than a one-day seminar to make the dream come true.

Still Brenda kept at it, because she'd been raised by a mother who had taught her that the only surefire way to fail at something was to quit.

On impulse, she rescued the writing brochure from the recycle bin.

"Okay, what else?" She held up another envelope, this one from Colonel Margaret Harkness. *Sail away for the holidays.* It was a printed invitation to her mom's weeklong retirement party. Brenda had known it was coming, but seeing the announcement in print made it all too real. She tapped her phone screen.

Her mother picked up right away. "Did you get it?"

"Looking at it right now," said Brenda.

"And you're coming, right?"

It was a question, but there was only one answer. "Sure, Mom. Can't wait."

"It's going to be a dream, pure and simple. A dream. We set sail out of Galveston on Christmas Eve, and it will be nothing but fun until we return on New Year's Day. It'll be the best Christmas ever."

Brenda picked up a pen and doodled on a picture on the back of an envelope; it depicted a massive yacht with a helicopter and water slides and couples dancing on the stern deck. She bit her lip to keep from reminding her mom that when it came to Christmas, Brenda didn't exactly have the best of luck. It might be dangerous to bring her and her bad luck on a Christmas cruise.

Cissy and Dilip would be on board, of course. Brenda would be treated to a whole lovely week admiring her perfect, newly pregnant sister, and Cissy's even more perfect husband. Brenda loved her sister. She even loved Dilip, yet she definitely didn't want to deal with the sense of yearning and failure she always seemed to feel around her happily married sister.

"It's going to be wonderful," her mother said firmly. "It'll change your attitude once and for all about Christmas." Margaret Harkness spoke in unambiguous imperatives. Brenda knew better than to argue.

But she also realized that being trapped on a big boat for Christmas was hardly the way to escape a holiday she'd never liked.

Don't be bitter, Brenda admonished herself. Her very accomplished mother had given thirty-five years of service to her country. She'd broken through glass ceilings. She'd conquered goal after goal. She'd moved the needle for women in the military. Her retirement was an event to celebrate.

The private luxury cruise had been in the works for months. One of Dilip's billionaire clients had provided a week on an Ocean Alexander yacht, complete with a full crew and an itinerary through the breezy, sunny Caribbean. There would be gourmet food, toasting and dancing. Shore excursions to Chichen Itza and Tulum, jungle canopy tours and dune buggy races.

At least it would be different from past Christmases with Grant's family. The Dickens clan was all about yuletide traditions. For the past eight years, Brenda had endured weeks of preparation and anticipation, her mother-in-law's lavish decorations and pointed questions about when Brenda planned to start a family. She had sat through the church pageantry, the endless carols, the Christmas specials playing on every TV channel and streaming service.

She had gone along with the whole process because it was important to Grant. Apparently, it was more important to him than she was.

Her mom nattered on a while longer about the once-in-a-lifetime cruise. "We'll be like that rich family on *Succession*," she said. "Only we'll be the nice ones, right?"

"Right," said Brenda, who secretly loved the villainous TV family on *Succession*. She found all the subterfuge and backstabbing to be fascinating.

"Oh, I'd better run," said her mom. "Lyle and I are meeting with the event planner about the party menu. Any special requests from you?"

Brenda smiled at the excitement in her mother's voice. "Naked waiter races?"

"I'll check."

"Just make sure they have all your favorites, Mom. You deserve it."

She rang off and turned to the dog with a sigh. He was curled up on his rug, enjoying a post-run snooze. "Can you believe it, Tim?" she asked him. "I'm going to be living like a bazillionaire for a week. How cool is that?"

At the sound of her voice, Tim gave her a side-eyed glance that somehow looked vaguely reproachful.

"I know, boy," she said, feeling a pang of regret, along with a niggling, deep-down feeling of resistance, which she quickly dismissed. "I'm going to miss you, too."

His relentless side-eye said it all.

"You'll be fine, I swear. You get to go back to the old house for a week, right? You're going to like that, I'm sure."

Grant had made a standing offer to look after the dog if she ever needed to go away. She hadn't taken him up on the offer yet. She knew it was selfish, but she had no desire to share her dog with her ex. Now she made a face, picturing Tim with the new girlfriend.

When the cheating came to light, Grant had sworn it wasn't serious, that the other woman hadn't meant anything to him. She was nobody, a bad impulse, a mistake.

Apparently, she had grown on him, because Brenda had heard through the grapevine that Danielle and Grant were still together.

She'd better be nice to Timmy, Brenda thought, *or else*.

Or else what? Gah, she was so powerless in this situation.

Tim kept gazing at her with sad puppy eyes.

"Look," Brenda said, "the cruise will be good for me. I need to get away. I'm lonely and jaded about Christmas, and I need to put the past behind me." She sighed. "Must be nice, being a dog. You just live in the moment. I bet you don't even remember the emergency vet last year. And you're not worried about tomorrow."

She opened the next envelope in the stack. "Looky here, Tim," she said. "It's the invitation to the annual Underdogs gala." She opened the fancy card printed on premium cream stock. She knew it was premium, because she had written the copy and ordered the print run herself.

Underdogs Unlimited was Brenda's first and favorite client. She believed heart and soul in their mission—finding safe homes for stray dogs and puppies. Not only did she manage their newsletter, she processed adoption applications, making sure each dog's forever home was the right match. She was also in charge of coordinating the dog transit process. Dolly Prentice was one of the drivers, and she claimed she never tired of unifying dogs with their new owners.

The organization had a remarkable success rate. The dogs they took in were never sent to shelters but to volunteer foster families. The pups never saw the inside of a concrete kennel. Thanks to the foster home system, Underdogs tended to be more calm and socialized than kennel dogs.

The other key component of the Underdogs program was that nearly all the adoptive families lived up north. The model program had begun in the aftermath of Hurricane Katrina. In the wake of the epic disaster, there were simply too many pets and not enough homes for all the strays. So the shelters in the South partnered with places in the North where adoptive families were more plentiful.

The partner organization of Underdogs was located in a small town called Avalon, in the Catskill Mountains of New York State. Once a month, a pair of drivers would load the dogs into a specially outfitted Sprinter van and head north to take the pups to their forever homes. Sometimes Brenda felt vaguely sorry for the dogs for having to live in all that snow, but maybe the dogs didn't share her aversion to snow and ice.

Such an ambitious enterprise took money. Lots and lots of money. Fortunately the nonprofit had many loyal patrons who gave generously each year, and the Christmas gala was their signature event. In a good year, they could raise a small fortune for the pups in one evening. It was the premier event of Houston's social season.

One thing that made the gala so special was the venue—Bayou Bend, the magnificent ancestral home of Houston's renowned philanthropist, the late Ima Hogg. Patrons paid $1,000 a plate to dine and dance like visiting royalty, to admire priceless art treasures, to sample a menu prepared by a celebrity chef, and to dance to the music of Carmen Batiste, one of the best band leaders in the business. Although people came to show off their gorgeous outfits and to dance the night away, they mostly came for the sake of the dogs.

Brenda admired the handsome, letterpressed invitation. She was good at what she did. The simple, elegant card was pure eye candy, and a tactile delight. It even came with a prestamped reply card, which was old-fashioned but too classy to resist. She picked up a pen to fill out the RSVP.

Tim wandered over and rested his chin on her knee.

She stroked his silky head. "Pop quiz, Tim," she said. "Who rescued whom? I don't know what I would have done this past year without you. I've got three invitations here. A cruise and a gala and a writing seminar. Things could be worse, right?"

Tim gently pawed her leg.

"Here goes nothing," she said. "It's the one and only Christmas party I'm willing to attend, right? It's for the sake of the dogs."

Her pen hovered over the *will attend* space. "Grant's going to be there, isn't he?" For the past seven years, Brenda had attended the gala with Grant, who was on the organization's board of directors. For him, the holiday event was steeped in tradition—and in Christmas excess. Brenda kept her focus on the purpose—to raise money for Underdogs. Although she was a fish out of water with the crowd of socialites, Brenda did like the people-watching and the gorgeous event space.

She set the pen down. "He's going to be there, and he's going to bring his new woman." Brenda cringed, imagining how that would feel, seeing her ex-husband with his girlfriend, the two of them looking blissfully happy together.

Brenda realized she could always stay away. She was learning that boundaries were a good thing. *No* was a good word. *No* was a complete sentence. There was no law that said she had to attend.

Why put herself through the torment of coming face-to-face with her ex?

Because she was needed. Because it was her duty. Because she was in charge of the team of service dogs that were going to be an essential part of the evening. She and Dolly had founded the Artful Dodgers—select rescue dogs trained by 4-H students to solicit donations throughout the evening in the cutest possible way. The patrons were always so enchanted with the perfectly trained dogs that they shelled out thousands of dollars, tucking checks and big bills into the dogs' signature tuxedo collars.

The evening wouldn't be the same without the Artful Dodgers.

Besides, staying home would be an admission of defeat. Of failure, even.

She wanted to make sure Grant knew he hadn't defeated her. That she hadn't failed.

With renewed conviction, Brenda made a vow. She was going to show up in a form-fitting couture revenge dress with designer shoes. No one would know the outfit came from a resale shop. She would show off her new hair, her sexy ankle tattoo, and her new sassy attitude. And most important of all, she had a secret weapon.

His name was Ryder Wynn. He was Carla's brother. Brenda had met him on a photo shoot for Carla's digital zine, and yes, his name was Ryder. Because of course it was. What else would you call your impossibly hot post-divorce boyfriend?

2

Somebody I
Used to Know

"How do I look?" asked Ryder as they approached the entrance to Bayou Bend. Decorative lights dripped from the live oaks like glowing Spanish moss. Papier-mâché turtledoves and partridges roosted in the shrubbery. *There is no escaping Christmas*, Brenda thought. *Not even tonight.*

"You look great. Amazing." She studied Ryder's flawless black-tie suit and shiny dress shoes. "You look like my extremely yummy boyfriend," she said.

"Oh, so I'm your boyfriend now." He tucked his hand against the small of her back. "Cool."

He was her boyfriend for *now*, Brenda thought. They had been dating for only two months. He was the ideal date, because she would never be tempted to fall in love with him. Her heart was safe.

Trotting at her side, Tim was adorable in his tuxedo harness and saddlebags for tips. At the reception area, Ryder straightened his jacket, squared his shoulders, lifted his chin at a proud angle, and strode forward like a conquering hero.

"And do I look okay?" Brenda asked, hurrying along in his wake.

"You look lovely," he said over his shoulder.

She quickened her pace to catch up with him. In the foyer, lavishly decked with boughs of holly, fairy lights, and pictures of rescue dogs in rustic frames, there was a tall pier mirror. Ryder paused to check himself again, and Brenda slipped her arm through his. They did look good as a couple. She'd splurged on a salon style and manicure, and the body-hugging dress looked expensive and sexy. Nancy had paired the ensemble with a simple cuff bracelet and chandelier earrings that were indistinguishable from the real thing.

"You sure you're ready for this?" asked Ryder.

"Nope, but I won't let that stop me." Brenda was actually fired up, keen to make her reentry into the world as a fabulous single.

He regarded her with kind bemusement. "Lead on. You got this, babe."

She had leveled with Ryder about tonight. This would be her first time to see her ex since the last, nausea-inducing settlement conference during which two expensive lawyers and a world-weary judge had finalized their divorce six months before.

Grant had bitterly disputed the prenup he had insisted upon when they first got married. He was established in business with a lucrative real estate firm. She was a recent college graduate with a sizable student debt. Fair was fair.

Yet at the divorce, Grant balked at a key clause in the prenup, one that declared her contribution to his business. He was forced to acknowledge her value in the company and rather than throwing her away like garbage, he was ordered to compensate her accordingly. His last-minute hissy fit had made the painful process even worse. For Brenda, the process was still painful, but she ended up with the wherewithal to begin again.

Tonight, Grant would see that she had moved ahead with her life. Although he had blown up their marriage, she had risen from the ashes to turn into a better version of herself. She kept her wounds hidden. Maybe they would heal in the dark.

She and Ryder moved into the ballroom, a glittering salon alive with classic sounds from the big-band era. Couples were dancing, groups stood around cocktail tables, and the Artful Dodgers in elegant garb moved through the crowd, cadging for more donations along with the 4-H volunteers. Brenda spotted Dolly and sent her a wave.

Dolly was retired and widowed, and she was as adept at training dogs as Brenda was. Tonight, Dolly wore a spangled red cocktail dress and earrings so big they looked like Christmas ornaments. Like a hummingbird going from flower to flower, she chatted up the patrons, cheerfully managing the service dogs.

Brenda glanced down at Tim. "Ready, boy?" she asked.

Tim's ears pricked up.

"I'm ready," said Ryder.

"Oh, I didn't mean—"

He grinned. "I've been dying to see your team in action."

Tim was adept at using his charm to separate wealthy donors from their money. He knew just what to do. He sidled up to a group of festively dressed people, his tail wagging like a banner. The delighted patrons stooped down to pet him and tuck a bill or a check into his saddlebag.

"If it's a good night, he'll end up with a few thousand in there," Brenda told Ryder.

"Amazing. My sister said you came up with this scheme and trained all the dogs."

"Dolly and I worked with high school students in the 4-H club. When I was a kid, I got into dog training. I wasn't so good at making friends, but it turns out I have a knack for working with dogs."

"I would've been your friend," Ryder said.

You wouldn't have known I existed, Brenda thought, remembering her awkward, bookish teenaged self. "I've always been drawn to dogs, and I got serious about learning to train them when I volunteered to be a puppy raiser for a Guide Dogs program. Check this out."

They watched Angus, a silken-haired Gordon setter, accept a large bill from a donor.

"Remarkable, babe. So you have a thing for dogs."

Brenda helped herself to a flute of Cristal from the tray of a passing server and savored the crisp, ebullient champagne. "They are the perfect companions," she said. "They love you unconditionally, they never judge you, and they never break your heart. They never cheat."

"Nice," he said. "But do they . . ." He leaned down and whispered a wicked suggestion in her ear. "You are so darn cute when you blush, Brenda Malloy."

"Down, boy," she said.

"Oh, I'm just getting started." He pulled her onto the dance floor as the band struck up a cool, brassy tune that would have made Brenda's grandmother swoon, back in her day. Ryder drew her into a close embrace, then reeled her out in a twirl that made her slightly dizzy, but garnered looks of admiration—probably for Ryder, with his swimming-pool-blue eyes and artfully shaggy, pop-star-blond hair.

After the dance, she went to check on Tim. He was doing his best, most irresistible tail wag . . . for Grant and the underpants woman.

BRENDA STOOD STOCK-STILL while too-vivid memories surfaced like fresh wounds. Christmas past suddenly felt more real than the present. Last Christmas Eve, the three of them had driven away from the veterinary ER, shell-shocked into silence. Timmy was groggy from the lingerie extraction. Grant was mortified at having been caught. And Brenda had sat motionless, holding on to her backpack for dear life while a block of ice had formed in her chest.

Grant had finally broken the silence to fumble through an explanation: "Look, it's not what you think—"

"On the contrary, it is exactly what I think," Brenda had snapped, finding her voice. "You took up with some woman. How long has it been going on? How long have you been sneaking around?"

"That's not how—"

"Oh, but it is. If you want to convince me otherwise, hand over your phone."

A tiny part of her held on to a shred of hope that she was wrong, even though she knew better. Still, she wanted Grant to offer some kind of plausible explanation. They were married. They'd been married for seven years, together for eight, ever since Brenda had joined his firm as a new college graduate. They were building a life together—first, a fine, too-big house in the Woodlands, a luxurious suburb hanging on the lush, bayou-fed edge of the Houston loop. They'd adopted Tim. They had been talking about starting a family, and she used to dream about the kids who would one day occupy a few of their five bedrooms.

The last thing on Brenda's mind had been the idea that Grant would cheat.

"You're not looking at my phone," he'd said, his voice taut.

He was acting weird. She couldn't tell if it was fury or fear. It was so strange to realize this person—her partner, her husband—was carrying on a secret intimate relationship right under her nose. Suddenly he was someone she didn't know at all.

"Yes, I am." She snatched the phone from the cupholder in the console of the car.

"*What the hell, Brenda?*" The car wobbled on the road as he made a grab for the phone.

"Watch where you're going," she snapped, holding it out of reach.

And that desperate grab told her everything she needed to know. She tapped the screen. "Oh look, you changed your passcode," she said.

The two of them had always shared the same passcode: 1224. Not the most secure arrangement, but it commemorated the Christmas Eve seven years before, when they had spoken their vows in a tree-lit ceremony. That night was supposed to erase her ill feelings about Christmas and give her a new start with the holiday.

"Everybody changes their passcode," Grant had growled.

"Not us," Brenda said. "Not unless one of us has something to hide."

"If you'd just listen for two seconds and let me explain—"

"Look out!" she yelled, catching sight of a deer ambling across the dark road.

He slammed on the brakes just in time. Tim, in his crate in the back seat, gave a small *woof*. It wasn't just one deer, but eight of them in a browsing herd, probably looking for someone's winter roses to graze on.

"Guess they're looking for Santa," Grant said in a transparently lame attempt at levity. "Ha."

"Yeah, Santa isn't coming." She turned the phone screen toward him. "Let's check your messages, shall we? Passcode."

"No way," he snapped. "You have no right to snoop through my phone."

"If you have nothing to hide, you'll unlock it," she said. "Up until recently, our phones were interchangeable, weren't they? We would check the grocery list and the calendar, scroll through each other's messages and photos and email when we needed to find something. But that all mysteriously ended, and I guess I never even noticed. Come to think of it, you turned off location sharing for some strange reason, didn't you?"

"I'm not going to be treated like a criminal," he said.

"Then don't act like one." She handed back the phone. "You know what? I don't need to see your text messages. I know what they say. Text messages from cheaters are all the same: *She doesn't understand me. We've grown apart. We want different things. The spark has gone out. The sex is virtually nonexistent.* That last bit is not for lack of trying on my end, by the way. You're the one who's been too tired, too stressed out, too busy with work. All those late meetings. How could I possibly make demands on you after such a long day?"

Grant's stone-cold silence confirmed everything she said.

Brenda refused to let up. Her normally even-tempered, controlled self stepped aside and she let her crazy out. She bombarded him with questions, demanding to know who he'd taken up with. Who had left her underpants where Tim could steal them and nearly die from swallowing them.

That meant the stranger had been in their house. In their bed.

The very notion made Brenda want to throw up. "Who is it, Grant?" she'd raged. "I need a name. At the very least, you owe me that."

A painful silence. "Danielle," he'd said at last, his voice taut with shame.

"Danielle from next door? Danielle who still lives at home with her parents? Jesus, Grant."

"Her mother has MS. She helps her out."

"By fucking the neighbor's husband? That's helpful."

Brenda would never forget the precise moment her marriage ended. The dashboard clock flipped to midnight.

She turned to the fine-looking, distinguished man she no longer knew and said, "Merry Christmas. I'm taking the dog."

SINCE THAT NIGHT Brenda had imagined this scenario several times—when she at last came face-to-face with Grant in the wild. She'd even rehearsed what she might say.

But faced with the actual moment, she forgot how to speak.

Tim went crazy for Grant, wriggling and whimpering.

Now Grant scooped up the little dog. "There's my boy," he said, and he actually sounded choked up. "There's my good, good boy."

Brenda noticed that her ex was wearing his only tux, the Armani one he'd bought for their wedding. He looked as tall, dark, and handsome as ever. It was as if the only change in his life was that he'd simply erased her—and replaced her with an exceedingly petite, gorgeous woman.

"Oh hey," Brenda managed to say, folding her arms across her chest.

"Hey yourself," Grant said.

They were in a standoff. She refused to fill the silence with niceties.

Grant was the first to cave. He used the dog as a prop, holding Tim against his chest like a shield. "Danielle, you remember Tim, right?" Then he made a nod in Brenda's direction. "And Brenda."

Danielle looked up at Brenda, who was a good six inches taller than her. Danielle's smile was full of confidence. "Such a lovely event for the dogs," she said. "And what a wonderful Christmas tradition."

Brenda studied the woman who, up until this point, had only ever been a pair of underpants to her. Danielle was not only petite; she was blond. With salon-enhanced eyelashes curling upward, and toothpaste-ad dental work. She wore a tiny dress and big jewelry. A flashy diamond ring glittered on her finger.

Oh. Apparently she had been upgraded from underpants woman to fiancée.

What did one say to one's successor? *Nice to meet you?* It wasn't nice. It sucked. *Hope you have better luck with him than I did?* No. Brenda didn't care what kind of luck they had. *Stolen any good husbands lately?* Not that, either. Grant was the one who was married and he'd let the cheating happen.

"And tiny Tim," crowed Danielle, taking the dog from Grant. "You're adorable!" She scruffed Tim's ears and planted a kiss on his head.

Grant had the grace to blush. *Sorry*, he mouthed over Danielle's head.

Brenda told herself she was over him. He couldn't hurt her anymore. He was just someone she used to know.

Then he said, "You look good, Brenda. Really." His tone was full of wonderment—or maybe puzzlement—as if he hadn't expected her to look so good.

Meaning he was comparing her to the way she'd looked when they were married. So, not a compliment.

"Big plans for the holiday?" he asked.

She offered an airy wave of her hand. "I'm going on an escape-from-winter cruise."

"You hate cruises," he said.

She had always felt too young for the shuffleboard, buffet, and floating casino crowd. "Maybe I changed my mind." Ironically, there was no winter to escape. Houston was usually perfectly warm in the winter. What she really wanted was to escape from Christmas.

"I hear you're seeing someone," Grant said.

"Ryder. He went to get us some drinks."

"Ryder? You're with a guy named Ryder?"

"We got matching tattoos." A slight exaggeration. They'd used the same tattoo artist.

His eyebrows shot up and he stepped back, looking her over. "Where?"

"Wouldn't you like to know?"

"Well, what's the tattoo of?"

"None of your business." She was determined to mask the fact that she felt lonely and empty, and her hot boyfriend had more interest in his Instagram followers than in a relationship.

"So how's that novel coming along?" Grant asked.

Touché, she thought. He still knew how to find her soft underbelly. "Really well," she lied. "It's being reviewed by publishers and literary agents."

"So, no takers, then."

He was such a dick. She couldn't believe she'd been married to him.

"*There* you are!" Ryder, her white knight, came up behind her and cupped his hands around her shoulders. "Hey, folks," he said with an affable nod. "Mind if I steal this gorgeous lady from you? They're play-ing our song. Our special song."

Grant's eyes narrowed and his face turned red as he took in Ryder's gym-perfect body and glorious mane of hair. Danielle gaped at Brenda's date. Brenda offered a tight, dismissive smile as Ryder promenaded her out onto the dance floor. She'd never heard the song in her life, but she flowed gratefully into his arms.

"Thank you," she murmured. "You have excellent timing."

"De nada. Sorry you had to deal with that," he said. "Was it bad?"

She sighed. "It was what I've come to expect from Christmas."

"Say what? Christmas is supposed to be everyone's favorite."

Brenda nodded. "Yeah, okay. I was just having a sourpuss moment." They finished the dance and had a little more champagne. There were things she could tell Ryder about her Christmas aversion. But now was not the time. And if Brenda was being brutally honest with herself, he was not the person she wanted to share these things with. He was a nice enough guy, and maybe they would grow into an actual relationship one day, but it was doubtful. The kind of connection and trust it took to share her heart—she wasn't even sure such a thing existed.

Except . . . as the evening progressed, Brenda furtively observed Grant and the fiancée. Danielle. They were horrible. They had cheated. The cheating had ruined her marriage and left her alone in the world. And yet, when she saw the two of them together, she sensed an unmistakable vibe between the petite, polished blonde and Brenda's ex-husband.

If her observation was correct, Danielle and Grant adored each other. Flat out adored each other with a total absorption that was pal-pable. They shared an intensity that made Brenda uncomfortable. It made her uncomfortable because it brought out a truth she had been hiding from for a long time.

She and Grant had never shared a love that deep. There had been love, that was true. There had been contentment and satisfaction. The sex was good enough. Their shared work situation was good. Life had seemed good. The world she had built with Grant had seemed nice and neat, progressing well.

When Brenda first met Grant, that had been one of the reasons she found him so appealing. He was grounded, and he offered roots and stability after her peripatetic childhood. He was *nice*. Nice looking, with a nice family and nice prospects for the future. So nice, in fact, that it was quite possible to mistake satisfaction for deep, soul-moving bliss.

She knew deep down that she wasn't cut out for the kind of crazy, chaotic love that made people want to write sonnets or indulge in romantic Christmas traditions, celebrating the holiday with whole-hearted belief and unfettered joy.

Her father had been that sort of person. The sort who believed Christmas symbolized everything good in the world, who squeezed every drop of joy out of the holiday. That, of course, had been his un-doing, and now Brenda wanted nothing to do with it.

Her notion that Grant was the right choice for her sprang from her belief that wanting something too much was dangerous. Grant didn't make the earth move. Who needed earthquakes, anyway?

The relationship had worked for them—or so she'd thought. Sure, cracks appeared with increasing frequency—a spat, a snarky comment, a wistful sigh when they watched a romantic movie's improbable ending.

At some point, apparently, the arrangement had stopped working for Grant. Certainly, he could have found a more humane, less humil-iating way to express his discontent to Brenda, but the result would have been the same.

She could not deny that he looked different with Danielle. More relaxed and animated. Utterly enchanted with the new person at his side.

Brenda wondered if he had ever been utterly enchanted with *her*. He'd been proud of her, she supposed, and satisfied that she fit so neatly into his life, including his work life. But enchanted? Utterly? Not so much. That sort of intensity would have made her uncomfortable, anyway. She didn't want anyone to be besotted with her, and she didn't want to feel a deep, obsessive, impossible love for any man. Because that kind of love was friable, and once lost, it left wounds that were too deep to heal.

She knew this about love, because she had loved her father with every tender fiber of her child's heart. And the loss, even twenty years later, still agonized her.

Fine, she thought. Let Grant drown in this glorious new love he'd found.

Yet as she watched them together, each aglow with adoration, Brenda felt an unexpected yet undeniable stab of envy. Against her better judgment, a part of her yearned for a love like that.

Good News, Bad News

"So there's good news, and there's bad news," said Dolly the next day. Brenda had met up with her at the Montrose dog park, a shady spot to sit while the dogs raced around. Dolly was one of the few paid staff members of the organization. She drank Diet Pepsi and spoke with a country twang. She and her late husband, Earl, had been independent long-haul truckers, and they had driven as a team for decades. Now Dolly was in charge of transporting dogs to their forever homes up north.

Brenda had her tablet computer with her, because they were making final preparations to organize the transport of the December dogs to the small Catskills town. She pulled up the spreadsheet with the dogs matched to their respective families.

"Start with the good news," Brenda said. "*Please.*" She picked at her manicure. She'd had it done especially for the gala. It had been part of her determination to show Grant she was better off without him. Even her nails were better. But the manicure was already chipping.

"Look at the amount we raised at the gala," Dolly said. "Can you believe it? We've met our funding goal for the next fiscal year."

"That's wonderful," Brenda said, watching Tim fend off the pack of puppies Dolly was fostering. She slapped at a mosquito on her thigh. Missed.

Dolly shook her head. "Your dog has the patience of Job," she said. "I'll be glad once these three are with their families. Anyhoo, yeah, great news about the funding. We might even get to expand our services. Save more dogs."

It was an unfortunate reality that pet shops were legal in Texas. This encouraged backyard breeders—inexperienced people thinking they could put their dogs together and make some money selling puppies. It rarely worked out that way. The puppies didn't sell, and the breeders dumped them on shelters or rescue organizations like Underdogs. Fortunately, there were three eager families in a small town up north who were going to give these pups a happy home.

"What about the bad news?" Brenda asked. Another mosquito landed, and she flattened this one, leaving a splat of blood on her arm.

"Scarlett can't drive the December transport with me. She blew out her knee playing pickleball, and she's out of commission for six weeks."

"Oh no," Brenda said. "That is bad."

"Tell me about it. I don't have anyone to help me get eleven dogs to their families in time for Christmas this year."

Brenda tapped her tablet to wake it up. "Then we'd better get busy finding a replacement."

"Oh, hon. I've been working on that all week. Do you know how hard it is to find somebody willing to drive eleven dogs two thousand miles to the frozen North? Somebody who knows dogs and can help with the unification process once we get there? And it's Christmas!"

Brenda shuddered and then opened her spreadsheet of Underdogs volunteers. "I can see how that would be a problem."

"I already went down the list," Dolly said. "It's a shame, because this is actually my favorite run of the year, the run to Avalon at Christmas."

"Eleven dogs? Two thousand miles? Snow? *That's* your favorite?"
Brenda shuddered again.

"Seriously, it's a wonderful holiday adventure. My sister, Penny,
and her daughter, Kim, live up there. Only family I have now that Earl
is gone. I love spending Christmas with them. Kim's got two little ones
and a great husband and a grown stepson. And the whole town comes
out to support Underdogs. They put on a big fundraiser at Christmas,
so that's quite a bonus, right?"

"We need all the help we can get," Brenda agreed.

"Glad you think so. We have to get the dogs up there." She showed
Brenda a file folder. "I have all their adoption applications here."

"I know. I sent them to you. Contracts signed, everything good
to go."

"But I need another driver. I can't do it alone."

Brenda drummed her fingers on the park bench, further damaging
the manicure. "I'll try to find someone who can help. Maybe place an
ad online?"

"Hey, I have to spend two thousand miles on the road with the other
driver. It can't be just anyone. And it's more than just driving. I need
a partner who knows dogs. Who can help with the adoptive families.
You and I both know that the way a dog is introduced to its forever
home is key, right? That's one reason we have such a good adoption
success rate, right?"

"Good point." Brenda drummed her fingers some more.

"Glad you agree. We're leaving day after tomorrow."

Brenda frowned. "Sorry, what?"

"The drive. I need you to make the Christmas run with me."

"*No.*" Brenda's reply was swift and firm. "Dolly, I can't help with
that. I've got my mom's retirement cruise coming up—"

"You'll be home in time for that. And even if you missed it, your
mom would understand," said Dolly. "I've known Margaret for years.
She gets it. When duty calls—"

"It's not my duty," Brenda objected. "It's . . . You're asking me to drop everything and hit the road with you. I can't possibly—"

"I know it's a lot, hon. I wouldn't ask if I wasn't desperate." Dolly handed her a Diet Pepsi from her cooler.

Brenda never drank the stuff, but for some reason she opened the bottle and took a sip. It tasted like some kind of seductive sparkly sweet elixir, imparting a weird kind of kick. "I swear, Dolly, I'd like to help, but—"

"Look at these families." Dolly opened the folder, even though Brenda was familiar with the contents. "Christmas will be ruined for them. They paid hundreds of dollars in adoption and transport fees. They're counting on us. Just look. There's a preschool that's taking two dogs. *Two.* And a senior retirement place. And a single dad with a little boy, and the day we arrive is his son's birthday. And here—an older lady who volunteers at the library, and a childless couple who—"

"Okay. Okay. I get it. I'm the one who processed the applications and checked all the references."

"Then you know," Dolly pointed out. "As the great Louisa May Alcott once wrote, 'Christmas won't be Christmas without any puppies.'"

"She never wrote that," Brenda scoffed.

"Those precious dogs," Dolly pressed. "Only days away from finding their forever homes."

Brenda felt ambushed. She couldn't imagine such a trip. A drive to the frozen North with eleven dogs? "I'm sorry, Dolly. I just can't. I get carsick."

"Those patches you wear behind your ear work great."

"I hate the snow. I hate driving on icy roads."

"It's nice and cozy in the van, and I'll drive the icy parts. Been doing it for years."

"I've never even driven a van."

"Well, that's just wrong. As an independent woman, you owe it to yourself to know how to drive anything—van, forklift, semi—"

"I've led a sheltered life."

"Driving a van is easy peasy. It's fully automatic, and it has four-wheel drive. And the Catskills are beautiful this time of year."

"And freezing."

"You'll be indoors. Wait till you see where they put you up when we get there. It's incredibly nice."

"As nice as an Ocean Alexander yacht with a full crew and staff?"

"And the town. It's gorgeous, located right beside the most perfect mountain lake you ever saw. It even freezes over in the winter. You can skate on the ice. And there's a ski hill—"

"Did I ever tell you why I live in Houston?" Brenda asked.

"Because you enjoy mosquitoes, traffic, and humidity?"

"Right." Brenda wiped the blood from her arm.

"Because your mom and sister live here. Because I live here."

"It's nice being close, but that's not the reason."

"Why, then?"

"Because I can't stand cold weather. When I was little, we were stationed in Alaska. Third and fourth grade. That's where we were living when my dad died."

"Oh, I'm sorry. I'm sure it was incredibly hard for you."

"And then we had two years in South Korea. Fantastic country but brutal winters. Just brutal. Also, we lived in Belgium at SHAPE where the sun went away half the year—"

"What's SHAPE?"

"Supreme Headquarters Allied Powers Europe. It's gray and cold and never stopped raining."

"If you think I'm going to feel sorry for you because you lived in Korea and Belgium at some fancy important military base, think again."

"My point is, I despise the cold and snow. The darkness and damp. Always have." That was a lie, and Brenda knew it. Before the Christmas Eve tragedy that had ended her childhood, she had loved the snow like any other kid. She'd loved sledding and falling backward into fresh powder to make a snow angel. She used to study the fascinating individual flakes that landed on her sleeve. Her parents took her and Cissy skiing, caroling door-to-door, cozying up with hot chocolate by the fire. The truth was, she had liked winter until Christmas had given her a reason to hate it.

"Welp," said Dolly, "in that case, you're just going to have to get over yourself. We leave day after tomorrow."

"But I just told you all the reasons I can't go."

"And I just shot them all down. Basically, you're afraid."

"What?" Brenda prickled with annoyance. "I am not—"

"And I can empathize with that, because fear is something everybody understands. It's out of your comfort zone. It's risky. It's a challenge to face the unknown. Listen, if there was any other way, I'd take it. I went through my whole Rolodex—"

"Nobody has a Rolodex anymore."

"I do. I'm old. Anyway, there's no one else who knows the process, and who knows how to handle the dogs—"

"That's it." Brenda snapped her fingers. "Tim. I can't leave my dog." Bingo. He was her ace in the hole.

"Of course you can't. He's coming with us. We can bring him along with the other eleven pups. Ha! The twelve dogs of Christmas. Kinda catchy, huh?"

Brenda shot her a look.

"I'm like a dog with a bone, ain't I?" Dolly said with a wink. She sipped her Pepsi and stared across the dog park, where Tim and the pups were rolling around in the dirt. "I really need you to come through for me, hon."

"Sorry, Dolly, but it's a no," Brenda said, even though she felt like a heel. Even though a nearly imperceptible inner stirring kept nudging at her. "A hard no from me."

Two DAYS LATER, Brenda was watching out the front window when her phone chirped with Cissy's ringtone.

"Are you seriously doing this?" her sister asked. "Ditching Mom's retirement celebration? Ditching us at Christmas?"

"I already talked it over with Mom. If the drive goes as planned, I'll be back in time. Mom is fine with it. She understands completely."

"Of course she does. Duty first, and all that. But *I* don't get it."

"Um, this isn't about you. Besides, you have Dilip. Mom has Lyle. You'll all be fine."

"It's a once-in-a-lifetime *cruise*," Cissy said. "You could bring that hot new boyfriend of yours."

"Ryder? He's not an option. For that matter, he's not much of a boy-friend."

"We can't have Christmas without you."

"Christmas happens with or without me. Believe me, if I could make it *not* come, I would."

"Aw, Bren. You have to let go of that old feeling. It was a horrible accident. It wasn't Christmas's fault."

No. It was my fault.

"Anyway, Dolly didn't mention this to me—she would never—but she needs the money she earns by doing the transport gigs for Under-dogs. If we don't pay her, she can't make the rent. When I realized that, I knew I had no choice. I can get over my aversion to snow for the sake of a friend. Mom agrees."

Brenda had slowly and reluctantly embraced the idea. In certain moments, she found herself looking forward to escaping the holiday overload for a while, and what better way to do it than a road trip with a bunch of smelly dogs?

And if she didn't make it back in time for the cruise? The prospect of skipping Christmas had a powerful appeal to her.

Cissy heaved a sigh. "Okay, fine. Whatever. I just hope you don't end up regretting this decision."

Timmy gave a *woof* as a tall white Sprinter van pulled up in front of the house. Brenda was familiar with the pet transport van, which was specially outfitted to accommodate dogs in crates. But today, the vehicle looked different. A set of reindeer antlers adorned the radiator grille. The Underdogs logo on the side had been decked with magnetic holiday greetings: *Jingle all the way to our fur-ever homes.* The side windows glowed with colorful fairy lights. Worst of all, holiday music flowed from the exterior speaker, loud enough that Brenda could hear it from the house. Christmas, it seemed, was stalking her.

Then Dolly jumped out, only it wasn't Dolly. It was somebody who looked like the Elf on the Shelf, complete with candy-striped leggings, pointy ears, a stocking cap, and jingle bells hanging from the ends of her pointy shoes.

"I think I already do regret it," Brenda said to her sister. "Gotta go. Wish me luck."

She left the house with Tim's leash and her suitcase and let herself out the front gate. The dog barked when he saw Dolly.

"My thoughts exactly," Brenda said to him.

"All set, pardner?" asked Dolly with a smile that seemed to radiate through her whole body.

Brenda looked her up and down. "Don we now our gay apparel? It's eighty degrees out. Aren't you melting in that getup?"

"Nah, I'll run the AC," Dolly said. "I had to get dressed at home because the first rest stop doesn't have a dressing room. What do you think of the ride?"

"It looks like it drove through the Christmas car wash and you got the superdeluxe treatment."

"Hah! Exactly. I was up late decorating it last night."

"Um, why?"

"Well, you know how you said how much you can't stand Christmas?"

"Yeah."

"That's how much I'm *addicted* to Christmas. All aboard the polar express!"

"Oh, boy." Brenda had already figured out that it was easier to give in to Dolly than to argue with her. Ignoring a feeling of foreboding, Brenda slid the side door open. A chorus of chuffs and whimpers and thumping tails greeted her. The dogs' crates were firmly in place and labeled with their names—most of them Christmas themed, which came as no surprise. But when Brenda saw their eager faces, her regrets evaporated.

"There *is* a small catch," Dolly warned her.

"Ah. A catch."

"You'll be driving the empty van home without me. My sister and I are flying to Miami after Christmas. It's an annual tradition with us. Are you all right with coming back all by yourself? Just you and Tim? Without the dogs to look after, it's really not such a bad drive."

Brenda thought about the long journey with only Tim for company, no schedule to keep, no one expecting her. "That sounds like heaven," she said.

Road Trip

It's the most wonderful tiiiime of the yeeeeearrr," Dolly sang in a full-throated mezzo-soprano.

Brenda grimaced and tightened her grip on the steering wheel. "Really, Dolly? Really?"

"It can't be helped," Dolly said. "I have a big role in the Christmas play this year, and I have to learn my part."

"What Christmas play?"

"The one in Avalon. It's the annual fundraiser for Underdogs North. They put it on at the community theater in Avalon every year, and the proceeds benefit the organization. Everybody loves a play, right? The whole town comes out to see it, and they raise a bunch of money. I've got a singing and speaking part this year, so I'll keep you entertained during the drive. You can help me practice."

"I'm new to van driving," Brenda reminded her. "You're distracting me."

"Nonsense. Music helps you focus. And you're doing great, just like I knew you would."

The van felt like a bus, but it handled surprisingly well. "You do have a fantastic voice," Brenda admitted. "Why would you use it as an instrument of evil?"

"Ha. You're funny."

"Seriously, you're so good. Move over, Lana Del Rey."

"Well, thanks for that. As I recall, you've got a fine set of pipes yourself. It was fun, doing the barbershop quartet with you at the summer fundraiser last year. We should harmonize like that again sometime. Like on this trip. I bet you know the alto part of 'Adeste Fideles.'"

"Thanks, but I'm good." Brenda did actually like singing and she did actually know the alto part. She'd honed her singing skills for choir and glee club all through high school and college. Since she was always the new girl wherever she went, it was good to have a skill that helped her fit in with a group. But she always tried to steer clear of Christmas songs, those nauseating melodies that refused to be shaken once they took hold.

"So this play," Dolly was saying as she cracked open another Diet Pepsi. "You sure you don't want one of these?"

"Yep. Sure."

"How about licorice? I brought my favorite licorice to snack on."

"Not a fan of licorice, sorry," Brenda said.

"Well, I really would like your help with my part in the play. This year's is really something. We've been rehearsing it on Zoom meetings. When we get together, boy howdy, it's going to be *good*. I will make sure you have a VIP ticket to the show."

"Oh!" Brenda glanced over at her. "Thanks, but that's okay."

"Come on, Scroogetta. You will love it, I swear. Let's turn that frown upside down."

"I feel hoodwinked," Brenda said. "You told me this trip is all about the dogs, but I think it's all about you."

"And *I'm* all about the dogs, so there," said Dolly. "Heads up. Our first scheduled stop is coming up in half a mile."

Brenda checked the map on her phone, which was propped on the dashboard. "I'm watching for it."

Each stop along the way had been preplanned with the precision of a battle campaign. There was a known nationwide network of rest stops for pet transport, complete with star ratings. The best ones had a fenced off-leash area, and trails for walking. Dolly had plotted out the route to include a break every four hours or so.

"I better get ready." Dolly flipped down the visor and freshened up her bright red lipstick and blush. She teased her hair up higher, then pinned on the little elf cap.

"Ready for what?" Brenda couldn't imagine why Dolly needed to primp for a potty break.

"Oh, honey," Dolly said. "You'll see."

Brenda glanced over to see Dolly putting a Christmas sweater on Tim. Brenda frowned. "It's seventy-five degrees out."

"I know, but he is so stinking cute in this sweater. I mean, look at your little boy."

Tim, ever patient, sent Brenda a doleful look. *Oh, buddy,* she thought, *what have I gotten us into?*

A few minutes later, she pulled off the road to a big, tree-shaded highway park. There were a good many travelers out, stretching their legs, using the facilities, getting coffee at a small kiosk.

"Here, put this on." Dolly handed Brenda a Christmas-themed knit cap.

"What for?" Brenda demanded.

"For me. Come on, you look like a Goth in all that black."

"I happen to like black."

"Well, I happen to like Christmas. So does everyone else."

"It has a jingle bell on it."

"Well, it wouldn't be a Christmas hat without a jingle bell, now, would it? Park there," Dolly suggested. "Close to the coffee stand."

When Brenda turned off the engine, the dogs snuffled and whined in their crates. Dolly reached for the console and switched the Christmas music to the outside speakers.

Brenda scowled at her. "What the hell—"

"Hush now. You'll see." Dolly hopped out of the van and set up a shiny red collection bucket next to a big tent sign that said PLEASE GIVE GENEROUSLY TO SAVE THE DOGS. There was a stack of donor receipts describing their mission and nonprofit status.

As Brenda was clipping leashes on the dogs, a guy in a cowboy hat and a tight T-shirt stopped and stuffed a bill into the collection bucket. She gave him a startled smile. "Hey, thanks."

"My pleasure, ma'am." He sauntered away toward a big, shiny truck.

"Okay, Dolly," Brenda said. "I get it now. Come on, boys and girls. It's showtime."

The process of uncrating was fairly orderly. They had already familiarized themselves with the dogs' personalities, and they were methodical about the potty and exercise breaks. Dasher, Dancer, Vixen, and Rudy were first, leaping and twirling as Dolly led them to the fenced off-leash area. Then came Comet and Cupid, a wiener dog and a chihuahua mix that would soon belong to the director of the preschool in distant Avalon. They were so cute that a group of admirers followed them to the fenced area, oohing and ahhing along the way.

After that came old Maddie and young Pearly May, a sweet Lab mix and a little white ball of fluff, both headed for a senior care community worker. Timmy stood guard beside the collection pot, wagging his tail for each donor who dropped off a tip and complimented his sweater.

Brenda leashed up Buzz, Dirk, and Olaf last, because they were a challenge. Dirk, a blocky, brindled Staffordshire terrier, was timid and musclebound, having suffered from a bad owner before he was rescued. He required coaxing and treats to lure him to the fenced area.

There, he did his business and retreated to the periphery, where he dug a hole and settled in to look around with suspicion. With Brenda and Dolly, he was affable, but he was not trusting. His adoptive family, the Cullens, had promised they had the skill and patience to draw Dirk out.

Olaf was a rarity for Underdogs—a boomerang. Olaf had already been surrendered twice. His first placement had failed because the adoptive family couldn't handle his energy level. A handsome husky–Norwegian elkhound mix, he was only four months old. The family that had adopted him had brought him back after a week, complaining that he was too active. Did they think a working-dog puppy would be easy?

His new owner was a firefighter and paramedic named Adam Bellamy. He was single and had a little boy. On his application, he expressed confidence that he and his son would be a good fit with Olaf. *Right*, thought Brenda, watching the dog zoom like a Tasmanian devil around the park. *Good luck with that, Adam Bellamy.*

Buzz, the lean greyhound retired at the age of two from racing, was not allowed off leash. Buzz was an escaper. He also showed a distrust of everyone and everything. His adoptive family, a couple named Eddie and Maureen Haven, claimed to be experienced with dogs and confident that they could make a fine home for Buzz.

As Brenda took the greyhound for a walk outside the fenced area, he tried his best to wriggle out of his harness, and he almost made it. "Hey there, whoa," she said, bending down to tighten the strap. "This is supposed to be an escape-proof harness. Maybe your name should be Houdini." She took out her secret weapon—a treat pouch with the smelliest training treats on the market.

That got the dog's attention. "Here you go, sweet boy," she said. "We just have to give you more training."

Buzz lunged at her with glee, practically bowling her over.

"A lot more training," she said.

Eventually, Brenda and Dolly wrapped up the rest stop—potty breaks all around, refreshed water bowls, cleaning out a few of the crates, reloading the dogs.

"I can see why you need a partner," Brenda said to Dolly. "This is a lot of damn work."

"Yep. Thanks again for coming, Brenda. Really. I couldn't do this without you. Wait here a minute. I'll go get us a cup of coffee."

Brenda and Tim waited by the donation bucket. She was amazed at how it had filled up with cash and even a few checks.

A man in cowboy boots and well-worn jeans approached her. "That's a fine-looking dog," he said, bending down to give Tim's head a pat. "Is he one of your Underdogs?"

"He was," she said. "We adopted him three years ago."

Tim wagged his tail, clearly judging the man acceptable. The guy was good-looking, with solid shoulders, a five-o'clock shadow, and a nice smile. "We. That'd be . . . you and your husband?"

Brenda still slipped sometimes, saying "we" instead of "I."

"Yes," she said. "I kept the dog. Ditched the husband."

The guy offered a gratifying laugh. "Love your hat," he said. "Makes you look cuter than a bug's ear."

"Um . . . Thank you?" Brenda couldn't suppress a blush. He wasn't hitting on her. But he wasn't *not* hitting on her. After the divorce, once she finally figured out how to make herself a priority, an unexpected change had occurred. Men had begun to notice her. To focus on her.

"Welcome, ma'am." The guy took a checkbook from his back pocket. "Tell you what. Here's my name and number, right here on this check. In case you ever want to get in touch." He handed her the check, which was made out for a hundred dollars.

"Thank you," she said again, with less skepticism. "That's really generous of you. There's a donation receipt on the back of this." She handed him an Underdogs card. "And here's how to get in touch, in case you ever want a dog."

"I might just take you up on that."

When Dolly returned with coffee in their reusable travel mugs, Mr. Tall Dark and Cowboy was sauntering away.

"Well, well, well," Dolly said, watching the man head toward a tool sales truck.

"Well, well, what?" Brenda bent down and extracted Timmy from the Christmas sweater.

"You know what. How's that boyfriend of yours, anyway?"

"Who? Oh, Ryder." Brenda shrugged. "He's fine. We have fun together."

"But he's not the one."

"Well, we exchanged Christmas gifts early, in case I'm not back from this trip, and he gave me a hot cocoa kit."

"Oh. Then he's definitely not the one." Dolly sighed as she tucked away the donations. "I'm sorry, hon."

"It's fine. I gave him a hardware store gift card." She cringed inwardly at how pathetic that sounded. "Which means I'm not the one, either."

DOLLY TOOK THE wheel for the next leg of the journey, a scenic stretch of the interstate through Hattiesburg, Mississippi, and northward from there. Whenever they found a busy rest stop, they put out their collection bucket and chatted up their fellow travelers. Guys flirted with both of them, and Dolly took it in stride while Brenda shrank into herself. But thanks to Dolly, there seemed to be no end to the holiday cheer they spread wherever they went.

"Clearly, I am not cut out for Christmas," Brenda said, using the jingle bell cap to wipe the sweat from her brow. She waved to a trucker who had tried—and failed—to get her number. "Or for relationships," she added.

"Who told you that?"

"I figured it out in therapy. While I was trying to stay sane through the divorce, I went into counseling. Thanks to the way I grew up, I never learned what a deep friendship was supposed to feel like. Losing my dad at a young age affected me in ways I'm still finding out. Grant was the first guy to pay serious attention to me, and I was like a stray dog following him home. I just needed someone—anyone—to see me."

"You're being too hard on yourself, hon. Don't do that. Don't let your divorce do a number on you. Not all marriages last forever. Breakups happen to the best of us. It's not a crime. It's not a reason to give up on love."

"I haven't," Brenda insisted. "It's just . . . I . . . Sometimes I think I'm not cut out for the kind of deep, crazy love you read about in books. Getting all tangled up with someone seems . . . risky and dangerous to me." Her therapist had urged her to strive for emotional fulfillment. Brenda wasn't even sure what that felt like—feeling life to the fullest, like a child filled with the wonder of Christmas. Struggling through the divorce had left her feeling flat, and she wasn't sure how to recapture the wonder—or if it was even a good idea to do that.

"Deep, crazy love isn't risky," Dolly said. "Your ex was not the right person for you to give your trust to. With the right person, it's the safest feeling in the world."

Brenda sighed and stroked Tim's soft, furry head. "Know what I've noticed since the divorce? Nobody touches your head anymore. And you don't touch anyone's head."

Dolly glanced over at her. "How's that?"

"Touching the head is a kind of intimacy you only share with a few people—your spouse, or a little kid you love. Maybe that's why Tim is so important to me."

"You're right, come to think of it," Dolly said. "All the more reason to look for a human whose head you want to touch."

"I'm skeptical." Yet a part of Brenda yearned for an intimate touch, a gentle hand cupping her cheek or brushing the hair from her face. It was true that the sex with Ryder was good, but that was due to the level of heat between them, not the level of emotion.

"What did Grant Dickens ever do to you to make you so wary?"

"Up until our dog choked on his girlfriend's underpants, nothing, really. It seemed like we did everything right," said Brenda. She stared at the wide fields of sorghum and cotton along the highway. The drive was pulling her farther and farther away from the holidays she needed to escape, and pushing her into an unknown world that somehow seemed safer. "It's strange that I can remember every minute of the past eight years, but I can't pinpoint precisely when things broke down."

"How'd you meet that guy, anyway?" Dolly asked.

"I was an intern fresh out of college, working for a small business journal, and I was trying to find a publisher for my first children's book. I have always, *always* wanted to write novels for kids in the middle grades, you know, those first chapter books that make a child fall in love with reading."

"*Charlotte's Web*," Dolly said. "*Henry Huggins. Harriet the Spy*. I loved those books."

"Me, too. Anyway, the internship didn't pay, and obviously no one was going to pay me to be an aspiring writer. I knew I'd need a job. Or a patron of the arts. So I went to him about a job."

Grant was ambitious and energetic. He had a real estate firm that included ownership in a chain of senior care communities, and he was damn good at what he did. His business was booming. "He needed an editor and head writer for *Habitation*—that's a luxury real estate magazine he published to support his marketing. Lots of glossy pictures and articles about the good life. Turns out, I'm better at cooking up articles about Italian furniture designers and ladies who love golf than I am at writing children's books. Anyway, I needed a job, and he had a job." She watched the seemingly endless road ahead, idly stroking Timmy's ears.

"And you fell in love," Dolly said.

"I . . . yes. We were colleagues, and then friends. And it just seemed right. It felt right."

"Hmm."

Brenda glanced over at her. "What's that supposed to mean?"

"Welp. Seems to me there's a bit of a gap between something that feels right and finding true love."

"I don't know. There's a lot to be said for not wanting something too much. That kind of wanting leads to disappointment. By the time I met Grant, I could see how compatible we were, and I *did* want to be with him—but maybe not too much. Just enough. Nothing over the top. No intense emotions. I'd say I wanted Grant just the right amount. That was why it seemed like we were so good together. It worked pretty well for us. Until it didn't." She sighed. "Seems like whenever I want something too much, I end up being disappointed. I really did love him, Dolly. Maybe not the way you felt about Earl, though. Does that mean I didn't actually love my husband?"

"Love takes lots of pathways. It's a different journey for every couple."

"I thought it was working for us. It *was*. We were a good team. We made a life together. Got a dog. Talked about having kids. But I guess it wasn't enough for him."

"Was it enough for you?"

Brenda was quiet for a while. They passed a library, its entryway all decked out for the holidays. The marquee advertised a children's reading hour. She thought wistfully of her unfulfilled writing dreams. What would it be like, she wondered, to be the author of a book that held children captive, filled them with the thrill of adventure, kept them company when they were lonely?

She had been so busy doing a great job for Grant that her own writing fell by the wayside. After a long day working on *Habitation*, it had been hard to shift to fiction in her spare time. She managed to eke out another book manuscript and send it off to book publishers, hardly daring to hope her work would see print one day. The rejections came back with depressing regularity.

Now that she no longer worked on Grant's magazine, she sometimes lay awake at night, wondering what kept holding her back from writing the sort of novel she could see so clearly in her mind, the kind of story her younger self used to stay up late reading with a flashlight under the covers after her mom declared lights out.

"Enough for me? That's a very confusing question," she said to Dolly.

"It's not meant to be."

"How long were you and Earl together?" Brenda wanted to change the subject.

"Thirty-six years," Dolly said. "We had our share of rough times, but most years were excellent. You'd think we would've tired of each other, all those hours in the rig. We never did, though. Talked about anything and everything. Sang in harmony—he had a fine baritone voice. Listened to books on tape on our long hauls, and played cribbage at the rest stops."

"That's nice, Dolly. I'm happy you had that. But sorry you lost him."

"Thanks, hon."

"How long has he been gone?"

"Five years now. I miss him every day. I'd never rule out meeting someone new, but . . . well . . . He set a high bar, Earl did. A mighty high bar."

Brenda wondered if that was the source of Dolly's boundless confidence and Christmas spirit—all those years with a man who set a high bar.

Dolly smiled wistfully. "I had the kind of love that lasts longer than life, I swear. He's been gone awhile, but the love is still right here with me." A thoughtful smile curved her lips. "I can feel it any time I need to. Even when I don't need to, it's always there. Maybe one day I'll find some kind of earthly love again, maybe not. But what I carry with me is right here." She gestured at her heart. "And it's perfect."

How could anything be perfect if it ended in such an epic tragedy?

Dolly flashed another glance at her. "You're looking skeptical again."

"I guess . . . well, what's the point of finding someone to love if it's going to hurt so much to lose him?"

"Oh, hon. We are all going to lose each other in the end. That's not the point. The point is what we find along the way. What we do with our hearts."

We protect them from harm, Brenda thought. *That's what we do.* Her whole life had been about moving away from feelings that hurt. Or feelings that filled her with the kind of childlike wonder and joy that tried to overtake her when she forgot to steel herself against them. Because the trouble with wonder and joy was that when those feelings were lost, there was nothing left but sadness and hurt.

THE DRIVE TO Avalon took them through America's beating heart, from the Deep South up through the Blue Ridge Mountains, past river-fed mill towns and sprawling suburbs and tiny hamlets with little more than a diner and a gas station. They spent the nights at pre-reserved dog-friendly motels. The accommodations weren't fancy, but a bed for the night was always welcome after a long day on the road. Dolly insisted on falling asleep with the TV tuned to a heartwarming Christmas movie, which Brenda endured out of respect for her friend.

The weather changed from balmy to blustery. During the long, boring stretches of highway, Dolly was relentless in practicing her part in the holiday play, trying out different ways to deliver her dialogue until the lines and lyrics were permanently embedded in Brenda's brain.

Dolly was unapologetic. "We have to get this part right," she insisted. "Take me through that bit again, the scene where Santa finds out that little Greta has stopped believing in him, and Sprinkles the Elf—that's my character—shows her where the real magic is."

Brenda scowled at the dog-eared printed pages of the script. "Again? Seriously? That's the cheesiest part."

"Au contraire," Dolly said with an airy wave of her hand. "This is the scene that'll win the whole crowd over. There won't be a dry eye in the house."

Brenda glared at the snow flurries darting directly into the windshield. "And this is a good thing?"

"Humph." Dolly cleared her throat and practiced the song again as they cruised along a scenic highway in southern Pennsylvania.

The very wrenching tune—"Don't Fight the Feeling"—was particularly annoying because despite her better judgment, the piercing sentiment triggered something inside Brenda every single time she heard the song. It had been made into a holiday classic by a child star, Eddie Haven, now middle-aged and Avalon's most famous resident.

They practiced until Brenda begged for mercy. "Don't we have a stop coming up?"

"We sure do," Dolly said. "Next exit."

The shoulder road led them through an old-fashioned village decked with a colorful Dutch or German theme. They pulled up to a broad green space with a fenced dog park and went through the exercise and potty routine. The cold bit at Brenda with sharp teeth as she waited for Buzz to do his thing. Living in Houston, she was ill-equipped for the cold weather. She had only one sweater and a light jacket, a pair of flimsy fashion boots and some dollar-store gloves.

Snow flurries whirled across the dog park, and she jumped from foot to foot, trying to stay warm while the dogs nosed around, taking their sweet time as they sniffed out the perfect spot to pee.

"Here, put this on." Dolly draped a cloak around her shoulders. It was red velvet, trimmed with white faux fur. "Hey, red is your color, girl."

Brenda didn't protest. Nancy, her stylist, would say *my eyes are bleeding*. But Brenda was grateful for the added warmth. The snowflakes thickened and within minutes, the area was covered in a veil of white lace. Watching the peacefully settling snow tweaked a long-ago memory in Brenda. There had been a time when she loved the snow. Her mother had been stationed in Alaska, and the first snow of the year was always greeted like a miracle—by the kids, anyway. The parents put on snow tires, laid in firewood, and braced themselves for bad roads. The kids looked forward to skiing, sledding, and making snow angels and forts until their fingers and toes were numb. Afterward, Brenda would head inside for a mug of her dad's hot cocoa, sipping it by the fire while he made silly dad jokes or read books with her and Cissy—old classics like *The Best Christmas Pageant Ever*, or newer ones like *Horrible Harry*, which made them laugh until their sides ached.

"... once we get up to Avalon," Dolly was saying.

"Sorry, what?" Brenda pulled away from the memory.

"I was just saying, we'll have to get you some warmer things once we get to Avalon. We'll be there tomorrow afternoon, right on time."

"Great," said Brenda, loading the dogs back into the van. "I don't know about buying a bunch of things for the cold, though. I won't need them in Houston."

"When you see my favorite boutique, you won't be able to resist." Dolly secured the last dog into a crate and slid the door shut. "It's called Zuzu's Petals, and it belongs to Suzanne Roberts."

Brenda recognized the name. "She's getting one of the dogs, isn't she? Single mom with a little boy, signed up to adopt Vixen."

"That's right. Maybe she'll give us a discount in her shop." Dolly sighed and scanned the snow-dusted main street. "I've always loved seeing all the different ways each place celebrates Christmas," she said. "Let's pop into the general store for a cup of coffee. It's one of my favorite stops on the schedule. It's where I found out about the character Belsnickel and the Christmas pickle tradition."

Brenda zipped up her too-light jacket and pulled her pashmina more snugly around her. She followed Dolly to the Middle Grove General

Store and Café. "How have I lived this long without knowing about Belsnickel?"

Dolly ordered candy cane hot chocolate piled high with whipped cream. She never seemed to remember that Brenda took her coffee black. "So, Belsnickel is like St. Nick's assistant. He goes around with a switch to hit the naughty kids, and a pocket full of treats for the nice ones."

"Hitting naughty kids is such a good idea," Brenda said with a grimace. "What could possibly go wrong?"

"It's all in good fun. Nobody really gets hit." Dolly handed her a glass ornament in the shape of a pickle. "I bought this for you. Hide it somewhere on the tree, and on Christmas morning, the first person to find it gets to open the first gift."

"Thanks," said Brenda, tucking the trinket in her pocket. "I'm not sure where Christmas is for me this year."

"Oh, I imagine it'll find you," Dolly assured her. "Christmas has a way of doing that."

White Out

On the final leg of the drive to Avalon, the scheduled arrival time was four in the afternoon. That would allow time to settle the dogs at the Shepherd Animal Hospital, where the pups would spend their first night. Dolly and Brenda looked forward to a hard-earned rest at their respective hosts' homes before tackling the unification process the next day. The families and dogs, so carefully matched by Brenda and the other Underdogs volunteers, would finally get to meet face-to-face.

"It's the coolest thing," Dolly said. "Seeing our little buddies with their new families. The owners are always so thrilled. I swear, there's nothing like it."

Brenda glanced back at the rows of crates. For the most part, the dogs had tolerated the long journey with remarkable patience. She was eager to see each one of them finding a home. She still remembered meeting Tim for the first time—a wriggling bundle of fur, wagging tail, and diamond-bright eyes. "You make me glad I came, Dolly. Really."

"You're a softhearted woman," Dolly said. "You just hide it extremely well."

The problem was, the weather didn't care about their schedule. In the early morning of that last day, they started hearing reports of a lake effect snowstorm gathering strength as it rolled across Lake Ontario. Cold Canadian air was moving over the open water of the huge lake, stirring up three inches of snow per hour. According to the latest report, the wind direction was delivering the heaviest snow directly to them.

"I'll take the wheel," Dolly said at the final rest stop, raising her voice over the gusts of wind. With the exception of Dasher, a Bernese mountain dog, the pups made short work of their business and were eager to get back to the van.

Brenda loaded Tim into his crate, garnering a look of resentment. "It's for your own safety," she said. "The roads are terrible."

"Earl and I used to drive all the time in this kind of mess," Dolly said. "We'll be fine."

Brenda aimed the heating vents directly at her. She checked the weather on her phone, but there was no signal, so she zipped the phone into her pocket and kept her gloves on. "Do you think we should shelter in place right here?" she asked. "Wait it out?"

Dolly chuckled. "Nah. That's the thing about a snowstorm. The longer you wait, the deeper the snow. The wind is causing it to drift. And we are truly in the middle of nowhere—thirty miles from the last town, and another thirty from the next town, which happens to be Avalon. We'll probably be a bit late, but we'll get there. Earl used to say, 'Don't watch the clock. Be the clock and keep going.'"

"Alrighty then. But I'll keep checking for a cell signal so I can call and let the animal hospital know we might be delayed by the storm. We should probably get in touch with our hosts, too. Mrs. Bellamy and your sister."

Dolly settled comfortably in the driver's seat and fiddled with the radio dial. "All storm, all the time," she said, quickly switching it to a Christmas playlist stored on her phone.

Then Dolly smiled at the oncoming snow. "I wouldn't worry about calling ahead. They all know cell service is spotty out here, and they're getting the white stuff, too. My sister, Penny, and my niece, Kim, always have a nice family dinner waiting at the end of my run, so we can take our time."

Brenda thought about her mom and Cissy, so excited about the tropical cruise. They thought she was crazy for doing this drive. She *was* crazy. "It'll be nice to meet them," she said to Dolly.

"Penny runs Fairfield House—a bed-and-breakfast on King Street. That's where I'll be staying. She started the guesthouse after her husband passed a long time ago. And Kim—that girl's like a daughter to me. And her kids are like my grandchildren. Earl and I never got around to having kids of our own. Too busy on the road." She hummed along with the Christmas music for a few minutes. "If I have any regrets in this life, it's that I didn't have a child or two. So I'm real lucky that Penny is happy to share her grandkids. Those three are something. One of them is a half brother who's in college now. Are you a baseball fan?"

Brenda frowned slightly at the random question. "Sure. Love the Astros."

"Kim's husband pitched against them in the World Series."

"Her husband is Bo Crutcher?"

"The very one."

"Wow. A regular celebrity. Maybe I'll get a chance to meet him."

"Sure, you will. We'll all get together after the dogs are placed."

"I might not have time," Brenda pointed out. "Settling the dogs in their new homes could take a couple of days, right? Then I'm going to need to hit the road. Whoa—look at that!"

A deer flashed across the road. Dolly applied the brakes gently and steered away from the animal. The van fishtailed slightly. "Dang. Feels like a sheet of ice under this snow." She glanced over at Brenda. "We got all-wheel drive. The weather might keep you here longer than you planned on, hon, and that's a fact."

"Lovely." Brenda blew out a sigh.

"Oh, honey, you don't need to be in a hurry. The next transport doesn't go out for four more weeks. We take the holidays off, remember?"

"Everybody takes the holidays off," said Brenda. "It makes no sense."

"No sense to pause at the end of the year and reflect? To connect with friends and family?"

"I don't need a holiday for that."

"Yet here you are talking about driving back right away to Texas alone instead of hanging out in Avalon, raising money for the dogs, maybe getting to know a new part of the world."

Brenda scanned the snow-covered hills. "Not a huge fan of what I've seen so far."

Dolly moved expertly past a couple of cars that had pulled over, their taillights glowing a faint red through a thickening blanket of snow. "Ice skating on Willow Lake . . ."

". . . freezing my ass off in a town where I don't know anyone," Brenda interjected.

"Making new friends," Dolly said. "Seeing me perform in the cutest Christmas play ever . . ."

I'd rather freeze in six feet of snow, thought Brenda.

"Hanging out at the Bellamy estate," Dolly said. "You couldn't ask for a better host than Alice Bellamy. She's a major benefactor of Underdogs North."

"I'd just as soon get back. Tim and I have things to do."

"Oh yeah? Like what? You missing that pretty boy you've been dating?"

"Maybe. I might be."

"Nah, he already gave you your gift—the hot cocoa set from the corner drugstore, right? You're a puzzle, Brenda Malloy. I can't figure out if you're running toward something or away from something."

"I'm not running at all."

"Good. Then you can stay in Avalon through the holidays. Watch the Christmas play. Help with the fundraiser. Trust me, when you see Alice Bellamy's place, you won't want to leave. I think you're going to like Alice, too. She can be prickly sometimes, but she and her husband, Rick, are huge supporters of Underdogs. They have been ever since she got her service dog from them. They have a big place on the lake with plenty of room for dogs. It's like a five-star resort."

"I'm sure it's lovely. I'm sure she's great. But it appears to be located in the coldest town in America. So no. As soon as we get the dogs all set up in their new homes, I'll be on my way." The thought of spending Christmas at some random truck stop among strangers had a perverse appeal to her. It would be just another day. Nothing special. No one expecting anything. No grim memories of Christmases past.

"Not if the weatherman has anything to say about it. Shootfire, it's really coming down now, isn't it?"

The final miles rolled past with excruciating slowness. The snow obscured the road, and the wind blew the white dust across the surface in undulating, snakelike patterns. They passed the occasional oncoming car or truck, but for the most part, it seemed they were utterly alone in a howling white tunnel. To Brenda, the oncoming flakes resembled the shift to warp speed in the Millennium Falcon, relentless and surreal.

After what felt like an eternity, a barely discernible green-and-white road sign indicated that Avalon was just two miles away. An old-fashioned covered bridge loomed ahead, with a sign that read SCHUYLER RIVER.

"Look at that, kids," Dolly sang out. "You're home at last! Let's make our spirits bright!" She cranked up the music, and burst into "Joy to the World" with extra vigor. Her singing was infectious—to the dogs. A couple of them joined in, and that incited a few more, and even Brenda cracked a smile at the howling.

"We are all punch-drunk from this drive," she said. "Pet transport is no joke."

"Yep, it's exhausting for all of us," Dolly agreed. "Earl used to say the end of the road gets farther away the more you worry about it. And ain't it the truth. I swear, I—"

"Deer!" Brenda yelled as a shadow leaped out of nowhere, seeming to float across the roadway.

"Holy shit!" Dolly swerved, narrowly missing the critter. The back of the van fishtailed. "That was close. I almost—*shit*." A second deer materialized and Dolly swerved again.

There was a muffled thump, and the van skated sideways, as if gliding on ice. Emitting a stream of curses, Dolly dialed the steering wheel in the direction the rear wheels were sliding. The second deer leaped over the bank.

The van kept sliding toward the steep riverbank. The brakes were useless on the icy, unplowed roadway. The van tipped, then slid on its side down the bank. The crates rattled. Airbags popped out, loud as gunshots. The terrified dogs yelped and yipped.

Brenda saw nothing but gray sky and white snow and the flat dark snake of the river. Through it all, "Joy to the World" was still blaring from the speakers.

PART TWO

Christmas is a necessity. There has to be at least one day of the year to remind us that we're here for something else besides ourselves.

—ERIC SEVAREID

In the Deep Midwinter

Turn up the music, Uncle Adam! 'Joy to the World' is my favorite."
Adam Bellamy's niece, Keeley, age five, stood with her brother, Matt, and her cousin, Will, in front of the somewhat sad, single-dad Christmas tree Adam had put up and decorated with Will. She took a breath, then belted out, "Let Hannah Major sing, let Hannah Major sing . . ."

"Maybe turn it down," said Matt, who was a year older and light-years more sophisticated. "Or at least get the words right. It's a dumb song anyway."

"No, it's not." Adam picked up his small son, Will, and held him aloft. "But we need to switch to 'Happy Birthday' tonight, don't we, Willy Wonka?"

"Yeah! Happy birthday to *me*."

Adam could feel his little boy's heart racing with excitement. Will's cousins, Keeley and Matt, had come over for dinner and presents, and the fun would begin as soon as their grandmother joined them. None of the kids knew about the surprise Adam had in store for Willy—a dog. In secret anticipation, Adam had geared up with a crate and soft bedding, bowls and leashes and a harness, and plenty of food. The young husky mix named Olaf was due to arrive this afternoon, and Adam couldn't wait. A boy needed a dog, and according to the woman at the rescue organization, the dog needed a forever home.

Willy felt sturdy and substantial in Adam's arms, yet Adam could still remember how fragile and weightless he had been as a newborn, just four short years ago. He'd made an early appearance at thirty-one weeks gestation, and that had been the start of a six-week ordeal in the NICU. Sometimes when Adam looked back on those stressful weeks, he realized that it might have also been the beginning of the end of his marriage to Suzanne.

Their marriage had been impulsive to begin with, foolishly based on the misbelief that an accidental pregnancy would result in a solid, long-term relationship. He and Suzanne had both tried their best, but ultimately, they had to accept that they couldn't force themselves to belong together. The mournful, depressing unraveling had begun soon after little Will was born. By the time the baby turned two, the marriage had already lived and died.

Per the parenting plan, it was Adam's turn to have Will for his birthday this year. Then Suzanne would have their boy at Christmas. They swapped the arrangement every other year. This was Will's normal routine and he took it in stride, but it was hard on Adam. Having his son only half the time made every moment matter twice as much.

Suzanne had kept the house and Zuzu's Petals, her clothing boutique in town. Adam had kept his job as a firefighter and paramedic, and he'd moved to the boathouse on his mother's estate. He shared his little boy with Suzanne and battled the postdivorce feelings of defeat and failure.

Eventually, he emerged from the fog and embraced a life he'd never imagined for himself—single fatherhood. More specifically, a single father living next door to his mother, which sounded fairly pathetic. But due to the nature of Adam's job, the arrangement made perfect sense. If he was called away for work, his mother or Rick could keep an eye on Willy. And it was the nature of his job that the unexpected happened on a regular basis.

Not today, though, Adam thought. He checked his watch, then looked out the window at the swirling snow. Today, Willy was having a dinosaur-themed birthday with his cousins, and he was getting a dog. Adam had found Olaf through a local organization called Underdogs. The transport service was due to arrive any time now.

It was something to look forward to. Will was going to go nuts. It was going to make his birthday extra special.

The elevator, which had been retrofitted on the exterior of the boathouse, made a buzzing sound. The kids dropped everything and raced to meet their grandmother and her service dog. Alice Bellamy glided forward in her wheelchair, Bella trotting at her side.

"Excuse me," she said. "I'm looking for my little grandchildren. Have you seen them anywhere?" She whirled her chair in a circle, looking around the room. "I don't see any little children here."

"Grandma!" Keeley danced around with glee.

"Ah, you there," Alice said in a dramatic, imperious voice, "take my scarf and mittens, please. I had to bundle up against this wicked storm." Matt took them from her and hung them by the elevator door.

"I have a special delivery for Mr. William George Bellamy," Alice said. "Has anyone seen him?"

"He's here," Keeley said, shoving Willy in front of her.

Will giggled. "I'm right here, Grandma."

"You? My goodness, I was looking for a tiny child and you're a big four-year-old boy."

"It's my birthday. I'm four years old," said Will.

"Hence, the special delivery," she said. "In my basket."

He scurried behind her chair and hoisted a frosty bottle of Dom Pérignon.

"Hand that to your father," she said. "I brought sparkling cider for you so we can have a toast."

"I like toast," Will said.

"She means the cheersing kind," Matt said.

Adam put the champagne and cider on ice and checked his phone again. Still no word from Noah Shepherd, who owned the animal hospital where the dog transport would arrive. Then he made a big deal of popping the corks and poured a glass for everyone.

"Cheers to sweet William on his birthday," Alice said, and they all clinked glasses. Bella barked and delighted the kids with some of her best tricks. The mobility assistance dog was not only a means for Adam's mother to live independently; she was also a tireless, lively companion.

"Let's let William open one gift while we wait for Mason and Faith to arrive," Alice said, turning to Adam. "Your brother and his wife are running a bit late due to the weather."

"One gift," Willy said, running in crazy circles.

"Open that flat box," Alice said, nodding toward the table. "It's a game you can play while you wait."

"Yay!" Willy grabbed the box and ripped off the paper. "What game is this?" he asked, checking out the pictures on the box.

"Twister!" said Matt, who could read. "It's Twister." He turned to Adam. "What's Twister?"

"Oh, that's a classic," Adam said. "Your dad and I and Aunt Ivy used to play it when we were little. It's kind of bonkers. Are you okay with a game that's bonkers?"

"Yessss!" the kids said.

Adam helped them set up the large plastic sheet with its colorful dots. He put a sticker on Willy's right hand and foot to help him keep track, because he was just learning left from right. He explained the process. "Shoes and socks off. I'll be the spinner," he said.

"I want you to play, Daddy," Will said. "Let Keeley spin."

Adam turned to his niece. "Are you okay with that? And then we'll switch places?"

The little girl nodded eagerly. Adam peeled down to bare feet, and Keeley called out the positions. Within a few minutes, Adam and his son and nephew were hard at it, roaring with laughter as they tangled themselves in knots and collapsed. Adam somehow ended up in a back-bend with his T-shirt covering his head, and he lost the game on the last move.

"Look at Uncle Adam's stomach," Keeley said. "It's covered in abs. You got *abs*, Uncle Adam!"

"That's 'cause he's dating again and he's been working out at the station," Matt said, blustering with authority.

Adam flushed and pulled down his shirt. "Dude, where'd you hear that?"

"Grandma said."

He shot his mother a look. "Seriously?"

"That nice woman at the physical therapy place," she said with a knowing look.

"Once, Mom. We went out once. Not a match." There was a lot more he could have said about the date, but not with the kids present. He grabbed the spinner. "My turn to spin." The kids giggled and twisted while he and Alice watched.

"Mason and Faith's kids are so great," Adam said. "They make me hope I'll have more of my own one day."

"Of course you will," Alice said. "You must. For a person like you, it's mandatory."

"Why do you say that? 'A person like me.' What's that supposed to mean?" His mother always managed to make him sound like he was in trouble—the common lot of the middle child.

"You're an exceptional father with so much love to give, and William is cut from the same cloth. You most certainly should have more children."

Oh. So he wasn't in trouble. "Not exactly simple for a single guy," he said.

"You'll meet someone," his mom assured him. "If not the physical therapist, then someone else. There's a lid for every pot. I mean, look at me and Rick. Perfect example, yes?" She and Rick, her soulmate, had met later in life, after Alice was widowed in the accident that had left her in a wheelchair. She had rebuilt her entire world from the ground up, and in the process, had found the love of her life.

"You're not a pot, Mom," Adam said.

"Maybe I'm the lid." She took a careful sip of champagne with her one functional hand while her service dog watched her every move. "This is delicious," she said. "Sure you can't join us?"

He shook his head. "Wish I could, but I'm on call tonight. Not on duty, though. I made sure I can be off for sweet Willy's birthday party. I'm off all next week, too."

"Well, then. Let's hope you won't be called away."

"The emergency gods would not be so cruel," he said. "I only get my kid on his birthday every other year." He checked his watch a third time. Lowering his voice, he said, "I thought by now I'd hear that the new dog has arrived. I hope nothing went wrong."

"Don't worry. Dolly Prentice has made the Christmas run for the past several years. She's a pro."

"Didn't you say the partner was new?"

Alice nodded. "Brenda Malloy. I'm hosting her. Longtime volunteer, but she's never done the transport run. She processes adoption papers and helps with the matching."

"I met her through email. She asked tons of nosy questions when I submitted my adoption application."

"It's her job to ask the nosy questions. She has to make sure you know what you're in for when you adopt a dog. I have her staying in the pink guest room."

"The one with the two-person jetted tub? Is she, like, ginormous?"

"Don't be rude."

"I'm kidding. When she sees your place, she's never going to want to leave."

"When can we have cake?" Keeley asked. Sweaty from Twister, she and the boys circled like buzzards around the table. In the middle was a three-tiered cake from the legendary Sky River Bakery, topped by a rearing T. rex with a candle in its claw. There were balloons and streamers around the cake, and a small stack of brightly wrapped presents.

"We want cake," Will and Matt chanted. "We want cake."

"Well, you're going to have to wait," Adam said.

Will's face fell. "Wait for what?"

"Don't look at me like that, buddy," Adam said. "It's good news. You just have to wait until after pizza."

"Pizza!" The kids did a victory dance around the kitchen bar.

Adam removed the three puffy-crusted pies from the oven. He knew it was way too much pizza, but everyone had their favorites, and he could send the leftovers to the station for the crew on duty. He served up the hot, gooey slices and gave himself an extra-large piece.

He'd been running around all day, getting ready for the party and the new dog, and he was starving. He was about to take his first satisfying bite when a familiar, ominous sound came from his phone. It was not the anticipated text tone from Noah, signaling that the dog had arrived at the veterinary clinic.

No, the notification coming from his phone was the unique, dreaded on-call tone telling him to report for duty. With a soft groan, he set the uneaten pizza slice back on his plate and took a deep, calming breath. This was the job he had signed up for. The job he loved. The job Suzanne used to complain about. When someone needed help, he had to go.

Both his mom and Will recognized the ringtone. They knew what it meant.

I'm sorry, Alice mouthed at him.

"It's my birthday," said Will, looking crestfallen.

"I get it, Willy Wonka," Adam said with false cheerfulness. "Let me see what's up with this call, and I'll try to make it snappy."

"Okay, man." Will's lip trembled, but he never objected when Adam had to go out.

He was such a good little kid, thought Adam. Sometimes he seemed too good to be true. Adam wanted Will to have a perfect birthday. He wanted him to have the best dog ever. He wanted him to have the whole world on a silver platter. It was not going to happen tonight, though.

Adam's go bag was already in the truck. He jammed on his plaid cap with the earflaps and headlamp. Something told him he was going to need a headlamp. Darkness came hard and fast in the Catskills in December.

He checked the summons from central dispatch. Rolled vehicle at the Schuyler River bridge. Danger of immersion. Possible multiple victims—fourteen. *Fourteen victims?* Shit. That was bad. Was it a bus, then?

So much for Will's birthday surprise.

Deep and Crisp and Even

"Hang on." The dispatcher's voice came in broken, staticky bits through Brenda's phone. "... if you can ... emergency signal so we'll have your position."

"O-k-kay." Brenda's voice made its way past her violently chattering teeth. It was lucky that her phone had been zipped into her pocket. She'd found it there amid the sharp, glittery splinters of Dolly's Christmas pickle, which had apparently smashed when the airbags deployed.

The van lay tipped on its side—the driver's side. Brenda found herself kneeling on the console and trying not to panic as she disentangled herself from the seat belt and shoulder harness. Dolly was pressed against the window, groaning softly and cussing through clenched teeth. The odor and powdery residue of airbags filled the vehicle, and some of the dogs were whimpering and scratching at the doors of their crates.

By some miracle, Brenda had managed to connect a 911 call on one flickering bar of service and with a violently shaking finger.

". . . many in the vehicle?" asked the dispatcher.

"F-Fourteen," Brenda said.

"Ma'am, did you say fourteen?"

"Yes, but they're . . ." The dropped-call tone sounded. "Hello?" Brenda said. "Ah, shit. *Hello?*"

Silence. Deep and cold and eerie. The engine was still running, and the headlamp on the passenger side shone into the gathering darkness. The dogs had initially yelped and whined, but within minutes, most of them had settled into nervous vigilance. Some of the pups chuffed and snuffled. A couple of them continued to paw at their crates, but the majority of them fell still, emanating a watchful energy.

That was something most people didn't know about dogs. When they were scared, they didn't yell and scream the way people did. They stayed mostly silent, perhaps emitting a growl of fear now and then.

Tim, in his travel crate somewhere behind Brenda, made his familiar nervous throaty sound and pawed at the latch. "Easy, boy," she whispered. She tried the phone again, but it didn't connect. "*Damn it.* Dolly?" she asked. "How you doing?"

"I'm doing," Dolly said, though her voice sounded strained. "I can't believe that happened. Never had such a thing happen in all my years of driving."

"Couldn't be helped. Those deer came out of nowhere," Brenda said. She shifted her weight on the console to check on Tim in his crate. She feared that any sudden movement could cause the van to slide down the bank.

Dolly didn't answer.

"You're awfully quiet." Brenda leaned forward and craned her neck. In the half light, Dolly looked pale, although that might be the residue from the airbags. "Talk to me."

"I'm here, don't worry. But damn. My leg hurts. Could be I broke it."

"Try to hold still," Brenda said. "Help is on the way. She said they have our location and someone's coming."

"Well, that's a relief," Dolly said, her customary cheerfulness returning. "Thank goodness we're so close to town."

"I don't know how much information went through to the dispatcher before the call dropped," Brenda said. "I'm going to keep trying."

"If you can get out, you should set the flares," Dolly said. "Even if they have our position, we'll be hard to spot in this weather, and it's going to be dark soon."

"We have flares?" This suddenly seemed important.

"There's an emergency road kit in the glove compartment. Can you get to it?"

Brenda shone her phone light and pressed the latch to the glove compartment. It fell open, and a jumble of items tumbled out. She grabbed a red plastic packet. "I found the flares," she said. "I'll try to get out and set them off." She stuffed the packet into her coat. "I've never used flares before," she said.

"N-n-nothing to it," Dolly told her. "There's a diagram and instructions, but you really don't need it. Just twist the cap off but don't lose the cap. It's your striking surface. Point it away from you and strike it like a giant match."

"I'll give it a shot. You sure it's okay if I leave you here?"

"How far off the road did we end up?"

"Not sure. I'm just glad we didn't end up in the river."

"C-can you figure out how to get out?" Dolly asked. "If you can't—or if you're hurt—"

"I'm okay. Completely freaked out but no injuries. I just pray none of the dogs are hurt." She shone her phone light at Tim's crate. His bright eyes stared back at her, nose quivering. Then she twisted herself around and found the door latch above her. Snow was already settling on the window. "Okay, here goes. Wish me luck."

Brenda unlatched the door and gave it a push. At first the door wouldn't budge, and her heart sank. She pressed harder, and it opened a crack, letting in a brutal gust of icy air. The door felt impossibly heavy. Shaking and straining with the effort, she gritted her teeth and managed to push it upward, getting it to open like a hinged lid.

"I'm out," she said to Dolly.

"You okay?" Dolly called. Tim gave a miserable whine.

"You betcha." Brenda was far from okay. She was freezing cold. Her gloves and boots were woefully inadequate, and a clump of snow had made its way into her jacket. "I'm going to climb up the bank to the road and set off the flares now. You sit tight. I'll close this door so you don't freeze." Next, she hoisted herself up and scrambled out, landing in a deep drift of snow that nearly buried her.

"Holy shit," she muttered, eyeing the river. Another couple of feet and they'd be in the water. Or on the ice. The van was only partially on its side, leaning against a pine tree that had stopped its fall. It was precariously close to the ice-edged river, so she didn't touch anything.

As she made her way up to the bridge deck, scrambling on all fours and grabbing tree branches for support, fresh snow filled her boots and the sleeves of her jacket. *I hate the snow*, she thought. *I hate Christmas. I hate my life. I hate everything.*

The sky was a leaden gray as the light faded. The merciless cold drilled into Brenda. In the glow of her phone flashlight, she read the directions. Hold the flare vertically, with the cap angled away from you. Wind behind you. Remove the plastic cap to expose the igniter. Rub the striker against the igniter. Caution: Aim it away from your face.

Her hand shook as she tried to remove the cap. She couldn't get a grip on it, so she removed her glove, holding it between her teeth as she rubbed the striker against the igniter. Nothing. She tried again, her fingers turning numb with cold and fear.

Get a grip, she told herself. Dolly and the dogs needed her help. She steeled her nerves and tried again. There was a fizzle, and then a bright red glow . . . for about two seconds. Then the flare went out. A dud.

Shit. Shitshitshit. She tried the second flare. The top made a sizzle like water in a hot pan, and then a bright glow appeared. This one stayed lit. *Yes*. Now what? Hold the stick upright and set it in the flare holder, according to the directions.

"I don't have a damn flare holder," Brenda said through chattering teeth. She looked around, seeing nothing but white and shadow. Big wind-driven flakes sizzled against the flare. She stuck it into a snowbank. It held for a moment, then tipped over. Although it was still burning, the thing was barely visible now. Brenda swore and lit the third flare. Though her fingers could barely function, she used the string from her jacket hood to tie it to the sign marked Schuyler River. That was good. The bright light reflected off the metal sign.

By the time she lit the fourth flare, she was nearly blind from the burning red lights. She set this one on the deck of the covered bridge, somewhat protected from the snow.

And then . . . what? Did she wait here? Go back to the van? Start getting the dogs out? She checked her phone again. Zero bars. She tried 911. No service.

Brenda was trying to figure out her next move when she saw a flicker of something in the distance. At first she thought it was residual glow from the flares. No. It was a glimmer of light. A car? Please be a car. Please be the emergency workers.

The approaching lights slipped away, and she wanted to cry. Then they appeared again, flickering red, white, and blue.

Brenda grabbed the first flare. Holding it aloft, she stumbled down the bank, sinking hip deep in the snow. She noticed that the engine had died. She opened the door a crack. "Help is coming," she yelled to Dolly. "I can see emergency lights in the distance. How are you doing in there?"

"I'm still doing," Dolly said, though her voice sounded uncharacteristically thin. "My leg hurts like hell, but not as bad as my dignity. Shootfire. I'm a professional driver. That should not have happened."

Brenda was relieved to hear her chattering away. She was even relieved to hear Timmy and some of the others whimpering when they recognized the sound of her voice. "You have to quit blaming yourself. You had to avoid hitting that deer," she said. "There's a layer of pure ice on the road."

She flashed an anxious look at the lights coming over a rise in the road. *Hurry*, she silently urged them. The van was tilted on its right side, so the sliding door was accessible. They would be able to get Dolly and the dogs out that way.

"They're getting close," she called to Dolly. "I'm going to climb up and wave this flare like a madwoman."

"G-good idea," Dolly said.

For the first time, Brenda heard a hitch of uncertainty in Dolly's voice. She climbed up the bank once again and held up the torch, waving it to and fro.

Two EMS rigs rolled across the bridge and stopped. Brenda set down the flare. A large guy in a reflective parka jumped out of the first rig and hurried over to her, turning on a headlamp. "Hi, what's your name, are you injured?"

"Brenda Malloy and no, but the driver hurt her leg and she can't get out."

Two more workers pulled a stretcher from the back of the boxy ambulance. The second rig pulled up, disgorging more rescuers.

"How many victims?" someone asked. "We can't get Life Flight because of the storm."

"It's just me and Dolly and the dogs." Brenda squinted as the strobing lights flashed in her eyes. She was trembling so hard she could scarcely see straight. "The driver's name is Dolly P-Prentice."

"Dogs?" a woman asked. "Dispatch said there are fourteen passengers."

"Twelve of them are dogs," said Brenda. "I tried to explain, but the call dropped."

"Holy shit." The woman scanned the van. "There are twelve dogs in that thing?"

"They're rescues, contained in travel crates. We were transporting them to Avalon. One of the dogs is mine."

"Cancel backup," the woman said into her radio. "We got this . . . I guess. I'll do the scene assessment. Your friend's conscious? Lucid?"

"Yes."

"And the dogs are contained?"

"Yes."

The woman and another worker made their way down the bank to the van.

Someone—large, bundled up, very male—led Brenda to the tailgate of the rig. "Ma'am, I need to check you out," he said.

"I'm okay," she said. "Just really cold and worried about Dolly. And the dogs."

The guy put a space blanket around her. She spotted a name tag on his reflective parka.

"Adam Bellamy," she said, reading the tag. She looked up at his face, strobed by the harsh lights. It was a good face—serious, square-jawed, eyes intensely focused on her. Impressive cheekbones. He was chewing a small piece of mint-scented gum and wore a thick plaid hat with earflaps and a jingle bell on top. It was a dorky hat, but she was envious of how warm it looked.

"That's me." Leaning forward, he shone a penlight into her right eye, then her left one. He smelled of snow and cold air.

"We've met. By email. You're waiting to adopt one of our dogs."

"That's right," he replied, leaning back to study her face. "So you're Brenda. Bmalloy@Underdogs.org. My mom is expecting you tonight. Alice Bellamy. Her service dog is a rescue from Underdogs."

"Oh! S-s-small world."

"Small town." He opened the rear door of the ambulance and held out his hand. "Can I get you to climb up here?"

She placed her hand in his. "My gloves are covered in snow," she said. "Sorry."

He helped her into the rig, and she savored the warmth of the interior. "Have a seat." He gestured at a side bench and removed the blanket. "Can you take your coat off for me? Need to get some vitals."

She slipped off her jacket. Her very inadequate jacket from Houston. He removed the goofy earflaps hat. Brenda saw him for the first time in full light, and the sight of him caused a hitch in her chest. Even in the glaring, clinical glow, he looked like he should be on a disaster-movie poster, with those big shoulders and that chiseled face. He was the kind of handsome she had always shied away from. Men who were that good-looking tended to leave her tongue-tied. He had the sculpted cheekbones and square jaw of a TV cowboy, with the added bonus of rich hazel eyes fringed by dark, enviably thick lashes.

He was looking at her, too, which made her duck her head in self-consciousness. Three days on the road with a vanload of dogs, an accident, and a scramble through the snow had undoubtedly laid waste to her last vestiges of personal grooming.

"Hold still a minute," he said.

Brenda steeled herself against the shivers while he shone a light into her eyes, checked her pulse and blood pressure, and noted them on an iPad. His probing gaze made her blush, even though it was clearly a professional assessment.

"I smell bacon," he said.

Her blush deepened. "Dog treats," she said. "Mandatory when dealing with a pack of dogs. Sorry about the smell."

"I like bacon. You sure there's no pain, nothing hurting?"

"I'm sure. Is Dolly okay?" She craned her neck to see around him.

"She's in good hands. Wait here. I'll see if they need a hand." He put on a headlamp and the jingle bell cap.

Brenda pulled her jacket back on. "I'm not waiting," she said. "I need to see Dolly." Holding the blanket around her, Brenda followed him out of the rig. A team of three extracted Dolly from the side door of the van. A cacophony of barking accompanied them up the bank.

"Kinda wild in there," one of the workers said to Adam.

Dolly was all smiles, thanking them and explaining how sheepish she felt about the wreck. She was on a gurney with a cervical collar and some kind of apparatus to stabilize both legs.

"Hey, you," Brenda said.

"Hey, yourself." Dolly was shivering hard and clutching her cell phone. She sucked on some kind of plastic pipe.

"What's that?" Brenda asked Adam.

"Nitrous. We call it the green party whistle."

Dolly said, "I could use a Diet Pepsi right about now." She sang a phrase from the latest Pepsi commercial.

"Is she altered? Like maybe she has a head injury?" Adam asked.

"Nah. She's always like this."

"They told me I won't be able to stay and help with the dogs," Dolly said.

"Don't you worry about the dogs," Brenda said. "I've got this, Dolly. Really. I'll make sure each and every one of them is all right."

She caught concerned looks flashing between the paramedics as they loaded Dolly into the first rig. One of them indicated a blood pressure measure.

"We're going to Valley Regional," one of them said to Adam Bellamy. "It's going to take three of us. You okay with the friend and the animals?"

Why three of them? Brenda wondered with a cold beat of panic. Why did Dolly need a team of three?

"It's fine," Adam said. "I'll radio the DOT crew for the snowplow and tow truck. They can help with the dogs. You guys head out. *Go.*"

They worked fast, and within a couple of minutes, Dolly was loaded into the rear of the ambulance. The harsh interior light washed her of color, except the blue of her lips. She lifted her hand in a weak wave. "Y'all take care, now," she said. Within seconds, the rig pulled away into the night.

"Why does she need a team of three?" Brenda asked Adam.

"It's standard."

"What's Valley Regional?"

"Trauma center," he said bluntly.

"Oh god. Is she—"

"Best place to get her cared for in a hurry," he said.

"Now I'm scared."

"You've been through a scary wreck."

"For Dolly, I mean. And the dogs." She started wading through the snow toward the van. Adam flipped a switch on his radio. "Hang on, and I'll come with you. I need to check in with dispatch."

Brenda stood shivering as Adam radioed the location of the van and explained that the other passengers were dogs. He was told that all the snowplows were out clearing roads, and the tow truck was off somewhere else in the county.

"I need to get the dogs out," Brenda said. "I have to make sure they're okay. They can ride in the ambulance, right?"

"What?" The bell on his cap jingled as he turned to look at her. "No."

She glared at him. "So you expect me to walk the rest of the way with all twelve dogs?"

"We're not putting animals in an ambulance rig. No way. On a night like this, that rig's probably going to be called into service more than once." He radioed again, negotiating with someone named Ray Tolley and convincing him to head to the bridge with a snowplow rig. "Fifteen minutes," he said. "The snowfall is tapering off, but it's getting colder."

"All right, let's start getting the dogs out." She shrugged out of the blanket, wincing as the cold hit her. Then she headed down the bank.

Adam followed close behind. "Twelve dogs, you say? *Twelve?*"

"Yep. Eleven rescues and my dog, Tim."

"That's a lot of dogs."

"And they all need help. I guess it's a new twist on rescue dogs." She was out of breath when she reached the van. "Okay, how are we going to do this?"

"Can't say I've ever evacuated a dozen animals before," he said, studying the van with an assessing gaze. "The vehicle seems stable. I guess we'll go in from the side here."

Brenda tried to dismiss a lurch of fear. She didn't know what shape the dogs would be in. They were all scared—that was a given. She prayed they were all right.

"Tim first," she said. "He's my best friend."

Adam nodded and aimed his headlamp at the van. "You got it. Tim first. Just point him out."

"The crates are labeled with their names," she said.

He opened the passenger-side door and lowered himself into the van. The dogs yipped and whined with excitement. "The creatures are stirring," he said. Then he rolled open the sliding door, and Brenda entered, staggering against him. His chest was like a solid wall, covered in a down parka.

"Whoa," she said, grabbing part of a seat. "What a mess. Oh, hey, babies." The crates were still secured in place. The chorus of barks and whines crescendoed. "Easy now, kids," she said. "One at a time. We need to find the leashes right away," she said to Adam. "They're in a duffel bag. A red duffel bag. There are three leashes, each with four ends."

She made her way to Tim's crate, lying on its side behind her seat. The moment she opened the door, he leaped into her arms, wagging desperately, pawing at her, licking her face and whimpering. "Oh, Tim, you're okay, right? Good boy. My good good very good boy." An unexpected rush of tears burned her eyes, and her voice broke. "Aw, Tim. Thank god you're all right." Flooded with relief, she buried her face in his soft fur. "Oh my gosh, I didn't see that coming," she said shakily to Adam.

"What, the tears? You're entitled."

Entitled? To fall apart? "He really is my best friend," she admitted. "You'll see, once you get to know Olaf. A dog has a way of stealing your heart. And . . . I nearly lost Tim last Christmas. He's pretty special to me."

"Oh yeah? What happened?"

She wished she hadn't mentioned it. "Disaster," she said. "You don't want to know."

"Oh. Well, one of these days, you'll have to tell me about last Christmas," said Adam.

No, I won't, she thought. She grabbed the leashes. Her hands were so cold, they scarcely functioned. "Tim and I will get out, and then you can hand the little ones to me. After that, we'll figure out how to deal with the three big ones. If any of them are hurt . . ."

"Brenda. One thing at a time. I've got this."

"Yes, okay." *He's a rescuer*, she reminded herself. No need to rattle off orders to this guy. "Can I hand Tim to you?"

"Sure," said Adam. His grip was assured as he cradled the little guy. "Hey, buddy. I got you."

She approved of his tone with the dog, but at the moment she was too stressed to compliment him. She exited the van and reached for Tim. She clipped a leash on him, which was probably unnecessary, since he was trained to stay by her side no matter what. He found a spot in the trampled snow for a nervous pee.

Then came Comet, the wiener dog. Adam held the wriggling dog gently, then sent him through the door. Brenda clipped on the leash. Comet seemed delighted with his newfound freedom and leaped around in the snow. Cupid the chihuahua was next, followed by Dirk, who grunted as Adam helped him out. "Pit bull?" asked Adam.

"Staffie," she said. "Staffordshire terrier. Similar but not quite the same. He's pretty timid. It's okay, Dirk, boy." She used a soothing tone. The dog shivered and whined, but he seemed to be unhurt.

Maddie, the sweet white Lab, had a shallow cut on her muzzle. Brenda very gently pressed a handful of snow on it, and Maddie sneezed. Rudy, a shaggy mutt, seemed to have a sore forepaw.

"How far away is the vet?" Brenda asked.

"Close. Maybe fifteen minutes. Hey, this is Olaf," Adam said, his headlamp shining on the crate tag. "Olaf, hey, boy. You're about to be my new best friend." He brought the wagging, sneezing husky out of the van. Olaf immediately leaped for joy and peed in several places before Brenda got the leash on him.

"You said you wanted a high-energy dog," she told Adam.

"That I did. My little boy and I love hiking and camping, even in the winter."

Hiking in the winter sounded like a form of torture. "Should be a good match, then," Brenda said. "He's going to need a lot of training."

Olaf bounded to the end of the leash and dug furiously into the snow, flinging it back on the other dogs.

"Really a lot," Brenda added. So many adoptive families miscalculated the time and effort and space it would take to settle a dog into its forever home. "He's also going to need plenty of patience and tons of attention."

"I don't mind a project," Adam said.

One by one, they got the dogs out of the van. When it was Dasher's turn, Brenda bit her lip with worry. "That one—the Bernese—weighs about a hundred and twenty pounds. Are you going to be able to lift her?"

"We'd better hope so." Adam opened the crate and lifted the big dog through the opening, straining audibly and then pushing from behind as Dasher scrambled through the opening.

"Thank you," Brenda said. "I couldn't have lifted that one on my own." She cast a worried look around the area. There was still no sign of a snowplow or tow truck. Brenda was trying to picture all the dogs crammed into the vehicle. Would that even be allowed?

"What's going to happen when the truck gets here?" she asked. "Are you going to be able to pull the van back onto the road? Will I be able to drive it?"

"Yeah, don't count on that," Adam said. "Your vehicle is going to have to wait until tomorrow. And it won't be safe to drive until it gets checked out by a mechanic."

"But what about all the dogs?"

"One thing at a time. Okay, here's the last one," Adam announced from inside the van. "Hiya, Buzz."

"Be careful with that one," Brenda advised. "He's skittish, and he's a runner. And since he's a greyhound, he won't be easy to catch."

"Got it. Okay, big guy. Let's get you . . . *Ouch*. Shit."

"Did he bite you?"

"He nipped."

Damn it. Brenda had her concerns about Buzz. He was not an easy dog. He was going to be adopted by couple who sounded great. The husband had taken up running—like a human greyhound, their application had stated. They claimed to have the time and the patience to manage the dog's behavior problems.

"There's a net muzzle clipped to his crate," she said.

"No need," Adam replied. "He's just scared. Aren't you, boy?"

"Keep hold of his harness," Brenda said.

"Got it."

Adam climbed out first, and then he turned to lift Buzz out. At the same moment, bright headlights washed through the darkness as a massive snowplow arrived. Its brakes gnashed, and then it backfired with a sound like a gunshot.

Buzz leaped out of the van as if he'd been doused with scalding water and raced away into the snow-covered woods.

The Chase

O h, shit," Brenda said. "Shit shit shit. Buzz! Here, boy. Here . . ." She handed all the leashes to Adam. "Hang on to these. Tim and I are going after him."

"The hell you are. The river is right below us and you could fall through the ice." He planted himself in front of her. "Let's deal with the others first. Then I'll help you round him up. You're not going off by yourself in the middle of a snowstorm."

"It stopped snowing," she objected, scanning the area. "Almost."

"And it's nearly dark. One thing at a time. Let's get this lot into the truck and then we'll deal with Buzz." He took the van keys from the ignition, turned off the lights, and closed the doors.

Brenda ground her teeth in frustration. He was probably right, though. She had no idea where she was, and dark shadows were creeping in from all sides. Her hands and feet felt numb, and she was cold to her core. "Let's do it," she said, taking the keys from him and zipping them into her pocket.

The big rig with its flashing lights was marked *Tolley's Towing and Snow Removal* with a phone number on the door. A tall, lanky man in a mackinaw jacket and cap with earflaps jumped down and surveyed the scene.

"Got a project for you, Ray," Adam called.

"No chance getting that vehicle out tonight," Ray said.

"That's what I figured." Adam held leashes in both hands. Tim ran up the bank and danced around the new guy. "Can we get a hand with these dogs?"

Ray rubbed his eyes and blew forth with an enormous sneeze. "Sorry, man," he said, taking a few steps back, "no can do. I'm, like, fatally allergic to dog hair."

"Seriously?" Adam asked.

"Hand to God. I swear I'd help if I . . . I . . ." Another sneeze.

Brenda called Tim to her side. Adam swore under his breath.

"Can you drive the ambulance?" Brenda called to Ray.

"What? Who are you?" He sneezed again and backed farther away from the dogs.

"The person you came to rescue," she said. "Think of me as a damsel in distress."

Adam regarded her and the brace of straining dogs. "You're no damsel."

"But I can use some help. So . . . the ambulance?" She turned to the tall guy named Ray. "Since the dogs aren't allowed in the ambulance, maybe we could put them in your truck."

"I can drive anything," he said.

"He's a cop," Adam said. "His family has a tow truck and snowplow business." Adam turned to Ray. "You take the rig back to town, then. We'll take the truck."

"With seventy-five dogs in it," Ray said. "Great."

"We'll get it disinfected," Adam said. "Or decontaminated, whatever."

Another explosive sneeze. Ray rubbed his sleeve across his eyes. "Damn. Yeah, I need to get out of here."

Adam tossed Ray a set of keys. "Drop the rig at the station, and then drive my car to the Shepherd Animal Hospital. We'll take it from there."

"Got it. I'm off, then. Truck keys are in the ignition. Don't mess with the salt spreader, okay?"

"Your rig is in good hands."

"So is yours." Ray boarded the ambulance and slowly pulled away.

Brenda stood back and eyed the cab of the truck. "We're going to fit all the dogs in that?"

"Unless Santa Claus swings by on an early run, it's our only option," said Adam. "Let's try to make this work."

"It has to work. I think you'll be surprised how many dogs can fit into a small space." But then Brenda felt a lurch of anxiety. "Are they going to suffocate one another?"

"Nah, this thing is huge. And to be honest, unless you want to leave the runaway behind, it's all we've got."

"What are we going to do about Buzz?" She looked around, but darkness swallowed everything beyond the light over the bridge and the truck's headlights. "He's a greyhound—very short hair. I'm afraid he'll get hypothermia."

Adam's jaw ticked. "Let's load up all these dogs, and then we'll go look for him."

Brenda nodded. She couldn't come up with a better option. At least the truck would be warm inside. It sat high above the surface of the road and had a roomy rear cab. They started with the puppies and small dogs, Adam handing each one up to her. The cab smelled of motor oil and something pine-scented, and she noticed a garland of greenery on the dashboard. The dogs squabbled and snarled as they filled every inch of the space. They managed to load in all the animals except Tim, who was perfectly trained, and Dasher, the largest in the group. The Bernese mountain dog was made for this kind of weather, and she seemed delighted to be in the snow.

"Maybe you should drive these dogs to the animal hospital," she suggested. "I'll stay here with Tim and Dasher. We'll keep looking for Buzz."

"No way. You don't know the area."

"True, but—"

"I'm not losing you, too."

In some other context, that would be superromantic, Brenda thought.

Adam climbed into the truck and cut the engine, then shut the door and jumped down. "They'll stay warm for a while," he said. "Let's go find your runaway."

Brenda tried not to think about how cold she felt. She handed both dogs' leashes to Adam. "Keep hold of them," she said. "Don't let go. I used up all the dog treats in my pocket. I need to grab more from the van."

"Hey, you shouldn't—"

She waved her hand and hurried down the bank, stumbling and getting more snow in her boot. With shaking hands, she opened the van and shone her phone light around until she found a pouch full of treats.

"High-value treats," she said, rejoining Adam. "Put some in your pocket. They're a trainer's basic tools. Yummy and smelly and irresistible to any dog. Buzz is very food motivated."

"Got it." He made a face when the smell hit him. "That's not bacon."

"Liver. Buzz loves it. I think I saw him take off in that direction." She pointed at a wooded area some distance from the road.

"So did I. Come on. We'll track him down. He left a trail."

Brenda unhooked Tim from his leash. "He'll stay with me," she said.

Adam adjusted his headlamp and handed her a flashlight. He paused and studied her. "You're freezing. How about you wait in the truck with—"

"No way. I'll be all right. I'm worried that Buzz doesn't know you, and he might not come to you."

"Even with these treats that smell like ass?" Dasher was nosing aggressively at his jacket pocket. Adam took off his muffler and tucked it around Brenda's neck. His body warmth, lingering in the soft knit, felt heavenly.

"Thanks," she said. "That helps."

"Don't get hypothermic on me. The symptoms can be subtle, like a pallor in the skin, even though there's high color in the cheeks. And a bluish tinge to the lips—"

"I know the symptoms. Lived in Alaska when I was a kid."

"You live in Texas and you used to live in Alaska," he said. "I bet there's a story there. You'll have to tell me about that one day, too."

He kept talking about "one day" as if she had all the time in the world. Typical guy. "I'll let you know if something freezes and falls off. I'm more worried about the greyhound freezing to death."

They started off in the direction Buzz had run, down the bank and along the curve of the river. The dog's tracks were faint and had disappeared in places, obscured by the wind-driven snow. Tiny flakes swirled in the flashlight beam.

"Where are we?" she asked Adam. "Is this somebody's property?"

"It's a hike-and-bike trail that goes along the river."

"Where do you suppose he went?" she asked.

"Beats me. Seems like he was spooked by that backfire."

"It's his breed. They're trained to race at the sound of a gun," she said.

Adam shone the light on the paw prints. They were far apart, a greyhound's long strides. "How fast do you suppose that dog can run?"

"Greyhounds can go like forty miles per hour," she said. "Some even faster."

"Damn."

"Where does this trail lead? Are there houses nearby? Anything?"

"Not much. Easement and floodplain. There's an old summer camp about a quarter mile in—Camp Kioga. It's closed in the winter.

Except . . . yeah, I think maybe there's a caretaker on the premises. It's just at the end, where the river flows into Willow Lake."

"What if we lose his trail?"

Adam didn't answer. She suspected he didn't have an answer. But he lengthened his strides. "You okay with this pace?" he asked. "Let me know if you need me to slow down."

"The pace is fine. I'm okay. Been training for the past year."

"Training for what?"

"The single life," she said. "Divorced." The word came out as an icy exhalation. "I took up running after my divorce last year, so I trained for a marathon."

"Good for you. I thought about taking up drinking after my divorce, but as you can probably imagine, it wasn't much help."

She knew he was single, because she'd processed his adoption application. The Underdogs organization required a lot of information about prospective families, including the ages of the people in the household.

"Oh, I tried that, too," Brenda admitted, "but I needed something I could do with Tim, so I switched to running."

"Good choice. Anyway, um, sorry to hear about your divorce."

"Happens to the best of us," she said. A platitude, but it was true. "I think I can say I have no regrets, and I learned a few things about myself in therapy."

"Yeah?" His tone went up. "You'll have to tell me about that one of these days. Maybe when we're not on a hunt for a runaway dog."

Another of his "one of these days" comments. He spoke to her as if they were already friends—which they weren't. But he did seem to be a good listener. She was going to be too busy for "one of these days" with him, but it was a nice thought—having a conversation with a guy who was a good listener. A rarity, in her experience.

"You have a little boy," she said. "I remember that from your paper-work. He's three, right?"

"William, and he's four, as of today. Actually, we were celebrating his birthday when the dispatcher called about your crash."

"Oh, my gosh. I hate that you had to leave his birthday party."

"Comes with the job," Adam said. "Even though he's so young, Will is used to me being on call. My mom is right next door, so she watches him whenever I'm called away."

Brenda wondered about his divorce. What were the circumstances? Did he have a hidden flaw like everyone else? Had he cheated? Had his wife?

None of your business, she admonished herself. Then she thought about the fact that she was going to be staying with his mother, Alice Bellamy, and that Adam would be next door. Brenda couldn't decide whether that would be awkward or intriguing.

She shook off the thought and focused on tracking down the runaway greyhound.

"Buzz," she called. "Here, boy! Buzz!" Her voice was muffled by the snow. She tried to whistle, but her chin and lips were so cold that she failed. They trudged deeper into the wilderness, shining their lights on the tracks Buzz had left.

Dasher and Timmy were loving the snow. The trail wound into a thickly wooded area. The snow was deeper here, which actually helped them, since Buzz had apparently churned a path through the drifts.

Adam shone his flashlight on another set of tracks. "Does your boy like chasing critters?"

"One would assume," she said.

The trail zigzagged through the trees, then culminated around one of them. It appeared that the dog had treed the animal—a chipmunk or marten, Adam guessed—then trotted off again. The tracks led them to a gate marked with a Private Property sign.

"I think this is the boundary of Camp Kioga," Adam said.

"Buzz went over the fence." Brenda pointed. She silently thanked her trainer for building up her stamina. Trudging through the snow was damn hard.

Adam opened the gate, and Dasher surged through, tugging the leash tight. Tim trotted at Brenda's heels. The footprints meandered past a couple of buildings shrouded in darkness and half buried in snow. Adam paused and pointed the flashlight at a vast, flat expanse of whiteness. "Welcome to Willow Lake," he said.

"It looks enormous." In the distance, she could make out glimmers of light. "Is that the town?" she asked.

"That's Avalon." He shone the light back on the trail. A few yards on, a second set of footprints appeared in a haphazard pattern.

"What the hell . . . ?" Brenda paused. "Those are human footprints."

"Must be the caretaker."

The dog's trail was chaotic, forming circles and figure eights. Brenda could picture Buzz moving toward the human and then feinting away. Then at a certain point, the paths converged.

"Over there." Adam pointed. "There's a light on in that building."

"Let's go." Brenda half ran toward the light. Timmy leaped and cavorted at her side. She stopped in front of an old-fashioned cottage facing the lake. Light glowed in the windows, and puffs of smoke rose from the chimney.

"Think we found your dog?" asked Adam.

"Lord, I hope so." She knocked at the door, and a distinctive *woof* sounded. "I believe we have." A sense of relief unfurled in her chest, and she stooped to pick up Timmy. Then she heard the sound of slow, measured footsteps, and the door opened a crack.

She hugged Timmy to her chest. "Hi there," she said, unable to see who she was talking to. "My name is Brenda, and I've lost a dog. I'm with Adam, uh, Bellamy."

"Mind if we come in?" asked Adam.

There was a hesitation. The door didn't move. Brenda glanced at Adam over her shoulder. He gave a shrug.

"The dog's a brindle-coated greyhound named Buzz," Brenda said. "Wearing an Underdogs ID collar. His tracks led us to you."

Then the door opened, very slowly. "Come on in, then. Bring your dogs in, too. It's bad out there." He was an older Black man in a plaid shirt and a sweater that was threadbare at the elbows, dungarees, and comfortable-looking furry moccasins.

Brenda tried to stomp the snow off her boots. A blessed warmth emanated from a woodburning stove. Next to the stove was an easy chair, a reading lamp, and a small table with a stack of books. On a braided rug in front of the stove lay Buzz, the dog that would not stop running. Apparently he'd found a place to stop. He thumped his whiplike tail on the rug.

"Lester Jones," the man said.

"Thank you for bringing Buzz inside," Brenda said. Her fingers and toes had begun to burn as they thawed out. She quickly explained about the accident and the transport.

"He came right to me," said Mr. Jones. "I got a way with dogs. Lost my Alma last fall. She was a fine Irish setter. Been lonely ever since. When this one showed up, I thought . . ." He shook his head. "Well, it's that time of year, you know? When miracles happen."

Not for the first time, it occurred to Brenda that Christmas didn't mean the same to her as it meant to most people.

"Mr. Jones, would it be all right for you to keep him until tomorrow?" Adam asked. "We've got our hands full with all the others tonight."

"I'll keep him for good," the man said. "Like I said, he came right to me. Maybe it was meant to be. We're already friends."

Brenda sent a worried glance in Adam's direction. They were probably both thinking the same thing. Buzz had been promised to someone else. But now was not the time to explain to the kindly old man how the adoption process worked.

They exchanged phone numbers all around. Brenda promised to return as soon as possible. She wasn't able to tell him exactly when that would be, though. Without Dolly, and with the van out of commission, everything Brenda had to accomplish felt like a crushing physical weight.

She ached to cozy up to the potbellied woodstove and thaw herself out, but that wasn't an option. With a wistful look at the contented dog, Brenda zipped up, tucked Adam's scarf around her neck, and braced herself for the hike back to the truck. They took off into the dark, snowy woods at a good pace, with Dasher and Tim bounding along with them.

"I'm worried about Dolly," she said. "Will you be able to get an update on her?"

"Sure. We can call Valley Regional for an update."

"I want to make sure she's in touch with her family," Brenda said. "She has a sister in town—Penny Fairfield. And her niece, Kim Crutcher. Dolly spends every Christmas with them up here."

"That's good. Her relatives can look after her when she's discharged."

"I'm still worried," Brenda repeated. "She's such a good friend, even though she drove me crazy singing Christmas songs the whole way up here. She called me Scroogetta. Now I'd give anything to hear her sing again."

"I bet you will, real soon. She was wearing her seat belt and the air-bags deployed. I'm sure she's getting good care."

Brenda shuddered. "And here I thought this would be a simple process. Drive the dogs to Avalon, introduce each one to its new owner, then head back to Texas. Easy peasy, right?"

"My whole job revolves around plans going wrong," Adam said. "I'm kind of used to it."

She sighed, emitting a plume of frost. "I should have known better. This isn't my usual role with Underdogs. I process applications. Make spreadsheets. Just this once, I agreed to fill in for a driver who got sick. Seemed like a great way to escape the holidays."

"Why would you want to escape the holidays? Oh, that's right. You're Scroogetta."

"Everyone is Scrooge compared to Dolly. She is obsessed with the holiday. Christmas is . . . complicated for me."

"You nearly lost your dog," he said.

"I lost my marriage instead," she told him. And then, maybe because it took her mind off how cold she was, she told him the story of Tim's obstruction and the sexy undies that didn't belong to her. Trudging through the dark winter woods, it felt good to unload the story on a stranger. A year after the event, the pain had given way to irony, and sometimes grim humor.

Adam said nothing, but she could sense him holding in his reaction.

"It's okay to laugh now," she said. "I mean, it's pretty ridiculous, right?"

He chuckled. "A unique story, for sure. But you and your dog are doing great, right? You can enjoy Christmas once again."

"That's not even the worst thing that's happened to me at Christmas," she blurted out.

"Really?" he asked. "What's worse than that? If that's not too personal a question."

She wasn't sure how much more she wanted to tell this guy. "It's not, but I'll definitely need alcohol and a long time to explain it."

The dogs spared her from answering further. When the pups in the snowplow cab saw them, they set up a howling.

"Here we are," she said, hurrying to the road where the big truck was parked.

Adam kept pace with her. "I'm impressed, Miss Malloy. You're not even winded," he said.

"Neither are you." She wondered if he was a gym rat. She had never been a fan of gym rats. The ones she knew were self-absorbed and, okay, boring.

"We work out at the station," Adam said. "The department requires it."

Oh. So not a gym rat. Just a guy doing his job responsibly.

"How are we going to do this?" she asked, eyeing the tall snowplow cab. The windows were hopelessly fogged and marked with nose prints.

"Well, I'm going to drive, and you're going to hold eleven dogs in your lap."

"Very funny," said Brenda.

"I'm not even laughing. Biggest task is this one." He nodded at Dasher.

"She weighs more than a hundred pounds." Brenda took hold of Dasher's leash and eyed the height of the cab.

"In this line of work, I've handled bigger humans. Open the door for me." He grunted with effort as he braced a foot on the running board and hefted the big Bernese. Dasher managed to scramble her way into the cab, and Brenda climbed in after her.

The dogs were jammed into the cab of the truck like sardines in a can. If Brenda hadn't been so cold and miserable, she would have found it funny. The entire rear bench seat, the console, and the floor were crammed full of restless, sneezing, snuffling dogs. Dasher sat in the front between Brenda and Adam. A couple of the little ones were at her feet. She held Tim and Pearly May in her lap.

"Sit tight," Adam said, putting the truck in gear.

"There's really not any other way to sit," said Brenda, wedged between two walls of damp fur.

"We'll be there in just a few minutes." He called ahead to the Shepherd Animal Hospital, and the vet, Noah Shepherd, said he and his assistant would be ready. Then Adam called the hospital and asked about Dolly. "Her family's there," he told Brenda. "She's having surgery."

"Surgery!"

"It was a compound fracture," he said. "Damn, those are wicked painful."

"She never let on how bad it was. She's the most upbeat person in the world."

"Sounds like the news is not great," he said. "But she's expected to make a full recovery. It'll take some time, though. Probably a day or two in the hospital, and then she'll be discharged to her family's place while she recovers. Your friend's going to be all right. We're all going to be fine."

"And the van?" she asked.

"One disaster at a time, okay? Let's deal with that tomorrow."

The cab warmed up, and Brenda welcomed the hot air wafting from the panel. The snow had finally stopped altogether, giving way to a completely clear, star-studded night.

"Wow," she said, staring out the windshield. "Is this what deep space looks like?"

"It's pretty dark out here in the country," Adam said. "A lot of people think of the city when you say New York. But most of the state is like this, especially up in the mountains."

Brenda studied the array of constellations and tried not to think about the heavy scent of wet dog that pervaded the truck. The drive took them along a winding road by the lake, and through a residential area that had just been plowed. The Shepherd Animal Hospital was located at what appeared to be an old farm—a former dairy farm, Adam told her. Ray Tolley's brother arrived in Adam's car, because the dog hair in the snowplow would be too much for Ray.

"Can you get it cleaned up and send me the bill?" Brenda asked, pulled every which way by the nervous, eager dogs.

"I'll take care of it," the guy said. "Looks like you have your hands full. I gotta go. Thanks to the storm, every available rig's been called into service."

Brenda took the dogs inside the clinic and met the vet and his assistant, a slender guy with a ponytail and tight jeans named Milo. She wondered if there was something in the water in this town, because there seemed to be a freakish abundance of good-looking men. *Focus*, she reminded herself.

"I emailed all their digital records to you," she said. "Do you have those?"

"We do," said the vet.

"Each dog's collar has his name on it." She indicated one of them. "Be careful with Maddie. She doesn't like slippery floors. And Rudy tends to bolt his food and puke, so he needs a slow-eat bowl, but that's still in the van. A couple of the dogs need meds for anxiety—especially Dirk. And I didn't bring his pills, either. Oh my gosh, everything's in the van."

"Brenda. Take a breath. The dogs are going to be all right," Dr. Shepherd said. "You've had a hell of a day."

"But—"

"We'll take it from here," Milo assured her. He was already leading the dogs to the back, one by one.

"They will," Adam said. "Next step on your journey is to get you and your dog home. My mom's giving you the pink guest room. And her cook makes a hell of a mie goreng."

His mom had a cook? And a pink room? "I like the color pink," she said. "And I've never heard of mie goreng but I'd have what the dogs are eating if you offered it to me. I'm starving."

He grinned, and his smile unbalanced her. "Donno and his wife, Vonnie, are from Bali. You're going to love their cooking. Let's load up and go. I'm taking Olaf home tonight. Been waiting for days to meet this guy."

Brenda was about to object. There was a strict process when delivering a dog to his forever home. The initial introduction was key to making certain the dog settled in properly.

Then she looked at Adam, who had left his son's birthday party, who had abandoned his EMT rig to load the dogs into a snowplow truck, who had trekked through the wilderness to find Buzz, who had managed to bring them all to safety.

Yes, she knew this man would make a fine dog owner.

"Can we borrow a leash?" she asked the vet. "For Olaf."

"He'll be the newest member of the Bellamy family," Noah said, handing her a nylon leash. "Be prepared to meet a lot of Bellamys while you're here."

"Keep a good grip on the leash," she said to Adam as they went to the door. "Olaf's a real scamp. He likes to—"

"Shit," said Adam. The instant they stepped outside the clinic, Olaf ripped the leash from Adam's hand, glove and all, and took off at a mad run across the parking lot.

"—race around," Brenda finished, watching the dog zoom through the snow. The snowplow driver had thoughtfully cleared the parking lot of the clinic, and the dog was scrambling joyfully up and down the piles of fresh snow.

"Olaf," Adam yelled. "Here, boy."

"He doesn't know that command yet," Brenda said. "He'll come if we ignore him."

"Typical male, eh?"

She flashed a smile. "Dogs are pack animals, and at the moment, we are his pack."

Adam led the way to a utility vehicle. It looked like an old Land Cruiser, boxy and practical. "You've done this before," he said.

"Not exactly this. I've trained a lot of dogs, sure. But I've never done the transport until now. I can safely say I'm not cut out for it. The transport part, I mean. Even before today, it was not my thing."

"You had a long drive. With a partner who wouldn't stop singing Christmas carols."

"And rehearsing her part in the Christmas play," she said. "Did I tell you that part?"

"You don't like Christmas plays?"

"Also not my thing," she admitted. "But thanks to Dolly, I've memorized the whole play."

"I am going to buy you that drink tomorrow. I need to hear more about this." He opened the rear hatch of the Land Cruiser. It was cluttered with man things—toolbox, fishing rod, cooler, cardboard box labeled "donations," a grass-smudged soccer ball, two sets of skis—one long, one short. In the middle of the back seat was a car booster seat littered with crumbs and small plastic toys.

"Not a pretty sight, sorry. I wasn't expecting company," he said with a rueful grin.

"I'm not judging. But I've heard you can tell a lot about a person from his car."

"Yeah? What can you tell about me?"

"Hmm, that you like sports, and food, and your kid. He's growing fast so, donation box. Oh, and maybe you're handy around the house?"

"The mystery is gone," he said with a shrug. He eyed the zooming husky, still bounding around the parking lot. "You sure that dog will come?"

Brenda took a treat from her pocket and patted the truck's interior. "Timmy, up," she said.

Her dog leaped high, clearing the bumper and landing in the truck.

"Good boy!" she said in her brightest voice, and she gave him a treat.

"Nice," said Adam. "But what about—"

Olaf sailed into the back of the SUV, and Brenda gave him a treat, too.

"Dogs," she said, "have the worst kind of FOMO."

"I can see that," said Adam, stepping back and closing the hatch.

"He's a handful," she said. "But he's sweet-natured and food moti-vated. That'll help with your training."

"Good to know," he said, retrieving his missing glove. "Climb in, and I'll get you to Hacienda Bellamy."

9

Welcome to Avalon

"E ver been to this part of the world before?" Adam asked.

"First time," Brenda said, scanning the frozen panorama. *And last*, she thought. Definitely the last. She closed her eyes, savoring the warm air blowing in through the vents in the dashboard.

"You're a Texas girl," he said.

She opened her eyes and glanced over at him. "For the past eight years, yes."

"So what's in Texas? Besides all your exes?" He sent her a cheeky grin.

"Only one of those, thank heavens."

"Okay, what else?"

"Warm weather. A little house I moved into after my divorce. Family nearby." Not much else. She hoped she didn't sound pathetic. And she wished she sounded more interesting. But the truth was, she didn't have a big career and important friends, or anything other than an ordinary life. "And a chance to work on my novel," she added. That wasn't something Brenda usually mentioned to people. With the dark road unfolding in front of them and the scenery sliding past, she just blurted it out. Then she cringed, waiting for him to make the usual oh-how-nice comments.

Instead, he said, "You're a writer. That's really cool, Brenda. What kind of things do you write?"

"I wrote a novel for kids. More than one, actually. They're chapter books," she said, "the kind I loved as a child. I've been trying to get my work published, but it's a tough field to break into." For some reason, she felt sheepish, admitting to an impossible dream, so she changed the subject. "Anyway, I'm planning on making Houston my forever home. I moved around so much as a kid. It's nice to land in one spot."

"You lived in Alaska."

So he *was* a good listener. Also, he had a square jaw with just a slight hint of stubble. "Military brat," she explained, trying not to think about the jaw.

"I see. Which branch is your dad in?"

"My mom. She was a colonel in the army. Just retired this year." She held her fingers in front of the vent, savoring the burn as they thawed out. "Have you always lived around here?"

"No. My family moved around a lot, too. But we have Bellamy relatives who've been in the area for generations. I met my wife here—now my ex—and we decided it would be a good place to raise our son." He drove with his wrist draped on the steering wheel.

Brenda noticed, because her dad used to drive like that. It was such a little thing, but it made her feel drawn to him. "Turns out it wasn't the best place for being married, I guess," he said.

"Sorry to hear that," she said. "It probably doesn't have much to do with where you're married, but who you married."

They passed a sign at the city limits that read WELCOME TO AVA-LON—A SMALL TOWN WITH A BIG HEART.

"You're here to experience a different kind of Christmas this year, then. Because of, well, what you told me." He gave a nod back toward Tim, who had poked his head up over the back seat.

"That's the idea," Brenda said. "One of the main reasons I decided to make the drive with Dolly was to escape Chris—" She broke off as he turned the corner onto what appeared to be the town square. Before her eyes, the scene looked like a Christmas card come to life.

The entire town was one giant explosion of holiday madness—the light-strung town hall with a massive, twinkling pine tree in the middle of the park. The streets were hung with swags of lights and greenery, and all the shops glowed with holiday displays. Christmas carols emanated from a gazebo, and an animated Santa in his sleigh waved endlessly into the night. At both ends of the main street, there were illuminated church steeples thrusting into the night sky.

"—mas," Brenda finished, gaping at the holiday excess.

"You like?" Adam asked.

"It's a nightmare," she whispered. "A legit yuletide nightmare."

"Yeah, it's a bit much. They go all out in Avalon. Wait until you see the ice castle display at the lakefront park. It'll blow your mind."

"Awesome," she said, feeling a leaden weight in her gut.

"People come from all over to see this town at Christmas. We're just a couple of hours from the city by train," he told her. "Turns out this place is a top-notch tourist destination for the holidays."

So. Her plan to flee from Christmas had thrust Brenda right into the belly of the beast. Lovely.

He drove slowly down a street lined with glowing candy canes. Golden light flickered in the windows of the small, neat houses. As they left the main part of town, the new snow lay undisturbed on the unplowed streets.

"Hope we don't get stuck," she said.

"The truck's in four-wheel drive. New snow tires. We should be all right. I kind of like making first tracks. More fun on skis, though. Do you ski?"

"When I was a kid," she said. "Up in Alaska." The final winter with her dad. He'd taken her and Cissy up to North Star Mountain and taught them to ski. She still remembered the heady joy of careening down the slopes, and the deep comfort of cradling a mug of hot cocoa in the lodge afterward.

"Maybe you can take it up again while you're here. There's a ski hill called Saddle Mountain."

"I doubt I'll have time," Brenda said. "I'm going to have to get the van sorted out, and then make sure the dogs are all placed in their homes. After that, I'll be heading back to Texas." Without Dolly in the picture, it seemed like a lot to accomplish. Brenda took a breath, trying not to feel overwhelmed.

Adam turned off the main road, passing through a lighted gate that opened and closed automatically. "Hacienda Bellamy," he said.

Brenda was unprepared for the grandeur of her host's home. Colored lights decked the trees lining the long driveway that led to an elegant manor house with formal stairs leading to a wide veranda. Lights glowed from tall French windows, each one decked with greenery and candles.

"You didn't tell me it was Downton Abbey," Brenda murmured.

"My mother likes living large," he said. "She's in a wheelchair, and she misses being a world traveler. I guess this is her way of bringing the world to her. Mom loves having company. You'll see."

He drove to a multicar garage, and a door opened automatically. He pulled into a well-lit space. "Your last stop of the day."

Brenda sighed. "And what a day it's been."

Adam let the dogs out the back of the SUV. Olaf and Timmy immediately set to peeing and cavorting in the snow.

"Will and I bunk in the boathouse over there." Adam gestured at a large, well-lit building at the edge of the lake. It was connected to the house by a covered walkway.

"Boathouse" seemed like a modest term for the place. It was easily the size of Brenda's place in Houston, set atop four bays that presumably housed the boats. "I should help you get Olaf settled," she said.

"Thanks, but I think I'd better learn to handle him on my own." Adam turned to where the dog was zooming around the yard. "Olaf! Here, boy."

The dog ignored him. He lowered his chin to the snow and rolled in it. Then he grabbed a string of lights from one of the bushes and ran madly until a spark flashed, and half the trees went dark.

"Oops," said Brenda. "He's a lot of dog."

"You aren't lying."

"Grab a treat," she said. "And have the leash ready. Then go down on one knee."

"Like this, you mean?" he asked, sinking down and looking up at her. "Last time I did this, it didn't work out so hot for me."

Brenda felt a strange flutter in the pit of her stomach, and she gave a short laugh. "You'll have better luck with Olaf. Once you win that dog's heart, he'll be loyal forever."

"No wonder people like their dogs so much." He called to Olaf again. This time, the dog raced toward him, practically bowling him over. He gave the dog the treat and clipped the leash onto the harness. "That's better," he said, ruffling the dog's thick fur.

"I don't mind giving you a hand with him," Brenda said. "Really."

Olaf lunged again, splaying his front paws on Adam's shoulders and knocking him over. "I appreciate that," Adam said, getting up and shaking himself off.

With Olaf straining at the leash, Adam lurched along the covered walkway. At the end of the path was an elevator—installed to accommodate his mother, he said.

Olaf whined in the elevator, then shook his whole body, flinging clumps of snow everywhere. The door slid open to reveal a large, open room with big ceiling timbers and a row of windows facing the lake. The kitchen and dining area connected to a living room filled with oversize Adirondack-style furniture arranged around a river rock fireplace. An older Asian man sat next to a lamp with an amber shade, reading the paper.

Olaf strained to explore the place, but Brenda showed Adam how to keep him in check with a treat and a firm grip on the leash. Tim was his usual well-behaved self.

"Oh, hey, Donno," Adam said. "Thanks for looking after everything." He introduced Brenda to Donno. He and his wife, Vonnie, lived with Alice Bellamy, taking care of the cooking, driving, and housekeeping.

"Willy is sleeping," Donno said. "Very exhausted from the party."

"Yeah, I had to miss half the fun." Adam held the eager young dog back so Olaf wouldn't jump on Donno. "Here's the other half."

"Oh, boy," said Donno, eyeing the dog.

"Thanks for cleaning up after the party," Adam said.

Donno nodded. "Cake was super extra delicious. It's on the table."

The dining table was brightly decorated with streamers and balloons for a kid's birthday party. In the middle was a half-eaten cake iced in crazy colors and topped with what appeared to be a dinosaur habitat. Donno turned to Brenda. "Come over to the main house. I'll make you something to eat, Miss Brenda. Alice has been waiting for you. Your room is all ready."

"That sounds fantastic," she said. "I'm going to give Adam a hand with Olaf, and then I'll be over shortly."

Donno studied her for a moment, then nodded and headed downstairs. Adam filled two bowls with water for the dogs, and they both drank greedily. Then he cracked open the door to a darkened room and gestured to Brenda. A slant of light fell over a small, slumbering form on a bed shaped like a rowboat. "My kiddo," he said. "He's going to be amazed when he wakes up and meets Olaf."

"That's so great, Adam. It's going to change his life."

"I expect it will. Let me show you all the stuff I have for Olaf. I've been hiding dog gear for weeks." He took her to the bedroom across the hall and turned on the light. There was a big bed made of peeled logs and another fireplace, and a bay window that jutted out over the lake. She noticed a stack of books on the nightstand and resisted the urge to check them out. People who liked to read were her kind of people.

Adam brought out the dog gear from a closet—a safety crate with soft bedding inside, a leash and harness, and a couple of toys. "His food's in the kitchen pantry."

"That's good. Poor dogs haven't eaten since this morning."

She showed Adam how to get Olaf into the crate. "It's all about rewards and leash skills," she said. "And a ton of practice."

"I'm on it." He paused and gestured down a hallway. "Would you like to, maybe, freshen up? Powder room's that way."

"You read my mind." She definitely needed the bathroom. Bad. She hadn't been since the last rest stop, hours ago. Catching a glimpse of herself over the sink, Brenda nearly gagged at the specter she made. White residue from the airbags made her look like the walking dead, although her cheeks were blotchy with cold-induced color. Her lips were chapped and had a weird bluish tint. Her clothes were covered in dog hair and probably worse.

There was a stiff brown spot on her hat, and when she took it off, she discovered an oozing gash above her eye. The cut started bleeding after she removed the knit cap. She hadn't even felt it happen during the wreck. Same with the livid bruise on her collarbone, which she saw when she unbuttoned her shirt collar. Her throat had been rubbed raw by the seat belt. There were new rips in her jacket and jeans, probably sustained in the wreck.

Brenda shuddered at the image of herself. She looked . . . exactly like a person might look after an accident and a trek through a snowstorm.

She came out of the powder room, holding a wad of tissue against the cut. "You're very diplomatic," she said.

"How's that?"

"By suggesting I needed freshening up rather than cosmetic surgery."

Adam studied her face, focusing on the bloody tissue. "In my job, I rarely see people at their best," he pointed out. He gestured at a barstool. "Have a seat. I need to take a look at that cut." He took out a well-stocked first aid kit and went to the kitchen sink and washed his hands. Then he set to work, his touch skilled and delicate as he cleansed the wound.

Up close, and without the big parka and gear, he was even better looking than she'd realized at first. By contrast, she had never looked worse.

"Sorry I didn't observe this face lac earlier," he said.

"You had other things to deal with," she said. "I didn't notice it, either, until I took my hat off. Is it bad?"

"It's not great. In better weather, I'd take you to the ER—"

"No. No ER, please."

"I'll do my best to clamp it for you. Maybe it won't even scar your pretty face," he said, gently brushing her hair back. He offered that cheeky smile again. "And if it does, you'll look badass."

"Badass works for me," she said.

With meticulous care, he applied three tiny clamp bandages. "I bet you'll heal right up." He cradled her head between his hands, maybe just a beat longer than she expected, as he studied his handiwork.

"Any other injuries?"

"Nothing else is bleeding. Not that I can tell, anyway. There's a bruise right here." She pulled her shirt aside.

He gently palpated the area around her clavicle. "Any pain here?"

"Um, no. No pain." He smelled of fresh snow and evergreen. The smells of Christmas. His hands were achingly gentle on her collarbone.

"Doesn't seem to be broken. That sometimes happens with a seat belt." He gave her a cold gel pack to hold on the bruise.

"Have you always been an EMT?" she asked.

"I'm actually a paramedic. Before that, I was an EMT while I was working on my certification. And before *that* I was a firefighter. Turns out I'm better with people than with fires."

"Well, I'm grateful for you and all your skills tonight," she said.

"Glad to help," he told her. "But I didn't picture meeting my new dog under these conditions." Then Adam stood up and touched his thumb to the bandages. "Not bad, if I do say so myself. So. Brenda Malloy, it's been a night."

"That it has. Do you think I should check on Dolly again? See if she got through the surgery?"

"You could call the hospital, but I don't think they work that fast."

"I'll call first thing tomorrow."

"She's in the best possible place tonight. Come on, I'll walk you and your dog over to my mom's. You are in dire need of a bite to eat and a nice comfy bed."

"That sounds heavenly."

"Okay, I'll just check on Will again and— *Damn* it. Olaf! What the hell?"

Brenda turned to see Olaf standing on top of the festively decorated dining table, licking his chops after consuming the other half of the birthday cake. She bit the inside of her cheek to suppress a smile.

"Welcome to puppyhood," she said.

Light on Snow

Brenda awakened to a fairy-tale world. The morning light after a massive snowfall created a glow with a special luminous quality. She noticed it immediately as she blinked awake in the elegantly appointed guest room in Alice Bellamy's house. As Adam had promised, it was pink. Extremely pink. The pure white of the light on the snow fell through the tall French windows and onto the deep pile duvet, highlighting the rosy hues of the decor.

Last night, Alice had greeted Brenda warmly and made her feel right at home. After devouring a cup of homemade soup and a grilled cheese sandwich, she had sunk into the pink jetted tub that was large enough for two people, maybe more. She'd scrubbed off the residue of the day's ordeal, and then she had relaxed in the lavender-scented bubbles while reading a juicy romance novel she'd found on a well-stocked shelf by the window. Afterward, she'd practically passed out in the luxurious bed.

Checking her watch, Brenda saw that she'd slept a full ten hours. She brushed the covers aside, padded across the plush carpet, and sat down at a small, neat writing desk in the corner. Helping herself to pen and paper, she started writing down ideas for a new novel. The children in her story might be facing the terrifying prospect of being lost in the wilderness. To survive, they would have to draw on their deepest resources of courage. The story came to life in Brenda's mind, and as she wrote, she was flooded with memories of the night before— the horror of losing control and the gut-churning sensation of the van sliding down the riverbank. Her pulse sped up, and her palms started to sweat. *Yikes*, she thought. Maybe this was what people meant by writing outside your comfort level.

Feeling drained after an hour of brainstorming the new story, she put her writing aside and went to the window. Tim emerged from under the covers and scurried after her.

She was overwhelmed by the sight of the lakeshore estate in the light of day, done up like an old-fashioned Christmas card. A vast, pristine blanket of snow sloped down to the flat, frozen lake. Swags of greenery adorned the wraparound porch and every balcony and veranda, and a full-size sleigh was displayed on the lawn, filled with a life-size Santa and a sack of brightly colored boxes and bows. Even the birdhouses had sprigs of holly and mistletoe.

"We're in Christmas purgatory, Tim," she said. "And we're stuck here until the van gets towed and repaired. Then I have to sort out the adoptions and god knows what else." Sinking down to the velvet cushion on the window seat, Brenda realized it could be a lot worse. Here, she was like a princess trapped in the luxurious guest suite.

"I hate the snow," she murmured.

Tim put his paws on the windowsill and wagged his tail.

"Yeah, you like the snow, you crazy little mutt."

The wagging accelerated and Tim whined. Down by the lake, Adam and a little boy emerged from the boathouse with Olaf. The dog went zooming around the yard, churning up the snow every which way. He barked at fake Santa in the sleigh, then raced joyously in circles. When the dog raced back to Adam, the small boy held out his hand, probably offering a treat.

"Bad idea, kid," Brenda said.

Olaf jumped up and knocked the boy into the snow. With one swift movement, Adam swooped his son into his arms.

Even from a distance, Brenda could see the boy's face was red, his mouth open in a howl.

"Somebody's got a lot to learn, eh, Tim?" She indulged in a leisurely stretch and caught a glimpse of herself in a tall oval cheval glass. There was a slight improvement over last night's disaster-survivor look.

Alice had given her a new toothbrush and loaned her an oversize Avalon Hornets baseball shirt to sleep in and some thick wool socks. Brenda's clothes, washed and folded, were stacked inside the door. It was a bit disheartening to put on the same clothes she'd worn during the long drive, but at least her things were clean. Giving silent thanks to whoever had done the laundry, she got dressed and fixed her hair. "I feel almost human again," she said to the dog. "How 'bout you?"

Tim cocked his head, then trotted over to the door.

"In a minute," said Brenda. "I need to make a call about Dolly."

She grabbed her phone, freshly charged up with a borrowed cord, and dialed the number Adam had given her—Valley Regional Hospital. They put her through to Dolly's room, and Dolly picked up right away.

"It's so good to hear your voice," Brenda said, relaxing at the sound of Dolly's chirping hello. "I hope I didn't wake you."

"Shootfire," Dolly said. "A girl can't get a wink of sleep around this place. Things have been beeping and pumping all night long."

"So what's going on? Are you all right?"

"I will be," Dolly said. "I had surgery last night on my leg."

"I heard. And you're all fixed up now?"

"Not quite. I might have a ruptured spleen."

"Dolly! What does that mean? Does it hurt?"

"It's not as bad as it sounds," Dolly said. "They say it's not severe in my case, and it'll heal with rest and time. In fact, they're going to discharge me today to my sister's place. I am so ready to get out of here."

"Oh, that's a relief. Is there something I can do?"

"Not just yet. Penny's son-in-law and grandson are already building a wheelchair ramp for me. They're making me wait to use crutches because of the spleen thing. Can you come and visit me there tomorrow? At Penny's? It's called Fairfield House B&B."

"Of course," Brenda said. "I can't wait to see you. Can I see you today?"

"There's a lot going on today, hon, including the fact that I'm on some pretty heavy-duty pain meds. Tomorrow's better. I'll text you Penny's address after I get settled in. I'm supposed to stay in bed. Which is going to be a problem for you. There's so much to do. The dogs—"

"Listen, don't worry about a thing, Dolly," said Brenda, wanting to defuse the tension she heard in her friend's voice. "Not one thing—do you hear me? Your only job is to get better. I'll cover everything that needs to be done."

"Ah, shoot, you know I'll worry."

"And you know I've got this. I swear, I will cover everything you were planning to do while you're here."

"Everything?"

"Every last thing. I'll deal with getting the van fixed and delivering the dogs to their homes. Exactly the way you want it done."

"Is that a promise?"

"That's a promise," Brenda said firmly. "Just don't worry about anything except feeling better."

"Thanks, Brenda. I know you don't want to hear this, but you are a true blessing of the season. You're saving Christmas for all those dogs and their families."

"Whoa. That's a lot of pressure."

"I saw you under pressure last night. You can handle it. And delivering the dogs? That's the best part of the job, anyway. Make sure you enjoy being a part of such happy occasions. You're going to love it."

Brenda looked out the window at Olaf teasing Adam, bowing down and feinting away. "Hope so," she said. "I'd better go." She caught a glimpse of her outfit—yesterday's clothes—and found herself wishing she could look nicer. Everything was so plain. So . . . black.

"Knock it off," she said to the mirror. "Nobody cares about how you look."

But she cared about the way Adam looked at her.

Flustered, Brenda stepped out into the hallway. There was a grand staircase and an elevator, and a railing that overlooked a grand foyer, decked with a fresh Christmas tree that was about fifteen feet tall. The smell of coffee and something baking scented the air, and there was bacon, and she almost fainted with a sudden wave of hunger.

She and Tim found their way to the kitchen. Donno held out a mug of fresh coffee. "Cream?" he asked. "Sugar?"

"Black," she said, cradling the warm mug in her hands. "Bless you." She savored the first sip, then went to the adjacent mudroom to let Tim out the back door, wincing when the cold air hit her. The little dog scampered around and found a cone-shaped bush to water. Then he bounded off to greet Olaf. The big dog was making a game of avoiding Adam's attempt to leash him. Brenda shut the door against the weather.

"What would you like for breakfast?" Donno asked.

"Oh! Whatever is convenient," Brenda said.

"Oatmeal with walnuts and fresh blueberries. And some of those cinnamon rolls I smell," said Alice, coming into the kitchen. Bella, her service dog, trotted at her side. Alice smiled at Brenda. "Sound good?"

"Sounds delicious." Brenda took a grateful sip of coffee. "Thank you, Alice. And thanks for everything last night, too. You've been incredibly gracious." Brenda genuinely liked her host. Alice was lovely, with light hair and blue eyes, and a generous smile.

"Of course. You had quite a day yesterday. Have you checked on Dolly?"

"Talked to her," Brenda said. "She might be discharged to her sister's home later, but her recovery is going to take a while. We were able to leave all the dogs—except one—at the vet clinic last night, and they've all got families waiting to adopt them. So I have quite a few things to take care of today, and I'm on my own."

"Nonsense," Alice said. "In a town like this, no one's on their own. We help each other out. My husband, Rick, can pitch in, and Adam's off duty for the next few days."

"I'll take all the help I can get, then."

Donno let Bella out for a run and gave Alice a cup of coffee, and she thanked him. She watched Adam and his little boy out the window. With a soulful gaze, Alice surveyed the view. Brenda could see the family resemblance between her and Adam—the fine bone structure, the thoughtful way they both seemed to have of looking after people. Outside, the kid started running around, and Olaf chased him down, knocking him off his feet. Even from a distance, they could hear the boy wailing.

"Adam's got his hands full with that one," Alice said.

"The kid or the dog?"

"Both, it seems. Willy reminds me so much of Adam at that age," Alice remarked. "Adam is my middle child, in between his much-too-responsible older brother and flighty younger sister. Adam was always willing to jump in with both feet, and with his whole heart. He loved making elaborate plans, and he'd be completely shattered when something didn't work out his way."

"Is he going to be shattered if Olaf turns out to be a challenge?"

"Oh, my heavens, no. Adam never shies from a challenging situation. I suppose that's why the divorce was so hard on him. He truly did try like mad to work things out, but . . . sometimes working things out is not the answer." Alice gazed fondly out the window. "Why don't you see if they want to come in for breakfast."

Brenda nodded, then helped herself to a piece of bacon and took a leash from a hook by the back door. She stepped into her boots, which were nearly ruined by the previous night's trek. To her surprise, a lovely warm sensation surrounded her feet. "Is this a boot warmer?" she asked.

"An essential piece of equipment around here," Alice said.

"Well, thank you. And thanks for the clean clothes. My suitcase is still in the van, so this is all I have to wear." Her laptop and all the dogs' paperwork were in the van, too, along with Dolly's things.

"My daughter, Ivy, is on her way over. She already has plans to take you shopping this morning."

"That sounds lovely, but I have too much—"

"—to do," Alice interjected. "And it will all get done. You'll feel so much better doing it in some nice warm clothes."

The last thing Brenda had the time for was a shopping spree, but she didn't want to offend her host.

"So go ahead and see if Adam and Will would like to come in for breakfast. I'm eager to meet their new dog."

"Olaf is a lot." The young dog was running circles around Alice's service dog.

Alice smiled. "So are Adam and Will. But we love them just the same."

Shrugging into her jacket, Brenda waded out into the snowy yard and waved at Adam. The morning cold penetrated her coat and boots, which had seemed more than adequate in Houston. In this climate, her outfit was completely inadequate.

Bella, the service dog, made a dash for the kitchen door. Tim and Olaf kept racing around the yard, exuberantly kicking up snow. "Any interest in breakfast?" Brenda called out.

"Always," said Adam. Carrying his son on his hip, he jogged over to her. Olaf eagerly trotted by his side. "Oh, now you want to come," he said to the dog. He set the kid down, and the little boy clung to his leg, eyeing Olaf warily.

"Law of attraction," Brenda said.

"This is Brenda," Adam said to the boy. "She smells like bacon."

"And that's not even the best thing about me," Brenda said. She smiled at the little boy, who was almost painfully cute. Apple cheeks and sandy hair poking out from under his knit cap. Big blue eyes like his dad's. The trace of a sleep crease on one cheek. "Hey," she said to him, "I think your name is . . . Bill."

"Nuh-uh," said the boy.

"Billy? Like Billy the Kid?"

"No!" He giggled.

"Well, you look like a kid to me. How about Will-I-am?"

"That's not a name. I'm Will. Will Bellamy."

"And you're four years old, as of yesterday," Brenda said. "Happy day-after-your-birthday."

"Olaf ate my cake."

"I guess if there's a cake, you have to put it where Olaf can't reach it until he's trained to leave people food alone. And you must be starving."

"I'm starving."

"I thought you were Will."

"I *am. And* I'm starving."

Brenda smiled up at Adam. "Two things can be true at once. Now. Check this out." She motioned to Tim, who gamely came to heel and sat perfectly at her side, earning a tiny taste of bacon. Then she showed the bacon to Olaf.

The dog went nuts, because . . . bacon. He reared up and poked his muzzle at her. She ignored him until he settled down. "When he comes over to you," Brenda said, "hold your hand closed around the treat like this. He has to learn to take things gently." Olaf eagerly licked her fist. She used her other hand to clip the leash to his harness. Then she gave him a taste of the treat, holding her hand down and slightly ahead, leading the dog to walk at her side. Olaf was bright enough to catch on quickly and trotted nicely at heel.

"Behold, the power of bacon," said Adam. "Miss Brenda says that when we're training Olaf, we need to use a treat he can't resist. Such as bacon."

"I like bacon," Will said.

"Then you're going to love this breakfast," she told him.

In the mudroom, she showed them how to get Olaf settled by keeping him on the leash and giving him a reward whenever he paid attention and cooperated. Tim and Bella eyed each other but maintained their distance. Both were trained not to engage without permission. Breakfast time was challenging for Olaf, since there was a veritable feast laid out on the table by Donno and Vonnie.

After breakfast, Brenda helped Willy practice the best way to hold and offer the treats. The little boy giggled as the dog licked his hand, then swirled around in circles, trying to figure out what he was supposed to be doing. A kid laughing and playing with his dog was the best sound in the world, Brenda thought.

"Grandma, I got a dog. Olaf! He's a *dog*," Will said, racing in a circle around Alice's chair with Olaf in hot pursuit.

"He's wonderful," said Alice. "Very handsome, and a fast runner."

Brenda saw Adam looking across the table at her, and a flush rose in her cheeks. "What?"

"Your forehead okay?" he asked.

"It's fine." She brushed back her hair so he could see. "The bandages held. The patient will live. Thank you."

He nodded. "I didn't mean to stare. Just . . . It's nice, seeing you in the daylight."

"When I'm not in roadkill disaster mode." It was nice seeing him, too, though she didn't mention it. He was almost too good-looking. Not like Ryder Wynn, whose appearance was so perfectly polished it was as if he had been created in a lab. Adam seemed more genuine. Solid. Open in his posture and expression.

"How can I help?" Adam asked.

"What's that?"

"You're worried about a million things. I can see it in your face. How can I help?"

"I . . ."

"Remember what I said," Alice reminded her. "Around here, every-body helps." Her phone rang. "Excuse me," she said, and she went to the next room, where Willy was playing with the dogs.

"She's right. Look, my mom can watch Willy until he goes to his mother's, and I'm off duty. Whatever needs doing, I can help."

Brenda folded her hands on the table and regarded him with genuine curiosity. She wasn't used to people simply offering themselves with no ulterior motive. Did he have an angle? What was it?

"I have a spreadsheet," she said and caught a look from him. "Yes, I'm one of those people."

"I can handle spreadsheet people," he said.

"But there's a problem. My laptop is in the van. My suitcase, wallet and ID, phone charger, everything is in the van. Oh my gosh, I should have grabbed everything last night."

"You had other things on your mind," he said. "Twelve dogs, remember?"

"Ten of them still need homes. One of them ended up with a stranger in the woods. We're going to have to get the van back up and running."

"Towing and repairs. That might take a while, though."

"Understood." She felt tension take hold in her neck and shoulders, where all the stress lived. "Last night, I used my phone to reschedule all the unification appointments," she said. "When I explained what happened, almost everyone was really understanding."

"Almost everyone?" he asked.

She nodded and scrolled through the email queue on her phone. "There was one couple . . . they seemed kind of put out. Cullen."

"The Cullens are getting a dog?" Adam took a quick sip of his coffee and looked out the window.

"You know them?"

"Yeah, I . . . Actually, no. Not really. I just know them in passing."

"You seem surprised that they're getting a dog."

"I am, a little. Maybe."

"Do you mind telling me why? I don't want to pry, but it's really important to make sure every dog ends up with a family that will keep him safe."

"They're okay." His gaze shifted. "This might be small-town gossip. I heard they're splitting up."

"Oh. Could be awkward, then." Brenda finished her coffee. "But I've been through a divorce. I can deal with awkward."

"What happens when an adoption doesn't work out?" Adam asked.

"I haven't encountered that situation yet." She felt the knot of tension gathering even tighter between her shoulder blades.

Adam got up and stood behind her. "Do you mind?"

"Mind what?"

"I can help you loosen up."

"Uh, sure." The offer surprised her, maybe in a good way. Although Adam Bellamy was a relative stranger, he seemed tuned in to her needs. Because he was a paramedic? Or because the vibe she sensed was mutual?

With gentle strokes, he massaged her shoulders. It was almost embarrassing, how tight she was back there. And it was surprising, how much she was enjoying his touch. "You have good hands," she said.

"One of my many talents."

Willy and Alice came back into the kitchen. Alice gave them a pointed look. "William, help me clear the table. When you're done, we can finish putting the train together."

"Okey dokey." The kid was not efficient, but he made up for it in enthusiasm. "I love the train. We got this train from Back Then," he told Brenda. "It belonged to my great-grandpa George. He's dead now, but the train still works."

"Cool," said Brenda. "Maybe I'll get to see it later." She stood and helped him with the dishes, feeling Alice's subtle but speculative gaze. Adam's mother had to be used to this, Brenda thought. Women falling under the spell of her son and grandson. Adam and Will were pretty irresistible. Their new puppy made them even cuter.

Brenda pushed away the thought. She didn't need a man, cute or otherwise. She needed help with the dogs.

They were just finishing up when a woman came in through the back door, bursting into the kitchen like a bright whirlwind. She wore a white parka and white wool stretch pants, tall faux fur boots, oversized sunglasses, and bright red lipstick. She looked like a ski resort model from the 1960s.

"Someone said there's a shopping emergency afoot," she said, stomping the snow off her boots onto a floor mat. "I'm Ivy," she said. "Alice's daughter. This one's far superior sister." She brushed back the hood of her parka and sent Adam a cheeky grin. "And *this* one's supercool auntie." She planted a kiss on the top of Willy's head.

"I got a dog for my birthday," Willy said.

"I heard. Is it this perfect little guy right here? Or this giant husky from the wilds of the Yukon?"

"Olaf," Willy said. "And he jumps."

"Lucky you," Ivy said. "A dog that can jump is pretty special." Then she turned to Brenda. "You must be the shopping emergency."

Brenda introduced herself, liking Ivy's brash energy. "I'm out of clothes," she said. "I wouldn't call it an emergency, though."

"Oh, being out of clothes *is* an emergency. I'd like to take you into town and help you find a few things to wear in this weather." She poured herself a cup of coffee and stole a cinnamon roll.

"That's really nice of you," Brenda said, "but I'm afraid I don't have much time."

"You have an hour or two," Adam said. "Probably all morning. It's going to take that long to deal with your van. Pretty sure all the tow trucks and snowplows are busy this morning. Tell you what. Let Ivy do her thing with you. I can already tell you, she won't take no for an answer. I'll organize the tow truck while you're gone."

Brenda was tempted. Her jacket and boots were no match for this weather. And it would be nice to have something a little more presentable to wear when she met the dogs' families. She looked from Adam to Ivy. "Thank you. That sounds fantastic."

IVY DROVE A white SUV that was filled with shopping bags and gift wrap. "Sorry about the mess," she said. "I'm just here for the holidays, so I've been rushing around with all the preparations. I live in Santa Barbara. I've got an art gallery there."

"Sounds nice."

"It's a living. What I really want is to make a living making art, not just selling it. I've sold a few of my own pieces, but not enough to call myself a professional." She sighed. "I don't mind working hard, but just once, I'd love to catch a break. How about you? My mom said you're from Houston."

"We're not so different," Brenda said. "I'm a content creator to pay the bills, but what I really want is to be a writer. I mean, I *am* a writer, but I haven't published anything yet. I write novels for children." She wondered if the bit she'd written this morning was any good. "I'd love to catch a break, too."

Ivy drove slowly past Santa's gingerbread cottage, which had a line of children waiting outside. "Maybe we should stop in and see the big guy about it."

"I've never had much luck with Santa."

Ivy drove into the town square and found a parking spot. By light of day, it was even more glaringly Christmassy than it had looked last night. People in bright winter clothes were strolling around, visiting the shops and cafés, taking pictures and pulling little kids on sleds. There was a line outside a place called the Sky River Bakery, and a cozy-looking corner bookstore. In the park in front of the town hall there was a bustling winter market, which seemed to be patterned after the Christmas markets of northern Europe. The area was filled with booths and displays of handmade goods, and a guy roasting something in a brazier over hot coals.

Ivy noticed her staring. "Ever try roasted chestnuts?"

"I'll pass, thanks," Brenda said.

"Not my favorite, either," Ivy said. "It's a tradition. This is a town with lots of traditions, as I'm sure you're finding out. Come on. Let's get you something nice and warm to wear." They crossed to a cute boutique called Zuzu's Petals. The windows displayed an abundant winter wardrobe—sweaters and capes, downy parkas and hats, mittens and boots.

"Fair warning," Ivy said. "This is one of those shops that makes you want *every*thing. Suzanne—Zuzu—has incredible taste."

"I'll try to restrain myself," Brenda said. "Since I live in Houston, I won't need much, right?"

"Oh, and just another heads-up," Ivy said. "Suzanne, the owner, is Adam's ex. Willy's mom. It's not superweird or anything, but I thought you should know."

"Noted," said Brenda, her senses sharpening. She couldn't deny a deep curiosity about Adam's ex-wife. The mother of that adorable little kid. Former wife of that very nice guy.

Ivy must have sensed the unspoken questions, because she said, "The two of them get along for Will's sake. They just weren't compatible. Not the right fit, even though they tried. But we all get along like adults. They've been divorced for about three years now." She sighed. "Mom and I are always hoping Adam will meet someone else. He loves being a dad, but I can tell he's lonely. I keep trying to set him up, but nothing ever pans out. Hey, are you single?"

"Yes, and I'm not looking to be set up." The reply came quickly, a defense maneuver.

"He's not your type?"

Brenda looked away to hide a blush. *He's totally my type*, she caught herself thinking. "We're geographically incompatible," she said. "Avalon is a long way from Houston."

"Hmm. Well, I won't give up hoping for a Christmas miracle."

Brenda had given up on miracles long ago, but she didn't say anything. The boutique was a good distraction, anyway. Ivy was right about the shop. The selection was dazzling. There were gorgeous sweaters in yummy colors, and warm pants and jackets, all nicely displayed. Brenda glanced at Suzanne, attractive and briskly efficient as she rang up a customer's sale at the counter. She wore a lot of makeup, expertly applied, and had bright red nails that made Brenda self-conscious about her own short, unpolished nails. She wondered why the marriage hadn't worked out. Then she wondered why she couldn't stop wondering about it. Honestly, it was none of her business.

With Ivy's help, Brenda found several pieces she suddenly couldn't do without—a pale blue angora sweater and dark wool slacks, fleece-lined leggings, a warm jacket, and a good pair of snow boots. She gave into her weakness for well-fitting jeans and a cashmere scarf as well. With an air of defiance, she added some undies to the pile—the skimpy, sexy kind, the kind Tim had swallowed last year. She never used to indulge in lingerie when she was married. Grant would have deemed it impractical. It was gratifying to know she didn't have to consider him anymore. She made her own money, and she was entitled to splurge on herself.

"This is way too much fun," she said as Ivy brought yet another top to the dressing room. "I won't be here long enough to wear all this."

"You look amazing in everything," Ivy said. "Are you an athlete or just naturally lucky?"

Brenda shook her head. "I started running after my divorce. Been working my ass off, training for a marathon."

"What about something to wear to the play?" Ivy said, holding up a bright red sweater dress. "You know about the play, right? Fundraiser for the dogs?"

"I know way too much about it," Brenda said. "Dolly practiced her part in the van all the way from Texas. I'm not planning on going, though."

"All right, I'll stop." Ivy helped her take her things to the counter and introduced her to Suzanne.

"Suzanne Roberts?" Brenda asked.

"That's me."

"Oh, you're *that* Suzanne. I'm Brenda Malloy. With Underdogs."

"My gosh, Brenda! You're bringing me a dog!" Suzanne exclaimed. "I saw your email this morning about the delay. Is everything all right?"

"It will be. The dogs are all at the vet clinic now. As soon as I get my van running, I'll start taking them to their new homes. Maybe later today. Tomorrow at the latest."

"That's so exciting. I can't wait to meet Vixen. My little boy is going to love her."

As they drove home, Ivy said, "I didn't realize Suzanne's also getting a dog. I have a feeling Adam doesn't know, either. I'm like an invisible wall. I don't know what each parent is telling the other, so I keep my mouth shut."

"Good policy. It'll be nice for Will to have a dog at each house."

"Will's the best. Love that kid." She glanced over at Brenda. "Are you sure you're not interested in my brother? Because, I mean . . ." As they drove up to Alice's place, they saw Adam and Will with both dogs in the yard. They were laughing and tumbling, throwing snowballs and chasing Olaf.

"Texas girl," Brenda reminded her. "Geographically undesirable."

"Gotcha. Well, I'm off, then. Good luck with all those dogs. I think it's fabulous, what you're doing."

"Thanks."

Ivy winked. "And now you'll look fabulous doing it."

"Wow, CHECK *YOU* out." As Ivy drove away, Adam gave Brenda a long gaze that made her forget how cold it was outside. "You're ready for anything now."

She executed a spin, modeling the new jeans and sweater, jacket and boots. The boutique bag swung wide, disgorging a pair of spicy red undies onto the snowbank. "Oops," she said, rushing to scoop up the garment, hoping he hadn't seen.

"And I mean anything," Adam said.

Oh. He'd seen.

"Watch what Olaf can do," Will exclaimed. "Just watch! Watch!"

"Did you teach him something new?"

Will took out a treat. "Olaf," he said. "*Sit.*"

The dog responded right away, plunking himself down in front of the boy.

"Good work," Brenda said. "What a lucky dog to have you for a teacher."

"Dad says he has to stay on the leash. Why doesn't Tim have to stay on the leash?"

"Because I worked and worked to teach him to stay with me and to come when I call."

"Can you teach Olaf?" asked Will.

"You and your dad can. It takes lots of practice."

"Can we practice now, Dad?" Will tugged at his father's hand. "Huh? Huh?"

"Sorry, man," Adam said. "I told Miss Brenda I'd help out with her van."

"Aw." Will dug his boot into a pile of snow.

Adam turned to Brenda. "I think we've got a plan with Ray Tolley."

"The snowplow guy," she recalled.

"And also the tow truck guy."

"I want to go in the tow truck," said Will, bouncing up and down and kicking up the snow. Olaf swirled around and tugged at the leash. "Can I go? Huh? Huh? And ride in the tow truck?"

"Sorry, buddy. It doesn't have a car seat."

"Aw," he said again, and his woeful expression was almost comical.

Brenda felt terrible, because her situation had already called the kid's dad away on his birthday. "I have an idea. I wonder if his car seat could be moved into the tow truck. Because we're going to need all the help we can get."

"Yesss. I want to help! Pleeeease!"

Adam regarded her with raised eyebrows. "That's nice of you," he remarked.

"I'm not being nice. I just think a kid needs all the time with his dad that he can get."

ADAM LOADED UP an extra snow shovel, and they met the tow truck at the site of the crash. By now, the van was half buried in snowdrifts. As she made her way down the bank, Brenda was grateful for the new boots. She brushed against a nearby pine tree, causing the upper branches to drop their load of snow on her. She came up sputtering, but grateful that she'd opted for the warmer clothes Ivy had urged her to wear.

"Careful there," Adam said. "The snow can collapse under a tree and trap you." He extended a hand and hoisted her away from the tree.

"Noted," she said.

"It's called a tree well," Will said. "It can bury you alive!"

"That doesn't sound like much fun," Brenda said. "I'll be careful."

She was impressed by the way the little kid pitched right in with his pint-size snow shovel. She grabbed another shovel and flung scoops of snow down the riverbank. The thought that they could have gone into the river made her heart skip a beat. What if they had? They would have been icebergs by the time they were found. The very thought made Brenda shudder. *I would never have gotten a chance to publish my book*, she thought. *I would never have had a child.*

There was too much she hadn't done. Too much she'd put off. Too much she'd forbidden herself to do. To feel, to experience. She had not yet made her mark on the world. Other than her mother and sister, there was no one who had borne witness to her life, whose heart would be changed by her passing.

"Thanks for your help," Adam said. "Ray and I are going to hook the cables to the tow truck's winch. How about you and Will watch from over there?" He gestured toward the bridge.

"Good idea." Brenda started up the bank. After a few steps, she noticed Will had stayed behind. She turned back to see him standing still, one hand extended toward her, his expression reproachful. "Oh, hey," she said. "Let me give you a hand."

They made their way up to the bridge deck. One of her spent flares from the night before protruded from the snow, and she picked it up in her free hand, shivering at the memory.

Will looked up at her. "You're real cold."

"I am. I come from the South and I'm not used to the snow. You look nice and warm in that snowsuit."

"Yep," he said cheerfully. His bright blue eyes widened as Ray climbed into the cab of the tow truck. "I like big trucks."

"Trucks are awesome," she agreed.

"Big trucks."

"We'd better step out of the way, kiddo." Brenda held out her hand. "They're going to try to set the van upright. See how it's on its side now?"

"I wanna go in the truck," said Will.

"You'll have a chance after they get the van up the bank," she said. "Let's watch from over here."

He grasped her hand, and she took him behind a concrete barrier. Adam gave her a thumbs-up sign, then stood back while Ray put the truck in gear and crept forward. The cables stretched taut.

Brenda clutched Will's shoulders. "Check it out."

"Yeah! It's cool. It's really really cool."

She held her breath while the cables strained. The truck's big tires churned forward. Slowly, the van tipped and then landed on all fours, shaking like a bear coming out of hibernation.

"Yay!" Will jumped up and down. "It worked! Yay for the truck!"

The layers of snow fell away from the van. Dolly's Christmas decorations were still intact, but they looked sad, somehow. Cold and sad and abandoned. Having a bouncy little kid by her side lifted Brenda's mood, though. She was encouraged when Ray and Adam managed to draw the van up the bank and onto the road.

"Great work, guys," she said, beaming at them both. "Can I get in and see if we're back in business?"

The driver's-side door was crusted with snow and dirt. Adam pulled it open and held out his hand while Brenda climbed into the driver's seat. She gave the key a turn, and to her surprise, the engine started as soon as she turned the key in the ignition.

"Incredible," she called to Adam. "I was not expecting that. Should I just drive it to the vet clinic?"

"Sorry, no," Adam said. "It might be too damaged to drive. We'll need to get it checked out at the shop."

She sighed, emitting a frosty breath. "Good point." She culled through the jumble inside the van and found her backpack and suitcase.

"Tell you what. You and Will ride with Ray and I'll meet you at the garage."

"How's that sound?" Brenda asked Will. "Want to ride in the tow truck with me?"

"Yes, yes, *yes!*" Will jumped around in a circle.

They secured his car seat in the cab of the tow truck. Will scrambled in and expertly clipped the belts. "This is the best day of my life," he crowed. "The best day in the world. The best day ever."

Brenda couldn't help smiling. "I like the way you think, kiddo."

"I'm not thinking," he said. "I'm just being happy."

"Well, that sounds even better," she said.

Date with a Spreadsheet

I'll look at your spreadsheet on one condition," Adam said to Brenda. He had hurried back from dropping Will off at his mom's. He wanted to catch Brenda before she made other plans.

"You have a condition?" she asked.

He tried not to look at her like a wolf eyeing a lamb chop.

"Making me look at a spreadsheet is asking a lot," he said. "So yeah. I have a condition. But you're going to like it. Let me take you for a drink and a bite to eat at Hilltop Tavern. I'll check out your spreadsheet there."

Adam could see her waver. He forced himself to give her time to consider the offer. He had only just met Brenda, but he already knew she came with a hard, protective shell around her. That, and the fact that she was independent, determined, athletic, and gorgeous, and he wanted to know her better. He wanted to massage her shoulders. Inhale the scent of her hair. Rest his hand on the small of her back as they walked into a room where he could introduce her to his friends. He wanted to—

"You want to take me and my spreadsheets for a drink," she said.

He actually wanted to do more than that, but he had to start somewhere. There was something about this girl. Something that awakened a part of him that had been slumbering for far too long. He had to get to know her. And if that meant sitting through her spreadsheet agenda, then he was willing.

"I do," he said.

"But—"

"Come on. It's been a long day and you need a break."

He liked the way she softened. Her neck and shoulders relaxed, and her mouth curved into a smile. "Deal," she said, handing him Olaf's leash. "I'll grab my laptop."

"Meet you out front in fifteen." He headed off to the garage, whistling in the cold air. His mom and Rick had volunteered to keep an eye on Olaf and Tim.

While Adam got ready, he gathered up Will's artwork from the dining room table—a picture of Olaf bravely fighting a dinosaur. *Miss you, buddy*, Adam thought. Will was at Suzanne's celebrating what they called Second Birthday. Normally, Adam struggled with loneliness on the days without Will. The kid filled his whole world with exuberant energy. His spirited nature knew no bounds as he rushed headlong into spontaneous play. Adam loved even Willy's sadness and frustration, because it usually stemmed from too much enthusiasm, too much imagination, too much excitement about even the smallest matter, like riding in a tow truck.

Some of the women Adam had dated didn't seem to know what to do around Will. They seemed overwhelmed by his playfulness. Some were even intimidated by it, or wanted to suppress it. What they ended up suppressing was Adam's interest in them.

On the dating apps he had tried, there were codes. "Loves children" too often meant she loved the *idea* of children. But when a child appeared in the flesh, in all his noisy, squirming glory, the enthusiasm tended to wane.

Brenda, on the other hand, seemed to be a natural with Will. She took genuine pleasure in indulging him, from including him in the tow truck adventure to helping him build a snow fort when they got home to showing him more tricks to practice with Olaf. Her interactions with him didn't seem to be performative or contrived.

It didn't hurt that she had a fantastic laugh, the kind that started softly and built to an infectious crescendo. It didn't hurt that she looked like one of the girls from the flagrantly un-PC calendars that hung in the locker room at the station. And it didn't hurt that she seemed to blush every time she caught him staring at her.

Adam warmed up the car and brought it around to the front of the main house. When Brenda came out on the front porch, his heart skipped a beat. She was a vision in snug jeans and new boots, a soft, fuzzy sweater that hugged her figure, a puffy jacket, and a hat that surrounded her face like a picture frame.

He jumped out and hurried to open the car door for her. "Wow," he said. "You look like a million bucks."

"Thanks. I feel like I spent a million bucks shopping with your sister. Ivy is such an enabler."

"Totally worth it," he said. "You look fantastic."

Brenda buckled up, looking out the window as they headed to town. "Thanks. I wasn't being very practical," she said. "I won't have a lot of use for winter clothes in Houston."

The one thing Adam didn't find attractive about her—she lived thousands of miles away. Not only that, she seemed eager to get back, claiming a pathological aversion to winter and Christmas.

The Hilltop Tavern was warm and buzzy with happy-hour patrons. Adam was glad he had called ahead for a booth table in a quiet corner. He greeted a few friends as they passed through the bar, garnering speculative looks from some of the guys. When he took her coat, his hands brushed over her shoulders, and she felt as soft and warm as a plush toy.

"I'm going to guess your favorite cocktail," he said, watching her settle into the booth and peruse the menu.

She smiled across the table at him. "I'm all ears. And I do have a favorite."

"Let's see . . . Not a cosmo. That's too predictable."

"Correct—cosmos are too sweet for my taste."

"Then I'm going to rule out a mojito and anything made with rum." He studied her face, thinking he'd never seen such pretty eyes on a woman. "I'm going to go out on a limb and guess it's a whiskey drink, like maybe a Manhattan or an old-fashioned."

"Old-fashioned it is," she said. "If it's made properly. Does that make me hopelessly boring and predictable?"

"Nope. You're an old-fashioned girl. I think it's sexy when a woman drinks whiskey."

"I had not heard that before."

The phone in his pocket made a quick, nearly silent buzz. He ignored it. "You're going to love Nadine's old-fashioned—the Orchard. It comes smoked with applewood."

"Now that," she said, "intrigues me."

"It'll soothe your cares away."

Adam ordered two of them. Each drink came under a glass dome with a smoking bit of applewood and a toasted marshmallow on a toothpick.

Brenda gasped with pleasure. "This looks amazing," she said. "Okay, I'm starting to like your freezing cold, Christmas-excess town a little bit."

"Hard to resist," he agreed and touched the rim of his glass to hers. "Cheers, Brenda. Consider this your proper welcome to Avalon."

She tasted the drink. Her shoulders relaxed visibly, and she gave a little smile. "Wow, that's delicious," she said.

"Delicious enough to tell me why you can't stand winter and Christmas?"

Her eyes shifted to and fro, the look of a trapped animal. "I didn't think you'd remember asking me about that."

"You said you'd tell me more about your Christmas hang-up if I plied you with alcohol. So, I'm plying. And just so you know, I remember everything from the first moment I met you," he said. "And maybe that sounds like a line, but it's not." It really wasn't. If Adam had learned anything from the demise of his marriage, it was to be honest with his feelings. "Anyway, I won't interrogate you. It's okay if you don't feel like sharing."

She gazed at him across the table. He could study those pretty eyes all evening. They were deep amber, the color of his favorite beer. In his line of work, he'd developed ways to read a stranger's expression. In Brenda's face, he sensed uncertainty, and a subtle, wavering urge to trust.

"Spreadsheet first," she said.

"Deal."

She moved around to Adam's side of the booth and sat next to him, taking out a pen and a manila folder. She smelled so damn nice. The girl smell. It had been a long time since he had been turned on by the way a woman smelled.

"I've got ten dogs to deliver," she said, laying out several pages of forms. "I need to map out a route to each home. But with the van in the shop, I'm going to have to rent something. Is there a place where I can find a big van in Avalon?"

"Nope, too small. You'd have to go over to New Paltz or Kingston, maybe." He could feel her tensing up again. She clicked and unclicked the pen in her hand.

"Listen, I meant what I said this morning. I'm here to help. I'm going to help you take the dogs to their families. We can use my Land Cruiser," he said. "It'll just mean multiple trips, but we'll get the job done."

He felt the tension ease from her as she leaned toward him. "Adam, really? Really? It's a big job. Are you serious?"

"Of course. I'm happy to help you with your dogs." *More than happy*, he thought. He wanted to spend time with this girl. He wanted to know her. It had been a long time since he had felt a spark of attraction this intense. Sure, she lived a million miles away, but he didn't dwell on that. He wanted to hang out with her. Bring back that smile that flashed every once in a while.

"That's so nice, Adam. Thank you."

"You seem surprised," he said.

"I'm just getting over a divorce, remember? I'm not used to guys being helpful. Or nice."

"I do remember those days," he said. "Took me a year after my divorce to trust someone being nice to me."

"Ah. So it's not just me."

"You're going to be okay, Brenda Malloy," he said. "Sooner than you think, I bet. According to my mother, I'm definitely nice. Also trustworthy. We can start right now by taking a look at the addresses, right?"

"Good idea. Since you know the area, you can help me figure out the new delivery schedule. Then I'll email all the forever homes."

The thought of delivering a new dog to each family was incredibly appealing to Adam. There was something so elemental and selfless in the urge to rescue dogs.

"You're frowning again," he said as Brenda studied her list.

"I'm thinking about Buzz," she said. "The greyhound that ran away. I phoned Mr. Jones today and explained that I'd need an extra day before I could come and get the dog from him."

"Let me guess. The old guy doesn't want to give that dog up."

"Exactly. And even though I explained that Buzz has been promised to the couple that chose him and paid the adoption fees, Mr. Jones has a finders-keepers mindset. He's sure it's a Christmas miracle. So this could get sticky. The folks who adopted him . . ." She found their name on her list. "The Haven family. They seem perfect for Buzz."

"Maureen and Eddie Haven?"

"You know them?"

"A bit, yes. Maureen's the town librarian. Big into community theater. Eddie's a musician. He was some kind of famous child star back in the day, but now I think he writes songs and produces music. They've got a couple of school-age kids. They seem great." Like most emergency workers, Adam knew more than most people about the private lives of people in the community. He knew who got in fights. Who drove drunk or high. Who was careless with hazardous materials. Who did lousy things to their partners or their kids. Families like the Havens, who had no record of emergency calls, were either safety-minded or plain lucky.

He wasn't at liberty to tell her what he knew about another family on her list—the Cullens. They were a troubled couple. Vance Cullen had a mean streak, mean enough that his wife had called for help more than once.

Brenda cradled her drink and stared at the list on the table. "Well, on the application, the Havens said they've always wanted to rescue a greyhound. Eddie has taken up running and his son is on the track team." Brenda drummed her fingers on the table. "They seem like the ideal family for Buzz. But now Lester Jones wants that dog."

Adam pictured the old man, alone in his cozy winter lodge, convinced that Buzz was one of the miracles of the season. "I bet Mr. Jones would reimburse them for the fees."

"The Havens want a dog," Brenda said. "Not a reimbursement. Do you think the two of them would be willing to have a conversation about this?"

"Seems like the next logical step," said Adam. "There's no shortage of dogs needing homes, right? Maybe Mr. Jones or the Havens would be willing to wait for a different dog."

"I'm going to visit Dolly first thing in the morning. She'll know what to do."

Adam's phone grumbled in his pocket. Another text message. He ignored it. "I have a feeling you'll be able to figure this out. So," he said, "let's see what we can do for these other dogs. And just so you know, what you're doing is awesome, Brenda."

She gave him that lovely-eyed smile. "Well, thanks."

"I mean it. You're giving these dogs a new life, and the families are getting a gift without price, right at Christmas. Say what you will about Christmas, but you're like the human version of Santa Claus."

The smile wavered. "I wouldn't go that far. That's the last thing I want to be."

He sensed that he'd struck a sour note. "Let's go down the list," he suggested. "Tomorrow's going to be a fine day."

The name *Suzanne Roberts* jumped out at him. Well.

"Suzanne Roberts is getting a dog?" he asked Brenda.

"She is. Vixen, a little spaniel mix." Her gaze shifted away from him, then back. "Suzanne is Will's mother, right? Ivy introduced us at Zuzu's Petals."

"Damn. I didn't realize she was getting a dog too." Adam's stomach churned the way it tended to do when it came to Will's other life. His son lived in two separate worlds, and sometimes—a lot of the time—that made Adam crazy. Half the time, Will was gone as though he didn't exist.

Brenda gave him a probing look. "Your little boy is getting two dogs. Seems like you're surprised by that?"

He nodded. "Suzanne didn't tell me. I mean, she's not required to, but I let her know about Olaf as soon as you approved my application. Anyway, that's . . . kind of one of our things. I never hold anything back, and she never shares. Even something as simple as saying she's getting a dog. It's like she keeps the whole world on a need-to-know basis."

"Oh! Well, that's . . ." Brenda seemed flustered. "Is it going to be awkward, you taking the dog to her place? I can do it on my own if—"

"It's all right," Adam said. "We actually get along better now that we don't live together."

"That's good. That you get along, I mean. And I think Willy is a pretty lucky kid to have two dogs, right? One at each place?"

"Sure," he conceded. "I like your positive attitude."

"Anyway, Vixen is a lovely little dog."

"Named Vixen?" He was skeptical.

"She looks a bit like a fox—her reddish coloring and white-tipped tail and black feet. But she's supersweet—about three years old, good with kids, good on a leash."

Adam knocked back the rest of his drink. Why couldn't Suzanne level with him about the dog? Because she was Suzanne. She held things back. Kept things from him, even things that didn't matter.

Frustrated, he forced his attention to the other dogs on the list. It didn't take long to organize the delivery schedule. "We have a plan, then," he said to Brenda. "Now, about your Christmas issue."

She shifted uncomfortably and sipped her drink.

"I don't mean to put you on the spot," he said. "You really don't have to explain yourself."

"It's all right. You held up your end of the bargain," she said.

"Is it about your trouble last Christmas Eve?"

"Oh, my marriage, you mean. Unfortunately, that started going south long before Christmas. I just didn't realize it." She took a healthy swallow of her drink. "That night only reaffirmed my reasons for avoiding Christmas." She turned toward him, and her eyes shone with distant memories. "When I was nine years old, I was the world's biggest believer in Christmas."

He smiled. "Weren't we all?"

She nodded. "Some of my friends were starting to have suspicions about the existence of Santa Claus, but I was a firm holdout. We were stationed in Alaska that year, and I knew with one hundred percent certainty that he was only a few hundred miles away."

Brenda rested her chin in her hand. "The reason my little sister and I were such true believers was that our dad made it his mission every Christmas to convince us that Santa was real." A wistful smile curved her mouth. "Each Christmas Eve, after we went to bed, there were indisputable signs. Sleigh bells coming from somewhere outside. The sound of reindeer hooves on the roof. A *ho ho ho* that sounded nothing like my dad. And in the morning there would be tracks in the snow— hoofprints and sleigh rail tracks that somehow magically stopped right where the sleigh took off into the sky. No wonder Cissy and I believed so hard."

"Your sister's name is Cissy."

She nodded. "Makes it easy to remember. She is two years younger than me. There was a kid at school, Jack Maynard, who claimed to have all this evidence that Santa didn't exist."

"Jack Maynard," Adam said. "There's always a Jack Maynard."

"Right? So that year, I was determined to prove it once and for all. I was supersecretive about my Christmas wish. I made a big deal of saying I wanted Santa to bring me a toboggan. I wrote a long letter describing it, and I insisted on taking it to the post office myself."

"Let me guess. You secretly changed your wish."

"Exactly. I even steamed open the envelope and replaced my letter with what I really wanted. A dog. We had been without a dog for a couple of years, and I yearned for one. My parents kept putting off adopting a new pet, so I figured I'd circumvent them by going straight to Santa. I knew it was a risk. But I went for it. I tried to stay awake on Christmas Eve. Lost the battle, same as I did every year. And then Cissy and I heard them. The sleigh bells. The hoofbeats. The ho ho ho."

Oh no no no, thought Adam, feeling a prickle of apprehension.

She took a deep breath and another long sip of her drink.

Adam caught Nadine's eye and signaled for another one.

"A couple of minutes later," Brenda said, "I heard my mother scream. It was a sound I'd never heard before. I can still hear that scream."

"Aw, Brenda." Adam's heart hurt for her. "What happened? An accident? Did he fall?"

She nodded. "He was on the roof, and he slipped. Hit his head on a concrete planter that was partially buried in the snow. They say he died instantly. Sometimes I worry that they said that just to soften the blow."

"Damn," he said, too easily able to picture the chaos. "I'm so sorry that happened. I wish I could go back and comfort that kid."

Nadine brought the second drink to Brenda, and she gratefully accepted it with a brief smile. "We were all in shock. I blamed myself. Maybe I still do. If I hadn't been so determined to challenge my own belief, he wouldn't have gone to such lengths to get me to believe, you know?"

"I don't know, actually," Adam said. "Your dad sounds like a guy who made it his mission to bring joy to his kids. As a father, I can totally relate to that." Adam had dedicated his life to being the kind of dad his own father had never been. Adam lived for Will's smiles, his random chatter, his unbounded exuberance.

"Oh, and here's a painful irony," Brenda said. "I did end up getting my Christmas wish. At about six in the evening on Christmas Day, a family friend came over with a chocolate brown Lab named Chaco. My dad's plan was to bring him out on Christmas morning and surprise us. Chaco was one of the best dogs I've ever known. I was crazy about that guy. Sometimes I think he was the one thing that kept me from going insane with grief. He lived until my sophomore year in college."

"I'm sorry, Brenda. And sorry I made you talk about these things." Adam got a lump in his throat, imagining her pain.

"Don't be. It's . . . it'll always be part of my story. I don't think I'll ever get over the guilt." She swirled her fingertip in a drop of liquid on the table, her expression bleak.

"Hey," he said. "I appreciate you telling me what happened. I'm sorry he died. But you were a true believer, like any kid. We all were at one time."

"But I pushed—"

"You didn't. Do me a favor. Imagine your father's death was simply a tragic accident, caused by nothing but horrible luck. Sounds like you had a fantastic dad. Maybe you could decide to forgive yourself for believing in Christmas."

She turned toward him, her gaze unfocused, tears pooling in her eyes. "I don't think I can do that."

He touched her hand briefly, though he wanted to hold on longer. "You know what I'd like to hear about?"

She frowned with a look of suspicion. "Now what?"

"I'd like to know how he *lived*."

He heard her breath catch. She blinked and then regarded him with softened eyes. "It's been a long time since anyone asked me that."

"I'd like to know what he was like. What was his name? Besides being an awesome dad, what else was he?"

She smiled and sipped her drink. "His name was Jonathan Malloy. He was a high school teacher and basketball coach. His favorite books were *The Iliad* and *The Odyssey*—really. He read them aloud to us even when we were little. He was a pretty good skier. He only knew how to cook a few things, so when my mom was on deployment we lived on pancakes and buttered noodles, fish sticks and fruit. His favorite season was winter. He loved the stillness of the snow. And he loved Christmas. I mean, he *loved* Christmas. He had an amazing singing voice, and his favorite carol was 'Adeste Fideles.'"

"Wow," said Adam. "Wish I'd known him."

"I wish the whole world could have known him. The world would be a better place. And maybe we'd all still believe in Santa Claus."

"Tell me more about your family. Mom was in the military. Your sister's name is Cissy."

"We're an ordinary family, I suppose you could say. Mom remarried when Cissy and I were in high school. My stepdad is in sales, and he retired this year, same time as my mom. We're just . . . like I said. Ordinary."

"There is nothing ordinary about you," he said, the words tumbling ahead of thought.

Her eyes widened, and she caught her breath, and a smile curved her lips. "Um, thank you?"

"I mean it." He touched his thumb to her worried forehead.

She swirled the ice in her glass. "Anyway. That is way too much information about me."

"Oh, it's not nearly enough. I could listen to you all night."

"I'll spare you. Tell me about *your* dad. Fair's fair."

"Trevor Bellamy. Youngest of four sons of George Bellamy. And actually, my dad died in the snow, too. An avalanche about ten years ago."

"Oh my gosh. That must have been a shock."

"Totally. He and my mom were both caught in the slide."

"That's how she hurt herself?"

"Yes."

"Adam, I'm sorry. What was he like? Trevor Bellamy."

"Not quite the family man yours was. Or maybe *twice* the family man yours was. My dad was . . . Well, to be honest, he was a two-family man. Turns out he had a woman and a kid in France."

"Oh boy." She cringed a little.

"It was quite a revelation, on the heels of our mom being injured. We've all made our peace with it by now. My half brother, Simon, works up at the ski resort, in fact."

"Families can be complicated," she said.

He couldn't stop staring at her lips. "Keeps life interesting."

Brenda nodded and looked away. Adam really wanted to put his arm around her. Take her hand. She was skittish, though. He could see the sadness and distress hovering around her, an invisible but tangible energy.

And his phone kept nudging him with text messages, which he ignored.

"Are you sure you don't need to check that?" she asked.

"There's a special tone for work, and one for Will's mom. Everything else is secondary."

"Your phone's been going off a lot," she said.

Oh. He was hoping she hadn't noticed the constant buzzing. "I know what it's about," Adam confessed. "I'm supposed to go to something at the station tonight."

"Well, good grief, then you should go to your something," she said. "I don't want to keep you from an obligation."

He didn't want an obligation. He wanted to spend more time getting to know Brenda Malloy. "It's not important."

"The expression on your face says it is. What's going on, Adam?"

"Like I said, it's a thing at the station tonight."

"Well, hell's bells, you have to go."

"I'd rather hang out with you."

"Look, you don't have to entertain me. You can drop me off at your mother's and—"

"I don't want to drop you off."

"I don't want to make you miss your work thing."

"Okay, I have a proposal for you," he said.

Her cheeks bloomed with a blush. "A proposal," she repeated.

"I wanted to ask you earlier, but I didn't want to put you on the spot."

"You're being very cryptic. Tell me more about this thing you're ignoring."

"The station's annual party is tonight."

"A Christmas party. Go ahead. You can say it. You're going to a Christmas party."

"It's usually not too Christmassy," he said, lying through his teeth.

"Just how Christmassy is it?"

"It's—you know—the usual stuff . . ."

"Let me guess—a big bowl of punch that involves cranberries and cinnamon. Ugly Christmas sweaters. A white elephant gift exchange. Cookies with sprinkles. And music that haunts your dreams."

Adam sighed. "I think you just filled the entire bingo card. I'm supposed to bring a white elephant gift and a dessert." He hesitated, then took a risk. "I know Christmas is not your thing. But . . . suppose you come with me."

"Adam, I'm grateful for your help, but—"

"If it's as bad as you fear, I'll take you home right away."

She regarded him for a long moment. Then she carefully put away her folder of paperwork. "Do I have to wear an ugly sweater?"

"There isn't a sweater in the world that could make you look ugly," he said. "What you're wearing is perfect."

Brenda caught her breath. Her teeth briefly touched her lower lip as if to keep in a secret.

"Last call for happy hour," Nadine announced from the bar.

"Another drink?" he offered her.

She smiled and shook her head. Damn, he could live on that smile.

"No, thank you," she said. "I am happy enough."

I Saw Mommy Kissing
Santa Claus

Despite her determination to avoid Christmas, Brenda realized she was about to be subjected to an abundance of holiday cheer. The two cocktails she had consumed at the Hilltop Tavern helped to ease her nerves about the situation. Or maybe it was the person who was dragging her, neither kicking nor screaming, to a party. She felt warm and relaxed as they drove to the station.

It had been tempting to insist that Adam take her home after happy hour. She could simply retreat to her luxurious pink guest room, curl up with her dog, and write the next chapter of her story.

But no. The least she could do was be an agreeable guest. He was going above and beyond to help her sort out the dogs, and she owed him a debt of gratitude. And—okay, yes, she thought—he was hot and exceptionally kind. A girl could do worse than flirt with a hot paramedic who was a good listener and who gave a great shoulder massage. A harmless flirtation. How dangerous could that be?

She knew it was harmless; her heart was safe with him. Safe from being hurt, because he would never own it. He'd never have emotional power over her. In a matter of days, she would be on her way back to Texas. She and Adam Bellamy would probably never meet again.

The tiniest wisp of sadness crept in, but Brenda shoved the feeling aside. She shouldn't have had that second cocktail. It made her vulnerable to sentiments that were better left alone—yearning and regret. A sense that something was missing.

She'd already let him see too much of her. During that reckless conversation at the bar, she had spoken of things she rarely discussed, like the story of losing her dad, and the way it had affected her.

Now she wondered what her father would have said to her about this situation. What advice would he have offered?

Twenty years after losing him, she still remembered his last words to her as he was tucking her in on Christmas Eve. She had been fretful: *What if it's not real? What if there really isn't a Santa?*

It's Christmas Eve, remember? her dad had said. *That's when the magic happens. Trust me. I know about these things.*

Brenda really did try to forgive her nine-year-old self for wanting something too much, but she couldn't escape the thought that if she hadn't wanted Santa to be real, her father would not have died that night. The point was proven over and over again as she grew up—a pattern. Whenever she wanted something too much, she wound up disappointed.

Every year after her father had died, she'd had to suffer through the sound of sleigh bells, the cheery greetings, the songs and joyous celebrations. As a girl, she'd wanted to scream at the other kids—*He's not real, Santa isn't real, he's just a lie. A dangerous lie.*

By the time she met Grant, Brenda had learned to temper her desires. For several years, the marriage had worked quite well. Until it didn't. The fact that everything had fallen apart at Christmas only confirmed her conviction that the holiday was her Kryptonite.

Adam pulled up at the Sky River Bakery, which bustled with shoppers perusing the display cases. "Be right back," he said. "I need to grab something for the potluck."

While he waited his turn at the counter, she looked around his car. It was a typical guy's car, with a cluttered console, papers and receipts stuck in the visor. There was a school picture of Will, whose wide, crooked smile made him look just like Adam, and a December calendar page with Will's birthday highlighted in bold. She noticed a flyer from the parks department with a couple of items circled—ice climbing, and conversational Spanish.

Stop snooping, she told herself, shifting her gaze out the window. *Stop wanting to know more about this person.*

Adam returned a few minutes later with a box. Brenda nearly fainted from the smell of cardamom, ginger, and molasses. "Gingerbread cookies?" she asked.

"Yep. You'd better try one now, because they'll disappear fast."

She sneaked one from the box, a ginger angel with wings of white icing. A soft moan escaped her before she could stop it. "This is delicious," she said. "It might be the best cookie ever."

"Yeah? Maybe it'll make you believe in Christmas again."

She savored every last bite of the cookie. It truly was a mouthful of pure Christmas, the perfect balance of spices and sugar, evoking the scents and flavors of the season.

"One thing is certain," she said. "You're going to be a hero at your party for bringing these."

"You think?" He smiled as he drove through the twinkling, picture-perfect town. "Well, thanks for coming along. You're a good sport. I know this sort of event is not exactly your thing."

"I'll be fine," she said. "This isn't even the first holiday party I've attended this year. There was one in Houston—a gala fundraiser for Underdogs."

"Well, I'm glad you survived. Hope it wasn't too painful."

"Oh, it was painful all right," she assured him. "My ex was there with the underpants woman. I found out they're engaged."

"Oh. Ouch," he said. "I'm sorry that happened."

"I figure if I can survive that, I can survive your Christmas part—" She broke off as he pulled up to the station. It was practically on fire with colored lights and decorations. On the rooftop was Santa's sleigh with a full complement of reindeer. Santa himself was waving from the chimney.

"—or not," she muttered under her breath.

"Yeah, sorry. Sometimes when we're on duty, we have a lot of extra time on our hands." He parked the car, then came around and opened the door for Brenda, holding her hand as she stepped out. She liked his strength and the way he smelled. She liked it a bit too much. She held the cookie box in front of her like a shield.

He went around back and fetched a couple of wrapped gifts, pausing to shed his parka and put on a sweater. Noticing her look, he grinned. "How do I look?"

"That sweater."

"I know, right?" He spread his arms wide and turned in a circle. The sweater was bristling with tinsel and blinking lights, and a nightmarish image of Santa locked in combat with Krampus.

"Is it bad that I'm not wearing one?" she asked.

"Nah. This one is ugly enough for both of us." He picked up a couple of parcels.

"You're bringing two white elephant gifts."

"I had an extra one in case someone new shows up."

"You rat!" She punched him lightly in the arm. "You planned for me to come to this thing with you all along."

"I wouldn't say I planned it," he said. "Hoped. I definitely hoped. Thanks for being my date tonight, Brenda."

"Whoa. This is not a date," she said. "I am not your date."

"Maybe," he said. "Maybe not. It all depends on how it ends."

Before she could react to that, Adam held the door wide for her. The party was already in full swing. The station house was jammed with people in their sweaters and sparkles, sampling the hors d'oeuvres and sipping red punch and prosecco in plastic flutes. The spread of food was eclectic—potstickers, wiener rolls, cheese balls, charcuterie and crudites, pans of lasagna and trays of sliders. Adam parked his cookies on the dessert table alongside cupcakes and brownies.

Against her will, Brenda was sucked into party mode. And she was forced to admit that it was a good party. The crew and their guests were filled with cheer, probably thanks to the spiked punch and free-flowing beer and wine. Adam introduced her around, and his friends seemed interested in talking to her, keen to hear about Underdogs. The white elephant game was ridiculous and hilarious, featuring bath salts, a snow globe, hairy foot slippers, tea towels with obnoxious sayings, flashlights and tools. She was impressed that Adam had brought something reasonably useful—a stocking cap with a blinking light for night visibility, and a water bottle with a built-in filter. After all the swapping was done, she ended up with a scented candle, and Adam was the proud owner of a new beer helmet.

There was a footrace involving spoons and plastic ornaments. The stakes were high because the loser of each round was forced to sing a karaoke Christmas song. And Brenda lost her round. "I blame those two drinks," she said to Adam.

"No excuses," he said. "You lost, fair and square."

She did a perp walk up to the raised dais, knowing that if she balked, she would be publicly shamed. Might as well get it over with.

The song that came up was one of the cringiest—"I Saw Mommy Kissing Santa Claus." She forced her way through each line, hamming it up to make the performance even cheesier, to the delight of her listeners. People joined in at the end and she earned a big round of applause. After making an elaborate bow, she scuttled down from the dais.

Adam put his arm around her and gave her a squeeze. "Well done. You have quite a set of pipes."

"Choir and glee club all through school," she said.

"Come on," he said. "Admit it. You do like Christmas. Just a little."

I like you, she thought, but didn't say so aloud.

Brenda was refilling her glass to recover from the singing ordeal when an older woman came over and introduced herself. "Elspeth Morton," she said, indicating her name tag. "It's really nice to see Adam with someone."

Was he *with* Brenda? Were they together? An explanation seemed too involved, so Brenda just smiled and said, "Thanks."

"So how did you two meet?" Elspeth asked.

"It was an accident," Brenda said.

"An accident?"

"Literally. We met by accident."

"Brenda . . ." Elspeth peered at her stick-on name tag and frowned. "Oh! You're *that* Brenda, then. Brenda with the twelve dogs."

"That's me."

"Well, now, Brenda." Elspeth nodded sagely. "It's good to meet you in person. I work in dispatch."

"Oh! Are you the one who took my call when we went off the road?"

"Yep, that was me. I nearly pissed myself when you said there were fourteen in the car."

"Sorry about the misunderstanding. And thanks for sticking with me even when the call kept dropping. I feel so lucky that you were able to keep track of our location."

"Is your friend all right, then?"

"She will be. She broke her leg, and they fixed her up at the hospital. She's going to her sister's house to recuperate."

"And the pups? Are they okay?"

"Yes, they're at the veterinary clinic waiting to be taken to their families tomorrow. Adam volunteered to help me deliver them since my van is out of commission."

"Well, then. I'm glad you two met, even under the circumstances. You're adorable and so is Adam, and I think you're going to be great together."

Brenda couldn't help being curious. "Have you known Adam long?"

"Oh, yes. Ten years, at least. Here at the station, we're all so fond of that guy. We've been waiting for him to meet someone."

"You have? Why is that?" Brenda realized it was probably none of her business, but she was inappropriately curious about Adam Bellamy.

"He's got such a big heart. He's been pretty lonely since his divorce. I've watched him chasing love but not finding it. All of us want to see him in love again."

Brenda's cheeks warmed with a blush. "Well, I'm sure he appreciates your good wishes. But I'll be heading back to Texas as soon as I—"

"You are going to love Avalon," Elspeth blithely assured her. "It's such a friendly, charming little town. Enjoy your stay. And good luck with those dogs. You must feel exactly like Santa Claus, bringing joy to those families at Christmastime."

It was the last thing Brenda wanted to feel like, but she smiled and thanked the woman for her good wishes. It turned out Elspeth wasn't the only one who assumed she was Adam's new girlfriend. His co-workers insisted that he was a catch—one of the good guys, a family man, he checked all the boxes. A couple of guys applauded *his* taste, which should not have pleased her, but it did.

"Why is everyone so keen to see people paired off?" she wondered aloud, when a woman mentioned that Adam was the best cook at the station house.

"All the world loves a love story," the woman said. "Especially this time of year, right?"

"I . . . Sure, yes. That's right."

WHEN ADAM DROVE her home after the party, Brenda was in an exceptionally good mood.

"What's that smile?" he asked, looking over at her.

"I wasn't smiling."

"Yes, you were. I saw."

"Probably because I'm having a much better time tonight than I did last night."

"That's an extremely low bar. Come on, tell me tonight wasn't as bad as the other Christmas parties you went to."

She shook her head. "Not even close."

"It wasn't that bad at all, was it?"

"Well, the food was good. The caroling karaoke, not so much."

"Yeah, sorry about that. You should have done a better job balancing the ornament on that spoon." He chuckled as they drove up to the house. "Well. Thanks again for coming along."

"Hey, the dogs are going to need to go out for a run," Brenda said.

"That's right. First things first."

First before what? she wondered.

Olaf, Tim, and Bella were waiting eagerly in the mudroom. The moment Adam opened the door, they bolted outside and raced across the snow-covered lawn. Under the lavishly starry sky, they ran around madly and did their business.

"Olaf slept all night in his crate last night," Adam said. "He probably would have slept longer, but Willy got up early. He was so surprised when he came charging into my room like he does every morning. I wish you could have seen that kid's face. He was blown away. Here. Check it out. I got a little video on my phone."

Brenda leaned in close and watched the bit he'd captured. Will, in Spiderman pajamas, focused on the crate. "That's a dog," he said. "A *dog*."

"He's all yours, buddy," Adam said. "Happy birthday." His hand came down and unlatched the crate, and the dog shot out. "His name is Olaf," Adam told his son.

"Yay! A dog! Olaf!" Will giggled and fell over, and Olaf bowed down and licked his ear. The video cut off as the giggles crescendoed.

"What a moment," Brenda said. "You guys have a friend for life."

"That's the idea. Hey, are you warm enough?" Adam asked, stepping close to her.

"I am. Now that I have the right clothes, it's actually quite pleasant out here." She tipped back her head and looked at the bright sweep of stars. "It's certainly beautiful."

"Yeah," he said. "It is." But he wasn't looking at the sky.

The way he was studying her made Brenda feel warm and a little breathless.

"I hope you had a good time this evening," he said, "your aversion to Christmas notwithstanding."

"I liked meeting your friends, anyway," she told him.

"Everybody loved meeting you," he said. "I could tell. I was getting high fives from my workmates."

"High fives for what?"

"You're . . . different from other girls I've known."

"Different in what way?" She narrowed her eyes in suspicion, picturing the very feminine, perfectly groomed Suzanne.

"In a good way. Don't look at me like that. I'm just saying, other women I've known don't do stuff like drive all the way from Texas to deliver a load of dogs at Christmas. They're not writing novels or helping pull vans out of the snow."

"All I heard was how much your colleagues like you," she said.

"Seriously? I hope they had good things to say about me."

"They did. They told me all your secrets."

"Uh-oh. I have secrets?"

"Apparently not."

Brenda paused and glanced over at Adam, catching a glimpse of that smile. "You throw a mean line drive in baseball. You play piano and you speak French. You make the best homemade chili at the station. You're a family man—" She broke off, not wanting to finish what she'd heard—that he was essentially a family man without a family.

"A family man, but . . ." he prompted.

"Elspeth the dispatcher thinks you—" She stopped herself again.

"She thinks I what?" he asked. "Come on, I can take it."

Brenda ducked her head. "She thinks you need to fall in love. I believe she said you've been chasing love."

Adam was quiet for a few minutes. Despite the cold, Brenda felt a flush of warmth. She shouldn't have said anything.

"Chasing love all my life," he said. "Maybe due to my distant-father issues?"

"Well, she didn't say that, but—"

"She's not wrong," Adam said after a lengthy pause.

"About . . . ?"

"Me. Falling in love. I do want that. Doesn't everybody?" He turned to face her. "Don't you?"

She took a step back. "The falling part is fun," she admitted. "But when you land, then what? The staying part—that's more challenging. As we both know."

"But with the right person, it's not impossible," he said.

"The reality of love is this—it's scary because of the risk of loss."

Adam took her hand. "I wish that wasn't your takeaway from what happened to your dad."

"It's n— Maybe it is," she admitted. "All I know is, I never want to feel that kind of pain again, Adam. And so far, I have managed to avoid it."

He tilted his head to one side. "Say, would you like to come up to my place for a drink?"

Yes, she thought with every cell of her body.

"I'd love to," she said. "But I can't."

"You can't. Why not?"

"Because a drink is never just a drink."

He nodded. "Good point. I guess what I'm really asking is if you'd like to come up to my place, and I'll make a crackling fire, and fix you a drink. After that, we'll sit on the sofa and talk some more, and then if I'm incredibly lucky, we'll start making out. Yep. That's what I'm really asking."

She let out a snort of laughter. "God, Adam."

"TMI?"

"No, it's just . . . Actually, I appreciate your frankness. But a kiss is never just a kiss."

"So you don't want to sit by the fire and make out with me," he said.

"To be honest, I might like that after all."

"Whoa. Whoa whoa whoa." Adam's hand found hers. "Did I just hear you say you'd like that? You'd like to kiss me by the fire?"

I'd like to kiss you anywhere.

Despite the cold, Brenda's face grew warm. "Maybe," she said. "I might have implied something like that. I blame the two cocktails and that red punch."

"Nah," he said. "It's because of my irresistible charm. Admit it."

It was because in the past twenty-four hours, she'd felt more excitement about a guy than she ever had before. All day, Brenda had been trying to dismiss the feeling, because it was so powerful. An attraction like this felt edgy. Dangerous. *Risky.*

"Well, you're just full of confidence, aren't you?" she asked.

Adam's smile was a bit wistful. "No. I'm not. I'm really not. I gotta admit, my confidence has been shaken. I tried like hell to keep my marriage together, because oh my god, it felt like the one job I was supposed to succeed at—to create a safe, stable family for my little boy—was the one I failed at. I failed at the most fundamental level. So, no. To be brutally honest, I don't have much confidence in the romance depart—"

Brenda stopped him with a kiss. It was pure impulse, one that had been building all evening, but suddenly she couldn't hold back. He was a perfectly fine guy who shouldn't be running himself down. And she'd been wondering all evening what it would be like to kiss him.

It was even better than she'd anticipated—soft and warm and sexy and deeply evocative. She lingered a moment, then pulled slightly away. "Shut up," she whispered.

"That was cool," he said. Then he grinned. "Better than cool. I'm seeing stars."

"Yeah?" She ducked her head, leaning into him a little. "Listen, you haven't failed at anything. You're doing all right, Adam. I can tell."

"You can tell."

"Your kid is great. Your dog is . . . well, he's not great at the moment, but he will be someday soon. You have a job, a home, family nearby, and if you can handle this climate, you have a good life."

"You're right. I've got plenty to be happy about. Should we give it a shot, then?" He tipped her chin up to face him and offered that smile again. "Go up to my place?"

A small laugh escaped her. At least he was persistent. "Sorry, no. I need to get myself organized for tomorrow. Ten dogs are being delivered to ten forever homes, remember?"

"I do. And I promised to help. But that's tomorrow. Tonight, we're on a date."

"I told you before, this is not a date."

"And I told *you* it all depends on how it ends. Not gonna lie. I'm superattracted to you. It's crazy, right? We just met, but I can't stop thinking about you. Not in a creepy way, but just . . . I think about the sound of your voice, and the way your hair curls around your face, and your big, serious eyes and how they change when something lights you up, and the way you laugh. And after that kiss, I have a lot more to think about. Sorry, I'm not being very smooth about this. I really want to get to know you."

"That's . . . I'm . . . flattered, Adam. I like you, too. But what you need to know about me is that this situation"—she made a vague gesture around the snowy yard—"is temporary. As soon as I can, I'm heading back to Texas. I need to get back to . . ." Her voice trailed off. She couldn't stop looking at his lips. His eyes. The fall of hair over his brow. "Um, I forgot what I was talking about."

He looked back at her. One corner of his mouth lifted in a half smile.

"Then don't talk. We do better when we're just kissing," he said and pulled her into his arms.

Dog Delivery Day

On dog delivery day, Brenda got up before everyone else. There was a lot to accomplish, not the least of which was to figure out what to do about Buzz, who was still in the winter lodge with Lester Jones. She took a quick shower, then slipped on her light robe and went to the kitchen. No one else was around, but she found a fresh pot of coffee and some cinnamon rolls, still warm from the oven.

"I could get used to this," she said to Tim. She put some of his kibble in a bowl and set it on the floor.

"Morning," said a cheerful, deeply resonant voice. Covered in fresh powder, Adam Bellamy paused in the mudroom to stomp the snow from his boots.

Startled, Brenda stood up straight and checked the tie on her robe. "Oh! Uh... yes. Good morning." All rational thought disintegrated at the sight of him. In a thick ski parka, well-worn jeans, and snowmobile boots, he looked ready for anything. Through the window, she could see Olaf zooming around the garden.

When Adam smiled at Brenda, his expression hid nothing. He checked out her bare legs, his gaze lingering with unapologetic intensity. That intensity seemed to emanate a kind of heat.

"There's coffee," she said, quickly turning away. "And rolls. I was, um, going to have a bite to eat and get ready for a big day. Are you sure you're up for this?"

"A hundred percent. It'll be fun, right?"

"I think so. We're both novices at this, but Dolly swears it's the best part of the process."

"We're all set. My mom said she and Rick will watch Olaf and Tim today."

"That's great." Brenda let Tim out the back. "Give me a few minutes to get dressed, and then we'll get started."

She practically fled from the kitchen, feeling breathless just from talking with him. She was ridiculous, a grown woman suffering from a schoolgirl crush. There was a very undisciplined part of her that wished she had taken him up on his offer to go to his place last night. Their kiss had only made her long for more.

She combed her hair and thought about applying some makeup. Adam's ex-wife wore makeup like a model. *No*, Brenda thought. *Focus.* Today was about the dogs. Maybe just some lipstick. She dressed in her new leggings and a thick tunic sweater and boots. Then she grabbed Dolly's suitcase, a supply of dog treats, and the folder of adoption papers and vet records.

Adam had cleared out his SUV to make room for a few dogs at a time. "All set?" he asked as she stepped outside.

The cold air took her breath away. "Yikes. This weather."

"You prefer Houston."

"It's almost always warm there." She started walking to the car.

"And you like a warm climate."

"Doesn't everyone?"

"I like the seasons." He held the door for her. "I like being near my son."

So there it was. The immovable obstacle. Adam Bellamy wasn't going anywhere.

FAIRFIELD HOUSE B&B was a colorful Victorian mansion with a wrap-around porch and intricate trim framing the windows. The place oozed vintage charm. And of course, Christmas decorations. There were sprays of greenery, twinkling lights, and old-fashioned ornaments. No wonder Dolly liked spending the holidays here.

A ramp made of raw lumber covered half of the stairs leading up to the porch. Brenda hurried to the door, eager to see Dolly.

An exceedingly tall guy with a ponytail and a goatee opened the door for them. "You must be Brenda," he said. "I'm Bo. Bo—"

"Crutcher," she said, tilting her head to look up at him. "Wow, I'm a bit starstruck. I saw you pitch against the Astros."

"Hope I did a good job," said Bo, stepping back to bring them into a foyer filled with rich woodwork, inlaid floors, and chandeliers. He stuck out his hand to Adam. "Hey, man. Good to see you again. It's been too long. Merry Christmas, and come on in. We've got a VIP in the house. My mother-in-law's out shopping so they left me in charge of the patient. And fair warning. She's not very patient."

"I heard that," called a familiar voice. "Get yourself in here, partner."

Bo took them to a light-filled suite on the main floor. Dolly was propped in the middle of an antique four-poster bed, surrounded by books and magazines. There was a bay window with a sitting area, and coffee service on a tray.

"This is Adam Bellamy, Dolly," Brenda said. "We've brought your things from the van. Oh, and I brought some of your favorite licorice and some Diet Pepsi."

"Bless you," Dolly said. "You're the only one who understands me." She favored Adam with a smile of delight. "And you're Alice's son. We brought you a dog."

"That you did, ma'am," Adam said. "Olaf is fantastic. He's going to love it here." He placed her suitcase on a bench at the foot of the bed.

"Hey, I could use your help," Bo said to Adam. "The kids just left for school, and I've got two toys to put together. It'll only take a couple of minutes."

"You got it," Adam said. "We'll let you two go over the plan for the day."

The second he was gone, Dolly started fanning herself with an exaggerated gesture. "Holy smokes, Brenda."

Brenda grinned. "I know, right?"

"And he's the one who's helping you with the dogs."

"Uh-huh. I doubt you'll remember this, but Adam was there the night of the wreck. He's a paramedic."

"Really? That's fantastic. But you're right. I don't remember. It's all a blur."

"I was so worried about you. And then there were the dogs . . ." She told Dolly about the crazy ordeal they'd faced, cramming the dogs into the snowplow cab and hiking through the woods in search of Buzz.

"So we might have a problem," she said. "I called the guy who found Buzz yesterday and explained to him how this works. He listened to what I had to say, but he doesn't want to let that dog go."

"Shootfire," Dolly said.

"Exactly," Brenda said. "I also spoke to Maureen Haven, the woman who's adopting Buzz. She said she and her husband are glad someone found him in the woods, but obviously they're not keen to give him up."

"Of course they're not. Imagine that. When the poor dog's racing career didn't work out, nobody wanted him. Now he's got folks fighting over him."

"Suppose we introduce the Havens and Mr. Jones and come up with a solution together. They all seem like reasonable people."

"Let's hope the spirit of the season brings out the best in everyone," Dolly said. "I imagine it will. Christmas has a way of doing that." She studied Brenda for a moment. "So . . . Adam Bellamy."

"What's that tone?"

"You know that tone. He couldn't take his eyes off you just now. And by the way, you do look amazing. You've already been shopping?"

Brenda nodded. "At his ex-wife's boutique."

"Gotta love the small-town life," Dolly said, her eyebrows lifting in curiosity.

"I have a life in Houston."

"But right now, you're here. Talk, sister."

"I kissed him," Brenda blurted out, then looked over her shoulder to make sure no one else heard.

"You did not."

"I totally did. And then he kissed me back. Last night, after the Christmas party. I had some drinks . . ."

"You had *drinks?* You went to a *Christmas* party?"

"He practically kidnapped me. There were people in ugly sweaters. Cookies and a white elephant game. Carol karaoke. It was hell."

"Shootfire. Here I was looking for some drama to stream on the TV. You're way more entertaining."

"I'm not. Adam and I are not . . . There's no Adam and I, actually."

"Except when you go drinking and partying together. Except when you kiss him."

"A small lapse in judgment."

"Hon, you are showing *excellent* judgment, if you ask me." Dolly beamed at her.

"He's going to help me deliver the dogs, and I'll be out of here as soon as the van's fixed."

"Maybe don't be so hasty," Dolly said. "Maybe this is the new thing you've been waiting for."

"I haven't been waiting for a new thing," Brenda objected.

"I bet you have whether you know it or not." Dolly gave her a wise look. "Waiting to fall in love. Waiting to be a mom. A stepmom. It's time to put the past away. You're ready, girl. You are so ready. You're ready to give your heart to someone who deserves it."

Brenda felt an unbidden beat of yearning, but she couldn't let go of the fear of a love so powerful that losing it might destroy her.

"Even if I was looking—which I am not—we're not a match. Adam's life is here. His kid, his family, his job. And mine's in Houston."

"You moved around all your life. Maybe there's another move in your future."

"To a place like this? No, thanks. When I finally settled down in Houston, I swore I'd never move again. Had my fill of that when I was growing up."

"Look at you. That outfit is fantastic. You are made for this weather."

"Dolly, I—"

Bo knocked on the door. He and Adam stepped inside. "Mission accomplished," Bo said. "Put together a dirt bike and a snow scooter. Are we interrupting?"

"It's fine," Dolly said. "Brenda was just telling me about kissing Adam."

Bo grinned. "Cool. Adam was just telling me about kissing Brenda."

Adam leaned in the doorway. His smile was unapologetic.

Brenda couldn't stifle a blush. "Hey," she said. "We've got dogs to deliver. Dolly was about to fill me in on the details."

"Your details are much more interesting," Dolly said.

Brenda shot her a glowering look.

"All right then." Dolly leaned back against the bank of pillows. "There are a couple of things you need to know about delivering the dogs, so listen up. The first drop-off will be to the preschool. The director is adopting the dogs, and they'll come to work with her every day. She wants them to show up when the kids are all there. She's taking two dogs, and it's a big deal." She held out folders marked *Comet* and *Cupid*.

"Hey, that's Will's preschool," Adam said. "Cool."

"They've been telling the children that there would be a special visit from Santa and his chief elf," Dolly said. "Bo was planning to dress up as Santa, weren't you, Mr. Bojangles?"

Bo rolled his eyes. "It was a weak moment and a strong-willed wife that made me do it."

"My niece, Kim, takes after me," Dolly said with a broad wink at Brenda.

"Well, as Santa, you're going to have to explain that you brought me and Adam along in place of the elf," Brenda said to Bo. "I'm sure they'll un—"

"You will be perfect," Dolly said breezily. "It'll be a great look for you, Brenda. I have my elf outfit all planned out. It's the same one I was going to wear in the Christmas play, and it is freakin' adorable. I mean *adorable*. It'll be even cuter on you. We're practically the same size. You're going to make a fantastic elf."

"I'm not your damn elf," Brenda said, stony-faced. "I'm not anybody's elf."

"Hey. A promise is a promise," Dolly reminded her. "Remember what you told me yesterday? Back when you were worried sick about me getting better? I think your precise words were 'I'll do everything exactly the way you planned.'"

"Yes, but I didn't realize—"

"Come on. This is for the dogs. And for the kids."

Bo turned to Adam. "Dude, I'll give you a thousand dollars to put on that Santa suit and take my place."

Adam offered an easy shrug. "Give that thousand to Underdogs and you've got yourself a deal."

"Yesss. Come on, man. I'll grab my checkbook. And let's get you into that Santa outfit." He and Adam ducked out of the room.

"Dolly, I swear," Brenda began.

"You did. Be a sport, hon. You wouldn't deny a bedridden woman her dying wish, would you?"

"You're not dying."

"The elf outfit is hanging in the closet." Dolly clapped her hands. "Oh my gosh, it's going to be great!"

"I CAN'T STOP staring at you," Adam said as they headed to the vet clinic to pick up the dogs. He honestly couldn't. In the striped stockings and form-fitting green dress, topped off with a jingle bell cap, Brenda was radiant. She was on fire. She was hotter than fire. "Seriously, I can't stop staring."

"I wish you would," Brenda told him, flipping down the visor and scowling at the makeup job Dolly had done on her. "I haven't been this conspicuous since . . ."

"Since you belted out 'I Saw Mommy Kissing Santa Claus' last night? That was pretty conspicuous."

"But at least I didn't look like an anime character while I was doing it."

"It's actually really sexy," he said, stroking his fake beard. "I mean, really."

"Knock it off. This is not sexy."

Yes, it was. It was definitely sexy. Everything about her was sexy. Adam hadn't been this drawn to a woman since . . . maybe ever. He couldn't stop thinking about the way she'd kissed him last night. He'd lain awake for a long time thinking about it.

"How's my outfit?" he asked, stroking the red velvet jacket.

"Ridiculous," she said. "But the kids will love it."

He turned into the parking lot of Noah's place, a tall white wooden house and a massive barn across the way.

"Our animal clinic in Houston doesn't look like this," she said.

"Noah's supposedly the best vet in the county."

"Well, I'm grateful to him for housing the pups."

When Noah came to greet them and burst out laughing, Brenda's grateful expression turned to a frown.

"Don't ask," Adam said. "It's for the preschool."

"Can I get a picture?" Noah lifted his phone.

"Sure," said Adam.

"*No*," said Brenda.

"Too late," Noah told them with a grin. "It's not every day Santa and his elf come to see me in person."

"We're probably going to scare the dogs," Brenda said.

Noah's assistant, Milo, brought Comet and Cupid to the reception area. He didn't laugh, but shook his head. "I never know who I'm going to meet around here," he said. "Dogs are ready. We had time to give everyone a bath yesterday."

All the young dogs seemed delighted and excited, particularly when they recognized Brenda's voice. The pups were as exuberant around her as she made Adam feel.

"Hey, you two," she said, getting down on the floor with them. "You're going home today! And look how pretty you are, all fresh and clean. And who put Christmas bows on everyone's collar? That's adorable."

She was adorable, thought Adam, the way she lit up around the dogs. He could watch her all day. He was damn glad he got to do that today.

The dogs came in all sizes, shapes, and ages. There was a little thing that looked mostly chihuahua, a wiener dog, a shaggy mutt, a boxer with a funny face, a little fluff ball . . . All of them headed for their permanent homes. What a cool thing Brenda was doing.

The first stop was Willow Lake Preschool, located near the town center. The teachers and aides had the children settled and waiting on their mats in a circle area, leaving plenty of space for the dogs to explore. In spite of her outfit, Adam could tell Brenda was excited to present the dogs.

"Come on," he said, holding the door for her. "Admit it. This is going to be rad."

"It is," she agreed. "I never get to see this part. So this is your little boy's school."

"Yep."

"This will definitely earn you some daddy points."

They each picked up one of the dogs and walked into the classroom. The children gasped and cheered. "Santa! It's Santa! And Miss Chelsea's new dogs!"

A couple of rows back, Will clutched his chest with excitement and whispered to the kid next to him.

Despite her attitude about the outfit, Brenda was all smiles as she presented the dogs to the teacher who was adopting them. She talked just a little about the best way to make friends with a dog, to offer treats and teach them tricks. Then the children took turns petting the dogs.

A kid tugged on Adam's pant leg. "You're not the real Santa," he said.

"I am today," Adam said.

"But not the real true actual Santa."

"Maybe not technically, my boy," Adam told him. "I'm just dressed like Santa. The real guy is superbusy right now, getting ready for Christmas Eve."

"Then who are you, really?"

"I'm Willy's dad." Adam loved the look of pride on Will's face.

"And who's that?" the kid asked, gesturing at Brenda. "Is she your wife?"

Adam looked over at Brenda, who was bending down to introduce a little girl to one of the dogs. Something about the word *wife* struck a chord. For the first time since his divorce, he felt the most intense sense of possibility.

"Not at the moment, but I wouldn't rule that out," he said.

Brenda sent him a quizzical look, and he offered a nonchalant shrug. After a few more minutes, they left the school together, stopping for a high five on the way to the car.

"You were great in there," Brenda said. "You're good with kids."

"Thanks. Just a few years ago, I never imagined myself having kids. Sometimes the things you don't plan turn out to be the best things in life."

The next stop on their route was the nearby Lakeshore Senior Center to deliver the little white fluff ball named Pearly May, and the fine-looking white Lab named Maddie. The director of the center planned to bring the dogs with her to the senior center every day.

"Let's keep the costumes on for the old folks," Adam suggested.

Brenda shot him a look. "You're not serious."

"If I were you, I'd wear that thing every damn day," he told her. "You have the most amazing legs—"

"Hey."

"Sorry. But think of the old folks. Think how happy they'd be to see the two of us all decked out for Christmas."

"All right," she said. "We can wear this getup for the senior center. But after that, I'm changing back into my regular clothes."

"Deal," he said.

BRENDA HAD TO admit that Adam was right about the old folks. The people at the senior center were as thrilled—though not as noisy—as the preschool kids, and they loved the outfits, too. Gathered in the common room with their walkers and wheelchairs, their cribbage games and craft projects, they were enchanted by doe-eyed Maddie and cuddly Pearly May.

In spite of the outfit and the excessive Christmas decorations in the place, Brenda couldn't help feeling touched by the residents' joy when they welcomed the two friendly dogs. Both dogs had been selected for the comfort they gave. A reporter and photographer for the local paper captured images of the dogs being cuddled in people's laps or resting their heads on a friendly knee. Brenda tried to shrink into the background, but the camera lens caught her and Adam in an unguarded moment, leaning in to watch the greetings.

"Hey, Daisy," Adam said to the photographer, a woman with a blond ponytail in a hoodie and skinny jeans. "Did you get my good side?"

She grinned at him. "All your sides are good," she said and held out her hand to Brenda. "I'm Daisy. Adam's cousin."

"I'm Brenda Malloy. I was told I'd meet several Bellamys while I'm in town."

"Yeah, the place is lousy with us." She took another picture. "Good job on the costumes. These will go up on the Instagram page right away, and some of them will run in the Saturday paper. They're doing a piece about the fundraiser for your organization."

"Oh, that's good. The play, you mean," said Brenda.

"My husband and I are volunteering this year—painting the scenery. Hope to see you there," Daisy said.

"Doubtful," Brenda said. "I'll be heading back to Texas as soon as our van is repaired."

Daisy looked from her to Adam. "Well, have a merry Christmas. You sure did spread a little joy this morning." She went to take a few more pictures.

"Are you single, dear?" one of the women asked Brenda. She was a tiny thing with purplish hair and Christmas ornament earrings.

"I am, actually," Brenda said, taken aback. "Why do you ask?"

"I have six grandsons, all of them single. I ought to introduce you to them in case one of them fits the bill."

Brenda couldn't help laughing. "That sounds great, ma'am, but I'm not from around here."

"Ah, that's too bad. You could have your pick of the grandsons, I'm sure."

Brenda held back another laugh. "Good thought. But we have to be going. Merry Christmas."

"I thought one of those old guys was going to grab you," Adam said as they left the place. "I'm not the only one who thinks you're sexy."

"Stop it. I can't wait to get out of this ridiculous thing," Brenda said as they headed to the vet clinic. There, they changed back into their street clothes and loaded up the next group of dogs.

Dolly's prediction of this part of the process turned out to be exactly right. The joy was palpable. No wonder she did this every Christmas. Brenda felt utter delight as the different families welcomed their newest members. The gasps of surprise, the happy tears, the cuddling touched her heart. Most of the dogs readily took to their new owners.

Adam watched the young boxer's family surrounding the sneezing, happy dog. "Can we do this, like, every single day?" he asked. "Because it is way more fun than doing emergency calls."

"This will never get old," she said to Adam, watching the boxer bounding across a snowy yard with three little kids.

"Agreed," he said. "In my line of work, I don't usually get such a warm welcome when I show up at people's houses."

When it was time to deliver Vixen to Suzanne Roberts, Brenda glanced at Adam, noting the tic in his jaw. "Is this going to be okay for you?" she asked.

"It's fine," he said. "My ex and I get along for William's sake."

The road to Suzanne's was steep and narrow, curved with switchbacks. There were warning signs about falling rocks, and a dramatic frozen waterfall suspended in time.

"It's pretty up here," Brenda said. "Is this where you lived when you were married?"

"Yep. It's the house where Suzanne grew up. We bought it from her folks when they moved to Florida."

As they stood on the front porch of the tidy, tastefully decorated house, Brenda cradled the little dog and pressed the doorbell. Suzanne came right away. She glanced at Adam and did a double take, then visibly composed herself. "Adam. I wasn't expecting you."

"Hey," said Adam with a slight nod. "I'm helping Brenda out with all the dogs today."

"Come in, come in," she said, sweeping the door wide. "Oh my goodness, Vixen!"

Brenda handed over the little dog, and Suzanne pressed her cheek into the pretty auburn fur. "She's wonderful," Suzanne said, and to Brenda's surprise, she teared up a little.

"This little dog is really sweet," Brenda said. "I know you're going to love having her. The first owners had to move overseas. They were heartbroken, but it helps that you're giving Vixen a new home."

The interior of Suzanne's place was painstakingly neat. The Christmas tree was a work of art, the ornaments color-coordinated and precisely placed. Expertly wrapped and beribboned gifts surrounded it. In the kitchen, there was a crate and bedding, food bowls, and a basket of dog toys. "Willy got everything ready for her this morning," Suzanne said. "He's going to love having a dog . . ."

She seemed nervous, nattering on and glancing at Adam, who didn't bother to hide his eagerness to leave. Brenda understood that there was no way around the sticky feeling of encountering your ex after a divorce. The person who used to be your whole world, who carried your most intimate secrets, your good habits and bad, who knew your taste, your touch, your body, was suddenly a stranger. Brenda always thought she would be a mom, but now she was grateful she hadn't had children with Grant. There were no strings binding her to a failed relationship from the past.

"I have to get to the shop," Suzanne said. "We're staying open late tonight. Vixen is going to be a shop dog—aren't you, girl?"

Adam was quiet as they drove away from Suzanne's house. "We saved the hard stuff for last," Brenda said.

"I'm usually in favor of doing that. Putting off something that's hard."

She studied him, unable to read his expression. He was too new to her. But she sensed the leftover tension from the visit to Suzanne. "I'm sorry that was stressful," she said.

"It's okay. I just think it's weird that she didn't tell me she was getting a dog. Or maybe it's on-brand for her. She tends to keep things to herself. Made it hard to know what she was thinking. I did a lot of guesswork when we were together."

"You seem like a person who is happy to say what's on your mind."

He grinned and draped his wrist on the steering wheel in that familiar way she'd noticed earlier. "If I say what's on my mind, then I don't have to remember anything. Our last two visits aren't going to be any easier," he predicted, checking his phone.

Brenda felt herself stiffen up, anticipating trouble. They were down to the final two—the Cullens, who wanted Dirk, and the Havens, who were expecting Buzz.

The plan was to deliver Dirk to the Cullens, and then visit Maureen and Eddie Haven, explaining why Buzz was still at Lester's place at the winter lodge of Camp Kioga. Brenda dreaded the meeting, because she was afraid Mr. Jones wouldn't want to give back the dog.

"One disaster at a time." She turned back and patted Dirk's head. "Let's get this sweet guy to his family and then we'll deal with the Buzz situation." She scratched Dirk under the chin, and he moaned in appreciation. "Can I ask you something?"

"Anything."

"That first night, when I mentioned the Cullens, you seemed surprised that they were getting Dirk. Why is that?"

"I . . . Well, not just Dirk, but any dog at all." Adam frowned at the road ahead. "This is tricky. I need to tell you something, but I also need to respect these people's privacy."

"Of course. I get it. I don't mean to put you on the spot. On the other hand, I need to make sure I leave the dog in good hands."

He took a breath. "There've been . . . well, a couple of calls to their place."

"Calls . . ." Brenda opened a document on her phone and looked at the Cullens' application, which seemed to be in order. Childless couple, single-family home, fenced yard, husband was a salesman and the wife stayed home. "Emergency calls? You mean like, domestic disturbance calls?"

"I wasn't on duty, but I do know that Noah's wife, Sophie, is Harriet Cullen's lawyer."

Brenda was aware that introducing a new dog into a troubled household was probably not the best situation, but there was no rule against it. People made bad choices every day. "Well, I guess we need to take Dirk to meet them and hope for the best."

Adam nodded. He didn't look happy. She sensed he wasn't telling her everything he knew, but she didn't press.

Harriet Cullen greeted them at the door. She wore sweats and her hair in a bun, scuffed tennis shoes and a wary expression. Brenda sensed an undercurrent of nerves as she stepped back and invited them into a living room that was neatly arranged, but smelled of cigarette smoke. There were framed posters on the wall from a few local Shakespeare productions in a festival called *Shakespeare on the Lake*.

The Cullen house was the first place they'd visited that was utterly devoid of Christmas—no tree, no decorations, no collection of cards, no candles. Brenda was surprised to realize she kind of missed it.

"Mrs. Cullen, I'm Brenda Malloy and this is Adam Bellamy. And here's Dirk, your new dog!"

"Please, call me Harriet." She gestured them into the living room and sat down on the edge of a wingback chair. Brenda and Adam took the sofa. Dirk plunked himself down on the floor beside Brenda, leaning against her leg. Harriet didn't offer much attention to Dirk. In fact, she kept her distance from the dog.

Brenda put on an encouraging smile. "This sweet boy has come a long way to meet you." She smoothed her hand over Dirk's bony head. Dirk made a contented chuffing sound.

"Um, yes, I realize that." Harriet's gaze shifted to and fro. Dirk wandered over to give her a sniff, and she flinched, holding herself away from him. The dog retreated back to Brenda.

"I . . . I don't know how to tell you this," Harriet said, "but . . . I'm afraid things have changed since we agreed to take the dog."

Brenda kept her expression neutral. "I see. Can you let us know about this change? I don't want to pry, but if it affects your adoption, I'll need—"

"I never wanted a dog," Harriet blurted out, and then burst into tears. "That was Vance's idea."

Brenda sent Adam a helpless look. He grabbed a box of tissues from a side table and offered them to the woman. She took a couple and pressed them to her face, taking a deep, unsteady breath. She looked shaken and fragile.

Brenda gave her a moment to dab at her eyes. "Oh my gosh, are you all right? Is there something I can do to help?"

"I'm sorry," she said. "I didn't see that coming. It's just . . . something very new. My husband has left me, and I was served with papers this morning." She gestured at a hall table in the foyer, stacked with mail. "I knew it was coming, but still. I can't even bring myself to open the envelope."

"Wow, that's really tough," Adam said. "Sorry we caught you on such a tough day, ma'am."

She nodded. "I suppose I should have contacted you, but frankly, it—this—was the last thing on my mind." She indicated the dog.

Brenda leaned forward, recognizing the shock and sadness in the other woman's eyes. "I get it," she said. "Listen, it's okay if Dirk doesn't work out for you. Things happen. Things change."

Harriet slumped back in her chair. "Thank you for understanding. I just don't see myself bringing a dog into the house. I don't even know if I'll have a house now."

Brenda nodded, remembering the rug-pulled-out-from-under-her sensation after she and Grant split up. Overnight, the world changed, and nothing was certain.

Adam cleared his throat. "Does your— Does Mr. Cullen still want the dog, then?"

Harriet's eyes narrowed. "I doubt it. Vance went to Florida yesterday. With his girlfriend." She nearly gagged on the word.

"Harriet, I'm so sorry you're going through this," Brenda said. "I know every situation is different, but you and I have something in common. Last Christmas, I found out my husband was cheating. I thought the world was coming to an end. But you know what? The world didn't end, and I'm still standing, and I've never loved my life more. So I guess now I can't thank him enough."

"I'm still at the world-ending phase. How'd you get past that?"

"This might sound crazy, but Underdogs was a huge part of that."

"You adopted a dog? But I don't even like dogs."

"I already had a dog. What I did was become involved as a volunteer. I'm not saying it was an overnight transformation, but it was a way to connect with people. I ended up doing a lot of other things I never thought I'd do. I trained for a marathon and started a small business. I finished writing a novel. I won't lie and say it was easy to get back on my feet, but I built a life on my own terms, and there's a lot to be said for that."

"I'll try to keep that in mind," Harriet said softly. "But what about . . . him?" She nodded her head toward Dirk, who had dozed off.

"He'll be fine," Brenda assured her. Her own dog had been a lifeline to sanity during her divorce, but everyone was different. "Please don't worry. I'll take him back and make sure you get a refund for your fees." The contract didn't call for that, but Brenda knew it would ease Harriet's mind.

"I appreciate that. Thanks for understanding."

Adam held out a card. "I'm with the county EMS," he said. "Feel free to reach out to me for anything, emergency or not."

She looked at the card, and then at him, and a slight smile softened her mouth. "Thank you." Then she looked flustered. "Sorry, I haven't even offered you anything. Where are my manners? Would you like some coffee? Something to eat? I don't have much in the house. It's been kind of chaotic around here."

"We have to be going," Brenda said. "But thanks." She dug in her bag and found a couple of the tickets Dolly had given her. "Not sure if this would interest you, but these are for the upcoming Christmas play. I'm told it's a yearly production. I mean, it's not exactly Shakespeare, but maybe you'd enjoy it."

Harriet's smile widened. "I might. I used to be really involved in community theater. Before I was married." She exhaled a long breath. "You've both been very kind. I'm sorry again about the dog."

Brenda and Adam walked Dirk back to the car and looked at each other. He seemed as rattled as she felt. "Holy shit, that was hard," Adam said.

"And now we've got a homeless dog," she said, shaking her head.

"Unless . . ." Adam stroked Dirk's head. "Are you thinking what I'm thinking?"

"Oh my gosh, I think I love you," Brenda said. A blush flooded her cheeks, and she bit her lip. It was a dumb thing to say, but she didn't regret it. "Um, that was just a manner of speaking because you're a great problem solver."

Adam nodded, giving her a sly grin. "So what I'm thinking is, maybe we could tell Maureen and Eddie Haven that you fed the greyhound too much, and that's why he looks like a hippo. How's that for problem solving?"

She elbowed him as they loaded Dirk back into the truck. "Not helpful. How well do you know them? Mr. and Mrs. Haven?"

"Enough to know they're nice folks."

"The town librarian and a musician, right?" Brenda felt hopeful, but skeptical. "They were expecting a retired greyhound. What will they think if I offer them a shy Staffordshire terrier mix?"

"Are the adoption fees the same?" Adam asked.

"Actually, no. The cost for a dog like Dirk is lower. It's sad, but we get too many dogs like him—pit bulls and staffies. So I suppose if the Havens agree to take him, they'll be getting a partial refund. God, this sounds like a long shot, doesn't it? And what if Mr. Jones doesn't have the funds for his adoption fee?"

"You're worrying about things that might not even come to pass. Also, I made Bo give me a thousand bucks to take his place as Santa today. I've got the check right here. That'll cover Buzz's fee."

"I need to be prepared in case the Havens insist on having Buzz."

"What about trusting in the spirit of the season? Human kindness and all that?"

"Right."

"You never know."

They went to the Havens' home, a place near the river with a big fenced yard and a couple of sleds leaning against the house. Maureen burst through the door to greet them. She was exceedingly pretty, with a bright smile and a spring in her step. "Hello!" she called. "Hello, hello! Eddie, come see! The dog people are here."

A tall, slender man with a ponytail, in black jeans, Doc Martens, and a Nirvana sweatshirt, joined them on the porch. "Adam," he said, holding out a hand. "Good to see you, man. You're in the dog delivery business now?"

Adam grinned. "Just helping a lady out." He introduced the Havens to Brenda, who stood holding Dirk's leash.

Maureen grabbed Eddie's hand. "Is that Buzz?" she asked, craning her neck. "Wow, he looks nothing like the picture."

"He's . . . Actually, this dog's name is Dirk. He's two years old, a Staffordshire terrier mix."

"Oh!" Maureen glanced at her husband. "Uh, where's Buzz, then? Where's the greyhound?"

"Would it be okay if we came in?" Adam asked.

"Of course! We've been expecting you," Maureen said. "I took off work early. We have play practice tonight, but not until seven." She turned to Brenda. "Eddie and I direct a Christmas play every year. Come on in. I made hot chocolate."

The house was filled with books and musical instruments. There were movie and pop music posters on display in the stairwell, and a bright country kitchen with a view of the river, a dog bed and feeding bowls in one corner. Maureen brought a tray of steaming mugs of chocolate to the front room, which featured a fireplace and floor-to-ceiling bookcases on three walls. In the front window, there was a Christmas tree hung with lots of handmade ornaments. A fire was blazing in the hearth, and the mantel was hung with stockings, one of them designated *Buzz*.

Brenda eyed the stocking nervously. "Well, as I told you on the phone, after Buzz ran away from the accident we had, he was found by a gentleman named Lester Jones. He's a caretaker at Camp Kioga. We had so many dogs to deal with that night, and Mr. Jones offered to look after Buzz."

"That was kind of him," Maureen said.

Dirk ambled over and nudged her hand, and she smiled and patted his head and neck. The dog gave a funny moan of delight and leaned against her leg.

"So you want us to go collect the dog from the guy?" asked Eddie, glancing at a clock on the shelf.

"That's what we need to talk to you about," Adam said. "Lester's an older man, kind of quirky. A loner. Said his own dog died not too long ago, and when Buzz showed up in the middle of a snowstorm, Lester took it as a sign."

"A sign that he gets to keep our dog?" Maureen stopped rubbing Dirk's neck. With a contented grunt, Dirk nudged her and she started up again.

"I'm really sorry this got complicated," Brenda said. "I could go pick up the dog from Mr. Jones. I'm sure I can make him understand. But something else came up today. Another possibility. The family that was supposed to adopt Dirk can't take him after all, so now we have a homeless dog."

"Dirk has no family," Maureen said, playing with his velvety ears and turning to look at her husband.

"Dirk has no family," Eddie said.

"Now, there's a chance we could persuade Mr. Jones to take Dirk and hand over Buzz," Brenda suggested.

"Or we could let him keep the greyhound and we'll adopt this guy," Maureen said. Dirk melted in ecstasy and turned belly up at her feet. "Honey?"

Eddie shrugged. "I didn't have my heart set on a greyhound. I was just drawn to his story. He peaked at a very young age and was forced into retirement."

Maureen sent him an adoring look. "Eddie had a huge movie career when he was five years old. Have you ever seen *The Christmas Caper?*"

"That rings a bell," Brenda said. She recalled the heartwarming movie, which resurfaced every year—a holiday staple. The child star had rocketed briefly to fame, and his had been one of the most recognizable faces in the country. She stared at Eddie. "It's a classic. Wow, that was you! This is such an honor."

"I'm still me," Eddie pointed out.

"Oh, I didn't mean . . ." Brenda flushed. "Sorry. You probably get that a lot."

"So what do you think?" Adam asked, cutting to the chase. "Will this guy work out for you?"

Eddie watched Maureen and the dog for a moment. "Sure," he said. "Let's do it."

Maureen sank down next to Dirk and cradled his face between her hands. His skinny tail quivered, and he sighed loudly.

"You guys are the best," Adam said.

"Absolutely the best," Brenda agreed. "Please, take all the time you need to get acquainted with Dirk."

Maureen dabbed at her eyes. "He's wonderful. He's going to love it here."

Over cups of hot cocoa, Brenda organized the paperwork, handing over the veterinary records. Eddie and Maureen sat on a rug in front of the fire with Dirk settled happily between them.

"He's wonderful," Maureen said again, beaming at the dog. "I think this was meant to be. You know, it seems like good things always happen at Christmas."

"You think?" Brenda tried not to sound skeptical. She felt Adam watching her.

"Sure," said Maureen. "We don't always see them coming, and maybe things don't look so good at first, but the season tends to bring out the best in everyone. Eddie and I first met at Christmas," she added. "We couldn't stand each other."

"Hey," he said. "I saw right through your Marian-the-librarian facade."

"And now look at us." She fawned over Dirk, giving him belly rubs.

"Thank you again. I'm really happy for you," Brenda said. "And I love this room. All these books."

"There are perks to being the town librarian," Maureen said.

"My wife reads books the way other folks breathe air," Eddie said, fondness shining from his eyes.

"I can relate," Brenda said.

"She's a writer," Adam told them.

Maureen's face lit up. "Wow, really?"

Brenda ducked her head. She wanted to hide. "An *aspiring* writer," she corrected. "I've written two novels for children, but they've never been published."

"Well, I hope one day they will be. Middle-grade readers are my favorite genre. That's when kids truly get addicted to reading," Maureen said, getting up and going to a shelf. "These are publishers' sample copies. They sometimes send them to me for feedback." She handed Brenda some books. "Here, take a few with you. For research."

"Are you sure? This is fantastic." She flipped through the pages, feeling a thrill of interest.

"I've made notes here and there, you'll see," Maureen said.

"She's being modest," Eddie said. "Several New York editors like to use her as an early reader because she's smart as a whip and has incredible taste."

She has an incredible husband, Brenda thought.

"So, like we said, this boy will do just fine," Maureen assured her, smoothing her hand over Dirk's wide, well-defined skull and holding Eddie's gaze with hers. "Don't you think?"

He regarded his wife and the dog. "Absolutely."

Brenda felt another rush of gratitude. "Y'all are amazing. Truly—amazing."

"We're not. We like to help," Eddie said.

"Give Mr. Jones our best," said Maureen. "Maybe we'll see him and the greyhound at the dog park one of these days."

"Oh my gosh, thank you so much," Brenda said. "I owe you, big time. If you ever need a favor . . ."

"Be careful. I might just take you up on that," said Maureen.

As they went out to the truck, Brenda felt giddy with relief. On impulse, she threw her arms around Adam. "They're keeping Dirk. They're keeping him! And Lester Jones gets to keep Buzz. I can hardly believe it all worked out."

"It's great," Adam said, holding her against him. "You gotta admit—I might be on to something. About the season."

Brenda gave a sigh of satisfaction, stepping back. Maybe Adam was right. Maybe there was something about the season—something that brought out humanity at its brightest and most kind. "My work here is done," she said.

"Almost," he said. "We have one more thing to do." He held the car door for her. "Let's go make a sweet old man happy."

The Best Place to Kiss

On the way home from Camp Kioga, Brenda rode slumped with relief in the passenger seat. Buzz and Lester Jones were inseparable, and he was more than delighted to settle the dog's adoption fees. "My Christmas miracle," he'd declared, all smiles.

When Adam pulled up to his ex-wife's shop, Brenda pursed her lips and cast him a worried look. Was he having second thoughts about Suzanne? When they'd taken Vixen to Suzanne, Brenda had sensed the tension straining between Adam and his ex-wife.

"What's up?" she asked.

"I need you to do something. Go inside and buy something nice to wear tonight."

"Adam—"

"It's not another party, I swear. I'm taking you out to dinner. To celebrate a successful day."

"Oh!" she said. "That sounds great, Adam."

"I booked a table at the Apple Tree Inn. It's the best place in town. It was voted Best Place to Kiss in the county. Gorgeous old Adirondack lodge, situated in an orchard by the river. You're gonna love it, but it's on the fancy side. So you should get yourself something nice to wear. I need to run a quick errand. Meet you back here."

"But—"

"Get something that's as pretty as you are," he called to her while walking backward, a grin on his face.

Date night. Suddenly the day was about to shift to date night. At the best place to kiss? Brenda couldn't quash her excitement. They'd had an incredible day. It seemed right to celebrate.

"I'm back for more," she said, stepping into Zuzu's Petals. "How's your new dog doing?"

"She's having the best day," Suzanne said. "How do you like her little jacket?"

"Adorable," Brenda said.

Vixen was under the counter chewing on a toy and wearing a gold lamé puffy coat. Suzanne beamed at her. "I can't wait to pick my little boy up from school today and introduce him to her. She's supersweet. Now. What can I help you find?"

"I thought I'd take another look at that red sweater dress," Brenda said.

"You're going to love it." Suzanne set her up in a dressing room that was tricked out like a boudoir.

The dress looked great. Suzanne added a pair of chandelier earrings. "These are on sale," she said.

"Well, then, I'd better get them." Brenda ran her hand over a buttery-soft pajama set. Lacy tap pants and a camisole with spaghetti straps. "So pretty," she said. "I have a weakness for nice pajamas."

"Then you should get those as well," said Suzanne. "I love that brand. They're supercomfortable." As she rang up the sale, she said, "Will told me you're staying with his grandma."

"While I'm in town, yes."

"He's convinced you have a magic touch with the other dog. The one Adam adopted."

Brenda laughed briefly. "Just a lot of experience. Olaf's a good dog. A good match for your little boy and his dad."

"Adam and I were supposed to be a good match. I hope things work out better for Olaf." Suzanne sighed. "I have so many regrets about my marriage. Sometimes I think—" She broke off, and then shook her head as if to reset her thoughts. "I'm sorry. I don't mean to dump on you."

"Oh!" Brenda tried not to seem flustered. "I'm divorced, too. I know how hard it can be." She felt awkward, given her feelings for Adam. "It was incredibly challenging to deal with when things fell apart with my ex."

"Do you, um, ever feel like asking him to try again?"

"Grant? *No.* He's already engaged to someone new." *Good lord*, Brenda thought. Did Suzanne still have feelings for her ex?

"Oh, that would be torture for me, if Adam found someone else," Suzanne said. "I mean, we've both tried dating other people, but for me, it's just been a distraction." She wrapped up the purchases and put them in a bag. "Now. Who's the lucky guy?"

Brenda nearly choked. "Um, there's no guy, lucky or otherwise," she said. "Just treating myself."

ADAM GAZED AT Brenda across the white linen–draped table at the luxurious, candlelit restaurant. Time seemed to stop when he looked at her in that certain way. She wished time *would* stop, because every moment brought her closer to leaving.

He swirled the wine in his goblet. "Remind me again, *why* are we talking about my ex-wife?"

"Well, it seemed like something you should know. At the boutique today, she said she has a lot of regrets. I got the impression that she wishes the two of you could give it another try."

"Oh, boy," he said.

Brenda couldn't read his expression. Was he annoyed? Frustrated? *Hopeful?* "I didn't know if I should say something, but . . ."

"It's okay," Adam said. "Not the first time she's brought it up. I feel bad, you know. I'm sympathetic. She and I both went through the same divorce, with all the same regrets and second-guessing. The difference is, I'm certain that there is no chance of a reunion. Especially now that I've met you."

She felt a flicker of nerves. "Adam—"

"No, let me finish. I like you, Brenda. A lot. I think I could fall in love with you."

"Well, you shouldn't," she said. In spite of herself, she felt a stab of emotion and winced. Stabbing was painful. Falling in love would only lead to pain. She wanted to shy away from the topic, but at the same time, she felt drawn to explore it with him.

"I realize we've only known each other for a matter of days," he said, "but you can't deny that something is happening between us."

"Only if we let it," she said.

"Why would we stop this? It's amazing, Brenda. I've never met anyone like you. Never felt this way about a woman."

She could say the same to him, but she didn't. She had always shied away from over-the-top, intense emotions. She had wanted Grant—but not too much. Not so much that losing him would destroy her. But this—whatever this was with Adam—was something different.

"That's a very romantic thing to say," she told him.

"I know, right?" He grinned. "I *feel* romantic about you. It's really cool."

After dinner, they went home together and let the dogs out for a run. Brenda had no memory of what she'd had for dinner. Some kind of wine. A dessert made with chocolate. All the other details were lost in the fantastic, frothy mess Adam had made of her emotions.

While Olaf and Tim romped in the yard, she looked up at the stars and inhaled the cold air, and Adam slipped his arm around her waist.

"You say you hate the snow," he said, "but you've got the best smile on your face right now."

"Do I? Maybe it's not as awful as I thought," she admitted.

"I can think of a dozen ways to have fun in the snow. I'm going to take you skiing. We could try skating on Willow Lake. Sledding. Touring the ice castle. Oh, hey—ice climbing."

"Now that," she said, "does *not* sound like fun."

"I'll make it fun," he said.

He could make anything fun. He could make sitting through an insurance seminar fun.

"It's late," she said.

He drew her closer. "I'm not ready to leave you."

She looked at the stars again. There was a three-quarter moon low on the horizon, its silver-white light adding a fairy-tale quality to the garden. "Suppose I go to my room," she said. "You could visit me there."

"Now that," he said, "is the best idea you've had all day. I need fifteen minutes to get Olaf settled at my place and grab a bottle of wine."

Brenda didn't allow herself to overthink the situation, or to talk herself out of it. The fact was, she wanted this night with him, maybe more than she wanted the next breath of air. After the divorce, she used to think she was lonely for sex, but after she hooked up with Ryder, she discovered that wasn't quite it. She was lonely for *connection*. She wasn't ready to leave Adam, either. And she wouldn't be ready to leave him when it was time to go back to Texas, but for some reason she refused to examine, she still wanted this night with him.

She went to her extremely pink bathroom and stared at the huge jetted tub. Then she freshened up, brushed her teeth, and put on her new pajamas. The soft fabric felt delicious against her skin. The lace-edged tap pants were extremely short. Self-conscious, she slipped on a bathrobe. Then she changed her mind and dropped the robe.

A few minutes later, Adam showed up with a bucket filled with snow, a bottle of champagne, and two glasses.

"Hey," she whispered, stepping back and holding the door for him.

"My heart just stopped." He didn't take his eyes off her even as he set down the ice bucket. "I opened the bottle outside. Didn't want to wake anyone." With a visible effort, he looked away from her and poured two glasses and they toasted. "To the dogs," he said.

"To the dogs." It was the coldest, best champagne she'd ever tasted.

"We're a good team." He put aside their glasses and slipped his arm around her waist, drawing her close. "You're wearing pajamas."

"Yes. I bought them today."

He bent to nuzzle her neck and whisper in her ear, "Why are you wearing pajamas if I'm just going to take them off?"

"Silly. Don't you know that's the whole point?"

THE MORNING CREPT in slowly, the pale light falling through the partially drawn curtains of Brenda's room. She opened her eyes, but didn't move. Adam slept in a heap, his body curved around hers, a warm and safe cocoon. She wanted to lie in this bed all day. She wanted to lie in this bed forever. Memories of the previous night floated through her brain. At first they'd been tentative, awkward—but earnest, finding their way to each other. There had been nervous laughter and sighs, and more champagne, and more lovemaking, the next time with increasing passion and assurance. And after that . . . An involuntary sigh escaped her, and she squirmed a little.

"Mmm." Adam stretched and pulled her snugly against him. "Morning, you."

"Morning." Flushed and restless, she turned in his arms. "I didn't mean to wake you."

"I don't mind. I especially don't mind waking up to you."

She lifted up on one elbow. Glanced at Tim, snug in his bed and in no hurry to get up.

"Adam."

"Yeah?" He brushed his lips along the curve of her jaw.

She stifled another sigh. "What are we doing?"

"Waking up together for the first time," he whispered.

"No, I mean, what are we doing?"

He tugged at the shoulder strap of her camisole and flicked it away, then bent down to nuzzle her neck. "Celebrating. Remember? Eleven dogs went to eleven homes."

Brenda forgot what she was going to say next. She forgot everything. She seemed to have forgotten—or maybe she'd never known—the sheer, pure fun of good sex.

Later, the light brightened, and Tim stretched and yawned. Brenda grabbed her phone to check the time and noticed that a message had come in. Her heart sank.

"What's up?" Adam asked.

"Shootfire, as Dolly would say."

"What's the matter?" Adam brushed a curl away from her cheek and placed a kiss there.

"Bad news about the van. The repair shop had to order some parts, and they're on back order. So the repair is going to be delayed."

"You can stay as long as you need to. Hell, stay forever. I'm sure my mom would agree. I like having you as my neighbor," Adam said.

I like being your neighbor, Brenda thought.

She slipped away and put on her robe and went to brush her teeth. The woman in the mirror looked flushed and a bit disoriented. *What are we doing?*

When she came out of the bathroom, she saw Adam, wearing only briefs, standing by the writing desk, checking out her notebook and pens. "You've been doing some writing," he said.

"I have. I had an idea for a new book, and I'm trying to get the story down." She flipped through the pages of the book, which was filled with blocks of writing, much of it crossed out and rewritten. "I make a lot of false starts," she told him. "Writing is one of those things that's actually harder than it looks."

"Are you kidding? Writing has always looked hard to me."

She felt a tug of yearning. "It's really all I've ever wanted to do."

"And you're doing it. That's so cool, Brenda."

"It would be even cooler if I could get a book published."

"You will." He pulled her against his broad, bare chest. "As long as you're stuck here, you could finish the book you're writing."

"I would love that."

Tim trotted to the door and pawed it.

"He needs to go out," Brenda said.

"I'd better go let Olaf out, too." Adam inhaled the scent of her hair. "I never want to leave here."

"Is it going to be awkward with your mother this morning?"

"Are you kidding? She'll want to high-five me."

"For sleeping with her houseguest."

"Truth be told, we didn't sleep much. It was awesome, by the way." Adam pulled on his jeans from last night.

There were few things more glorious, Brenda observed, than a shirtless man in faded jeans. She tried not to stare.

"Anyway, my mom likes you," Adam was saying. "I can tell. She's a typical mom in that she wants her kids coupled up and settled down. I bet your mom's the same."

"You might be right. She was thrilled when my sister got married, and then I did a year later. I think she was more disappointed in my divorce than I was."

"Think she'd like me?"

Brenda scoffed a little. "Everybody likes you, Adam." She hurried into a set of sweats and thick socks. "I'll meet you outside with the dogs."

A few minutes later, they stood in the cold morning air, watching Olaf and Tim zooming around, chasing each other.

"They're already best friends," Adam said.

She nodded. "Didn't take long, did it?"

"Tell me about Tim."

She beamed. "Tiny Tim. I spotted him on the Underdogs website, and something about him just told me he was the right match. Most of the dogs are sent north, but I made a strong case for adopting Tim, and I was approved. We've been besties from the day we met."

"He's a great dog. You're a good trainer."

"I adore him. He's only three years old, but I'm already dreading the day he leaves me." The thought made her shiver and move closer to Adam. "That's a dog for you. A little tragedy waiting to happen. And yet we keep doing it, over and over again."

"Maybe don't dwell on that. Because the dog sure as hell doesn't."

Olaf had found a stick and was taunting Tim with it.

Brenda shivered and stuffed her hands in her pockets. "Loving a dog shows how dangerous it is to love a person."

"What? Jeez, Brenda."

"I mean it. The joy and the pleasure—they're addictive, and when you lose them—"

"Hey." Adam put his arm around her. "When you fall in love with the right person, you get all that joy and pleasure, only it lasts a lifetime. We just haven't found the right person up until now. But when I look at you, I think maybe we have."

She pulled away and looked up at him. "This is a fantasy, Adam. It isn't real. Real life is messy and there are hard times and things fall apart and people get hurt and . . . and I'm afraid to risk it."

"There's a bigger risk in *not* taking the chance," he said. "Like, suppose you miss out on something that might be exactly what you've been looking for all your life?"

"You don't know what I'm looking for," she shot back, feeling defensive now. "If I've never had it, I can't miss it."

"Seriously? Damn, Brenda—"

Her phone rang, and she fished it out of her pocket. Maureen Haven's name came up on the screen. "Sorry. I should take this," Brenda said.

He scowled at her. "To be continued."

"Maureen," she said, picking up the phone. "Is everything okay with Dirk?"

"Oh yes, he's fine. He's fabulous. This is something else. Remember how you said you'd return the favor?"

"Of course. How can I help?"

"Well, I need a favor."

A Friend in Need

Diet Pepsi?" Dolly offered when Brenda arrived at Fairfield House, Tim trotting at her side. Dolly sat propped on the bed like a queen, her leg on a satin pillow, papers scattered across the coverlet.

"Um, no thanks," Brenda said. Dolly and her Diet Pepsi.

"Well, there's a cold one on the nightstand in case you change your mind." Dolly patted the bed. "Come on, Tim. Come see your old friend Dolly."

The dog leaped onto the bed and immediately tucked himself in next to her. "I just love this little guy," Dolly said, stroking him. "Maureen'll be here shortly."

"What's up?" Brenda asked. "She said everything is okay with her dog. Hey, do you think they might want another one?"

"We'll see. What's up with you?" Dolly cocked her head. "You look incredible, by the way. Is that outfit new?"

"I bought a few things," Brenda said. "I definitely didn't pack enough sweaters for this trip. Didn't know I'd be exiled to the frozen North."

"Well, you look fantastic. And it's not just the clothes."

Brenda ducked her head. "Could be the cold weather."

"You're blushing," Dolly said. "Ha! I swear, I can tell you've been up to something."

Brenda stared at the floor. "I've been having . . . an adventure. Yes. I guess you could call it that."

"An adventure. With Adam Bellamy?"

Brenda tried to fend off a smile. Even just the thought of him made her smile. "Let's talk about something else."

"Humph. You could do worse than end up with a hunky paramedic."

Maureen showed up in a bluster of books and papers, a distracted expression on her face. "Thanks for coming on such short notice, Brenda."

"Of course."

"Diet Pepsi?" Dolly offered.

"Not today, thanks. Caffeine would only cause my head to detonate. There's more bad news about the play. My script supervisor is sick. It's almost impossible to manage a production without a script supervisor. It's a volunteer position, but we have no volunteers."

Brenda thought for a moment. "What does a script supervisor do?"

"Oh, hon, that's not the right role for you," said Dolly.

"Well, I just might know someone."

"How do you know anyone in this town? Besides Mr. Tall-and-Sexy Bellamy."

"You forget, I've been running around delivering dogs. And now I'm stuck here waiting for the van to be fixed." She explained about the parts delay as she scrolled through her phone and found Harriet Cullen's number. "Let me check. It's someone who might be looking for volunteer opportunities, and I think she's interested in theater."

When Harriet picked up, Brenda stepped into another room for privacy. "Is that dog all right?" Harriet asked. "I really didn't mean to make extra trouble for you."

"He's great," Brenda said. "He's with a wonderful family. I should have called sooner to tell you that. And to see how you're doing."

"I'm not so great," Harriet said. "But I'm still here. Trying to come up with a reason to get myself dressed and out of the house."

"Now that," Brenda said, "is something I might be able to help with." She explained Maureen's dilemma and asked Harriet if she'd be willing to help out.

A few minutes later, she strutted into Dolly's room, smiling from ear to ear. "I found you a script supervisor," she said. "I'll send you Harriet's contact information and you can meet with her. I think she'll be great. She's a Shakespeare buff, and she could use a little holiday cheer."

"Well, that's fabulous," Dolly said. "One of your adoptive families?"

"No, but I met her yesterday." Brenda didn't want to explain that Harriet had rejected Dirk. "Anyway, she said she would be delighted to help. She's between jobs at the moment, so she has lots of time."

"Thanks, Brenda," said Maureen. "Harriet used to volunteer at Shakespeare on the Lake years ago. You just took one thing off my list."

"I'm happy to pitch in," Brenda said.

"It's good that you're happy," Dolly said, "because we need you to help, too."

"Didn't I just do that?"

Maureen and Dolly shared a look. Then Maureen said, "I was up all night worrying about this. It's kind of a disaster. Every seat is sold out. We'll be playing to a packed house. But you see, we can't do this play without Dolly. I was almost ready to cancel the whole thing, because the story doesn't work without Sprinkles the Elf. But then she shared something with me. She said you've been helping her learn her part."

A prickly feeling crept up Brenda's spine. She eyed the other women suspiciously. "During the drive up from Texas. It was a way for us to pass the time."

"We have a big ask," Dolly said.

"A huge ask," Maureen said. "Dolly has a key part to play in the production. I tried to rewrite the part without Sprinkles, but it just won't work. Trust me, I tried." She lifted her glasses to reveal the circles under her eyes.

"Hon, we need you to be the understudy," Dolly said. "You're the only one who knows the part. I realize it wasn't much fun for you to run me through my lines and cues, but the part sank into that brain of yours. I could see it happen."

"What you saw was a damn migraine," Brenda said, "from going over and over—"

"You're perfect," Dolly interrupted. "We already know you look incredible in the elf costume. We already know you can sing."

As she pictured herself dressing up like an elf and performing before a packed house, Brenda felt the color drain from her face. Her throat dried. No. Not that. Anything but that.

But then she remembered Maureen's kindness in lending her books for research. She thought about Dirk and Buzz, and the fact that Maureen could have caused no end of trouble for Underdogs. She thought about Dolly, saving dogs by the vanload, year after year. In the face of all that kindness, Brenda realized she was doomed.

"I swear I'll be your friend for life," Maureen said. "I'll return any favor . . ."

Before common sense kicked in, Brenda grabbed the bottle of Diet Pepsi from Dolly's nightstand and twisted it open. She took a long, scintillating pull, then set down the bottle, and wiped her sleeve across her mouth.

"Okay," she said. "I'll do it, then. I'll do her part."

AFTER HER FIRST table read of the Christmas play, Brenda yearned for something stronger than Pepsi. Thanks to the van trip with Dolly, she was familiar with the script, but as they ran through the story, terrible doubts crept in. The whole point of the play was to affirm and celebrate the season. And to convince the audience that Santa was real and Christmas was magic.

But for Brenda, Christmas had always been a season haunted by pain and regret. How was she going to convince an audience that Christmas was some kind of magic bullet that would heal the soul? How could she fool a packed house into believing something she herself didn't believe?

She was pacing in her room, glaring at all the tender affirmations she was supposed to speak, when her mother called from Houston. "I just saw your text message. Brenda, what's going on? You're supposed to be back in time for the cruise."

"I'm still waiting for the van to be fixed." She explained about the out-of-stock part the repair shop was waiting for. "I can't just ditch the van. It might be . . . a while."

"A while. What's a while?"

"Could be a couple of weeks."

"A couple of weeks? You'll miss the cruise entirely."

"I realize that. I'm really sorry, Mom."

"Here's an idea! Suppose you fly home for the week so you can come along with us, and then return at a later date to pick up the van? There's no point in you sitting around waiting."

"I'm . . . actually, I'm needed for something here."

"You're *needed*. For what?" Her mother sounded skeptical.

"Dolly had a part in a play they're putting on, and she can't do it because of her injuries. And I'm her understudy."

"A play? Like on a stage with curtains and a costume and an audience?"

"It's an annual thing up here. There'll be a packed house, according to the organizers. The proceeds are for the benefit of Underdogs."

"Well. A play. That doesn't sound like you."

"You're right. It doesn't. But I made a promise. I told Dolly I'd do everything she's not able to do."

"Tell me about this play. What kind of play are you talking about?"

"It's community theater." She realized she had to level with her mom. "A musical called *Jingle All the Way*."

A long silence.

"Mom?"

"You're performing in a musical Christmas play."

"I am. It's supposed to be Dolly's role. It's silly, and goofy, but I'm committed."

"Are you all right? You sound funny."

"I'm . . ." Brenda bit her lip. She had so much to talk about. "Mom, I might have met someone."

Another long silence.

"Mom?"

"Someone who's better than a cruise?"

Oh, hell yes.

"It's all really new." So new, in fact, that Brenda still wanted to keep the details to herself. She needed time to sort through her feelings.

"Oh, sweetheart. I'm glad. I mean, I'm sad that you'll miss the cruise, but you know we've all been waiting for you to find someone. So he might be *the* someone. Who is he? What's he like?"

He's like Christmas back when I used to believe in Christmas.

THE VERY NEXT day, Brenda attended the first run-through of the play at the community theater. Thanks to the hours in the car with Dolly, she was able to belt out the songs and speak the lines on cue. But even to her own ears, the words fell flat. She met with Maureen at the end of the evening. Over warm butterscotch toddies at the Hilltop Tavern, they went over Maureen's notes.

"You're a lifesaver," Maureen said.

"I'm nuts for getting roped into this. My own mother doesn't know me. Sorry my delivery was so awkward."

"Come on. It wasn't so bad. You sing so beautifully."

"I don't. But your musicians could make an alley cat sound good. I didn't realize I was going to be performing with Eddie Haven." The band was called Inner Child, and ironically, she had already met each member. Eddie was on lead guitar and vocals. Bo Crutcher played bass, Dr. Noah Shepherd was their drummer, and Ray Tolley, cop and tow truck driver, manned the keyboards.

"We're pretty lucky to have all this talent in our little town. Anyway, you have a strong, clear singing voice. You sounded wonderful." She paused. "Maybe you could practice some different inflections in your dialogue . . ."

Oh, here we go, thought Brenda. The dialogue. As Sprinkles the Elf, her role was to persuade a poor, bereft little girl—a girl who had lost all belief in Santa Claus—that the real gift of Christmas was the joy the season brings to everyone's hearts.

"I'll work on it," she said. "I have to admit, Christmas has never been my favorite time of year. It has . . . unpleasant associations for me."

"I'm sorry," Maureen said.

"For the sake of the play, I'll work on it," Brenda told her.

"There are some techniques you can try," Maureen suggested. "Most people tend to rush when they're speaking lines. Try pausing, and then feel the words before you speak them."

"Feel the words. Got it." Some of the words Sprinkles was supposed to say made her cringe, like *The joy of Christmas is in brightening others' lives and easing others' burdens*. And *The magic that makes Santa real is in everyone's hearts*. For Brenda, it was impossible to feel the words without a dark tinge of cynicism. "I'll keep practicing," she said. "The little girl who plays Greta is fantastic, by the way. She reminds me of me at that age." In the play, poor Greta had suffered too many disappointments at Christmas, and the experience had turned her into a total skeptic.

"She's great, isn't she? And you. You're an angel."

"I'm not." Brenda handed her a tote bag with the books Maureen had loaned her. "Thanks for these. I loved reading them. I felt like a kid again, hiding out with my books. And I learned a lot from your notes to the editors. It's so cool that they look for feedback from you."

"I can't call myself an expert, but I've been a children's librarian all my adult life. And here's what I know. When it comes to writing for kids, you have to go for it. They can spot phony sentiment a mile away, and they know when you're holding out on them, when something is being held back. With the book groups I lead here at the library, I call it the nectar. Something sweet and flowing. I know it's not easy for a writer to put her heart on paper. When I was younger, I was pretty buttoned up myself. I got over it, though. Wasn't easy, but it was worth it."

"How did you get over it?" Brenda asked.

Maureen smiled. "I fell in love."

"You'll have to tell me about that someday."

"I will! Anyway, it's fun to share with people who are in the business," said Maureen.

"I *aspire* to be in the business, but so far, I'm on the outside looking in. Publishing seems to be a very tricky process. I've sent my book manuscript out so many times, but it keeps getting turned down. More times than sheets in a cheap motel, as Dolly would say. It's disheartening."

"Getting the right story to the right editor is incredibly challenging. Sometimes I'm surprised that it works at all, but a good book will find its way into the right hands. Have you had any useful feedback?"

"Sure, but so much of it is contradictory. I'm afraid I haven't been writing the right story. Or maybe I haven't written it right. There's something missing. Or too much of something. Anyway, I started a brand-new story when I came on this trip. And . . . this one feels different. Like I might be onto something. Might just be wishful thinking, though. It's so hard to judge when I'm in the weeds."

"I'd love to read it. That is, if you ever feel like sharing."

Brenda stared at her. "Are you kidding? You'd read it?"

"Books are my life. And I've been accused of being too honest, sometimes, when a publisher asks for my opinion on something new. But if you can handle me being blunt as a spoon, maybe I could give you some helpful feedback."

BRENDA FOUND HERSELF with time on her hands, a rare occurrence. Her clients were mostly shut down through the holidays. Adam had a multiday duty shift. It seemed that circumstances had taken away all her excuses, and it was time to finish the new book she was working on. She did just that, writing in a white heat of inspiration. There was something so compelling about bringing the story in her head to life. She typed up a final copy, then went over it a half dozen times.

This one might be good, she thought. It was something a little different. Something fresh. Finally, she saved her latest draft and stared at the laptop screen, hoping that maybe this would be the one to turn her from aspiring writer to author. Then, before she lost her nerve, she attached it to an email message to Maureen Haven and hit send.

There was a soft knock at the door, which was open to the hallway. Adam stood there, leaning against the doorframe. He had a subtle beard shadow and a smile on his face, and her heart seemed to flip over in her chest.

"Shift's over," he said. "Did you miss me?"

Yes. *Yes.*

"I kept myself busy," Brenda said. "I finished writing my children's book."

"That's cool. Good for you."

"I just did a scary thing. I emailed it to Maureen Haven. She offered her services as first reader."

"I bet she's going to love it. The whole world is going to love it."

Brenda couldn't suppress a smile. "I think that's known as toxic positivity. Just saying something is going to turn out well doesn't make it so."

"How about instead of toxic positivity, we call it confidence? I still can't believe you're a book writer. It's awesome."

She shuddered and closed her laptop. "Is it five o'clock yet? I might need a drink."

"It's only three. You need to get out. Let's take Willy and the dogs to the sledding hill. Might as well enjoy last night's snow. And then later, maybe, we can enjoy something else."

"I know this will come as a shock to you, but I really can't stand the snow."

"But you like me, right? And you like dogs and little kids. Come on, my mom keeps extra ski pants in the mudroom. You can borrow them. We've got a good hour of light left, and then we can take Will to get something to eat afterward."

"Twist my arm, why don't you."

He stood behind her and treated her to a shoulder massage. "Nope. But I'd like to . . ." He whispered a suggestion that made her blush. "You did something good. Time to get out of your own head for a while."

Adam wasn't wrong. Just the act of gearing up for sledding helped Brenda shift gears. They picked Willy up from his preschool, and when he saw the sled and his snowsuit, he nearly exploded with excitement.

"The sledding hill is awesome," he told Brenda. "It's rad. Wait until you see!"

Willy wasn't wrong, either. The hill was a steep, smooth fairway at the local golf course. It descended into a small valley, then sloped upward again, creating the perfect ride. They went whipping down the hill on a long sled and tumbling out laughing at the end while the dogs ran alongside them, barking joyously.

The day filled Brenda with memories of long-ago winters when she was a girl. She could still hear her dad laughing as he challenged her and Cissy to make one more run.

"I love your smile," Adam said. "What's on your mind?"

"Just remembering my dad," she said.

"He loved the snow."

"He did."

"Tell me something you did with him."

She gestured at the hill, swarming with kids and sleds and dogs. "You're looking at it. Oh, and snow angels. You know, there's an art to it."

"Yeah? What's your technique?"

"It was my dad's technique." She took his hand and led him to an area where the snow hadn't been disturbed. "See, the trick is to make the design and then get up without making a hole in the snow. Spoils the effect, you know." She stood facing him. "Here. Take my hands, and let go when I lean back."

Brenda fell onto the soft, fluffy snow, and she was filled with the frozen scent of it. She drew her arms and legs through the soft powder, and then reached for Adam again. "The trick is to help me up without disturbing this amazing design."

He pulled her up as though she weighed nothing and lifted her into his arms. Over at the top of the hill, a couple of women stared at her and then leaned in to talk.

"Who are those women?" she asked Adam.

He shrugged. "Some moms from Willy's preschool, I guess."

"I think they're gossiping about us."

"That," he said with a laugh, "was hardly gossipworthy. But this is." He kissed her, then set her down.

"Whatcha doing?" Will asked, running over to them.

"Snow angel," Brenda said, gesturing at it. "What do you think?"

"I want to make one!"

He ended up making three, and then insisted on Adam taking a turn. Adam fell backward, and as he flailed his arms and legs, Olaf rushed in and made off with one of his gloves.

"Dang," he said. "These are my favorite gloves." He yelled at Olaf and ran after him, but that only made the dog more determined to keep it away. They managed to persuade the dog to come back, but the glove was long gone, probably hidden until the spring thaw.

"That was fun!" Willy crowed as they headed back to the car. "That was the best fun ever!"

"It was," Brenda admitted. "It's been a long time since I had fun in the snow."

"How long?" Willy demanded.

"Really long. Since I was a kid. I used to love sledding and snow angels."

He reached for her hand and Adam's, and they swung him up in the air. Now it was Willy's turn to be that happy kid.

A Friend in Deed

"Y ou keep making me do Christmas stuff," Brenda accused Adam
when he picked her up for night skiing at Saddle Mountain, the
ski hill near Avalon.

"This isn't Christmas stuff," he said.

She looked around the lodge, which had a massive lighted tree in the
front and carols blaring from hidden speakers.

Adam offered an innocent shrug. "How else am I going to get you
to like Christmas?"

"Maybe don't force it on me."

"Well, this is skiing. It has nothing to do with Christmas. People do
it all the time."

"Fair enough." She buckled up her stiff, rented ski boots and followed
him outside. A couple of deep booms sounded in the distance.

"Avalanche control," Adam said.

"Are we going to be able to get back down the mountain?"

"Sure. But if not, I don't think it would be bad to be stranded with
you." He placed her skis on the ground. "Ready for this?"

"I haven't gone skiing in ages. What if I break something?"

"I'm a paramedic. I know what to do about that. Come on. We'll start with the bunny hill."

The hum of the chairlift and the clatter of cables brought back memories. Brenda's parents had both been good skiers, and even after her father was gone, her mom had taken her and Cissy skiing at least once a year when they were growing up. The run down the snowy hill was exhilarating, and it was just what she needed after her very intense meeting earlier in the day with Maureen Haven about her book. The dramatic sweep of stars overhead and the far-off twinkle of lights along the lakeshore took her to a different world, a different frame of mind.

In spite of her reservations about the dangerous emotions she was feeling, Brenda savored every minute she spent with Adam. Something between them just clicked. The world seemed brand-new. Yet sometimes she felt as if they'd known each other forever. When she was back in Houston, she would remember him as the best thing about this trip.

They stayed until the lifts closed, then went into the lodge to warm up. "That was fun," she said, cradling an Irish coffee between her hands. "It felt good to get out and do something physical."

"Then let's not stop now. Let's go back to my place and play Twister. Willy got a Twister game for his birthday."

Brenda was involuntarily titillated by the suggestion; the thought of winding her limbs together with Adam's was undeniably appealing. But she shook her head. "I had a very long meeting with Maureen today about my writing."

"Tell me," he said. "She finished it?"

"My very first reader. I was a nervous wreck. She's a master librarian."

"Let me guess. She loved it. Said you're a genius."

"Not even. She said it was a privilege to read my book. She said I have top-notch writing skills. She said the plot and characters in the story are charming."

"Maureen's supersmart. So I'm sure she's right about you."

"She also said the emotional impact is muted, and my writing is too restrained."

"Well, if you ever need help undoing your restraints . . ." He moved closer to her and put his hand on her thigh.

"Adam."

"Sorry. I know this is important to you."

"Thank you for knowing it's important. Books were my refuge when I was little. They still are, to be honest. But see, this all goes back to my contention that when you want something too much, you're setting yourself up for disappointment."

He touched her hand. "I don't think there's such a thing as wanting something too much."

"When I was going through my divorce, I learned in therapy that there are emotional hurdles I haven't cleared. I suppose it applies to my writing, too. Deep down, I guess I know what's missing. I have to write about big feelings, the kind that scared me as a kid, and still scare me. The kind of sensations that make me feel like I'm drowning."

"Feelings about your dad," Adam said quietly.

It was freaky, how he'd homed in on that.

"I want you to do something for me," Adam continued. "I want you to close your eyes, and go back in time, and forgive that little girl for believing in Santa Claus. It wasn't her fault. It was never her fault." He slipped his arm around her. "I'm sorry for what happened all those years ago. I'm sorry you lost your dad in such a horrible way. But I'll never be sorry for falling in love with you."

"This is it, everybody." Backstage at the community theater, Maureen addressed the cast. There was a low roar from the crowd shuffling in to find their seats. Music drifted from the PA system, and ushers and volunteers collected extra donations from the patrons. "We've all worked so hard," Maureen continued, "and we have a sold-out house. Now it's our time to shine. Let's put on a show!"

Brenda ran her finger around the collar of her elf costume. She was already sweating.

"You all right?" asked Harriet Cullen. Armed with her clipboard and cell phone, she had done a fine job as script supervisor. "Need anything?"

"I'm all set," Brenda said. "Just nervous."

"We all are," Harriet said. "It's normal, right?" She moved on to organize the people who were playing the toys that would magically come to life.

Brenda had struggled with her part. It was easy enough to remember the lines, but delivering them was the challenge. She had to look Greta in the eye and convincingly explain the special magic of Christmas, leading into the biggest, most sentimental song of the production, the song that would finally turn little Greta into a true believer.

It helped that the audience was friendly, made up of locals and tourists out for a family holiday night. She recognized some of the people who had adopted the dogs, and it filled her with satisfaction to know she'd had a part in bringing something so special into their lives. There was VIP seating for Adam and Will. She glimpsed them from backstage, their hair slicked back and their Christmas sweaters adorably ugly. Adam said he was falling in love with her. He'd *said* it. She was still reeling from that.

Right away, the upbeat music, under the leadership of Eddie Haven, had people tapping their feet and sometimes even clapping their hands and singing along—an element that was encouraged. The big moment for Sprinkles the Elf occurred at the end of Act Two. Brenda knew her speech as though it had been embroidered on her brain. As she faced the little girl who played Greta, something came over Brenda. She was haunted by something Adam had said to her—forgive that little girl for believing in Santa Claus.

When Brenda started to speak, the moment took her by surprise. And she spoke not from the page she'd memorized, but from her own heart laid bare. And she didn't feel as if she was addressing Greta, but another little girl from long ago, her nine-year-old self. *If you listen very hard, you'll hear the promise on the whispering wind. Sometimes the greatest gifts can't be seen or touched, but those might just be the ones that last forever. Even when someone leaves us, the love remains. You get to keep it forever.*

When she finished speaking, there was a beat of silence in the house. Brenda froze, wondering if she'd made a horrible mistake. Then there was a collective murmur from the crowd followed by applause as the chords swelled to introduce the big musical number. Brenda dared to scan the audience, and she was amazed to see a few people dabbing at their eyes, while others cheered. Dolly Prentice and Alice Bellamy, in wheelchairs near the front row, beamed with pride.

The rest of the production passed in a blur. The jubilant finale was followed by curtain calls, rounds of applause for the musicians, and for Maureen. Armloads of flowers were delivered to the stage, and the production ended with a Christmas carol sing-along.

Brenda rushed to the backstage changing area, already tearing at the elf costume. "Lord, never again," she said to Harriet, who stood by with a supply of makeup wipes and clothes hangers.

"You were wonderful," Harriet said. "You reminded us of how Christmas can transform a person when they need it the most. I believe the phrase is 'not a dry eye in the house.'"

"Well, thanks. I'm just glad it's over." Brenda hurried into her street clothes. "And thanks for helping out with the production. You've been great."

"I should be thanking you," Harriet said. "Getting involved in the play was the one thing that kept the holidays from totally sucking this year. I'm on the permanent volunteer list now. See you at the after-party?"

"Not me," Brenda said. "I have a date with two adorable guys." She sent Adam a text and met him and Will in the parking lot outside. They went for ice cream, feeling lucky to find a booth at the crowded café. She looked around the warm, bustling place, at the faces of the children and grandparents and friends, and she understood that winter didn't always have to be cold, especially when it was encased in the closeness of families.

"I want sprinkles on mine," Will said. "Lots of sprinkles."

"Does Sprinkles the Elf approve?" asked Adam.

"Please. I'll be happy if I never hear that name again," Brenda said. Then she noticed Will looking at her. "Hey, not really, kiddo. Did you like the play?"

"Uh-huh."

"What was your favorite part?"

"The toys. They came out of the boxes and they were *alive*."

"That was cool, wasn't it?" Brenda said.

Will nattered on, speculating about his own toys coming to life and making a soupy mess of his ice cream. Adam gazed across the table at Brenda with a smile on his face. "Loved every minute of it," he told her. "I knew you had it in you."

She smiled back, thinking that this might be a perfect moment. No more play practice. No more Sprinkles. Just this sweet little boy and his dad. She wanted to hold it in her heart forever.

"Ready, Willy?" Suzanne arrived, brushing snowflakes from her coat. Beautifully groomed, smiling down at the little boy, she smoothed her hand gently over his head. Adam had explained to Brenda that it was changeover day—the day his son went home with Suzanne. And just like that, the mood shifted. Adam stiffened, Will wiped his mouth on his sleeve, and the light moment was gone.

"Mom! Mom! Guess what? Guess what?" Will bounced out of his seat. "We went to a *play*, and Brenda was the elf!"

"She was? Well, that's pretty special." Suzanne regarded Brenda with chilly speculation.

In that moment, Brenda recognized Suzanne's feelings. She offered a half-hearted smile, feeling impossibly awkward. Adam had loved Suzanne, and then he'd stopped. They were playing out Brenda's worst fears about falling in love.

"Yeah!" Will jiggled in his seat. "And the toys came to life! It was so cool."

"We'd better be going," Suzanne said. "Remember, we have a new little dog to take care of now, and she's waiting for us at home."

"Vixen! Can she sleep in my bed again? I love sleeping with my dog."

"Then I guess you'd better sleep with her." Suzanne flashed a look at Adam. Then she bent down and helped Will get his jacket on. He insisted on bringing the play program, the ice cream coloring page, and the ticket stub in his pocket.

"'Bye, my buddy," Adam said with forced cheerfulness. "I'll pick you up at your mom's, okay? In three sleeps." He gave Will a hug, and the little boy clung hard to his neck. Suzanne stood by, her expression carved in stone.

There would always be complications, thought Brenda.

Complications

The van was nearly done at last. The repair shop told Brenda it would be ready on the day before Christmas Eve. "Oh, that's good news," she said when the mechanic called her.

But at the same time, her heart sank. With the repairs done, there was nothing to stop her from leaving. No reason for her to linger like an unwanted houseguest. She had done what she'd set out to do—delivered the dogs to their forever homes. Now the van was needed in Houston, and it was her job to drive it back.

Not so long ago, it was all she wanted—to drive away from this godforsaken arctic town to the warmth and security of Houston, to the new life she'd made for herself there.

When she phoned Adam to tell him, he was quiet for several long moments.

"Adam? Are you there?" she asked.

Silence. Had he hung up on her? Dropped the phone in disappointment? She sighed and set down her phone. Maybe he needed to mull over the idea for a bit.

Brenda went to the closet of her room and took out her suitcase. Then, one by one, she started folding things to put in it. Since her arrival, though, she'd acquired too many clothes to all fit in the small roller bag. They were clothes she'd never need in Houston's climate. She should pack up all the winter things and take them to the charity box at one of the churches in town.

"I've been looking forward to this day since I got here," she said to Tim, who was lazing on a pillow on the window seat. "Haven't I?"

The dog cocked his head, then rested his chin between his front paws.

"Then why is the prospect of leaving so depressing?" she asked.

Tim gave an elaborate yawn. Then his ears pricked up, and he scampered to the door, tail wagging.

There was a soft knock, and Adam came in. "I have a better idea," he said. "Spend Christmas with me."

Brenda recoiled from the idea. Grant's family had subjected her to a relentless Christmas assault, year in and year out. Adam was not Grant, she reminded herself. But Christmas was still Christmas.

She resumed the chore of folding her clothes, creating a separate pile for the winter things. "Your mother told me your entire family goes all out for the holidays every year."

"Guilty as charged. Look, I know you don't have a lot of love for Christmas, but how about giving it another shot?"

She didn't want to drag him through all the reasons she was soured on Christmas; she'd already told him all that. But he deserved an explanation. "Look, I know I dressed up like an elf and delivered dogs and performed in the Christmas play. But that doesn't mean I've changed my mind. This is supposed to be my way of escaping the holidays. Not a trial by fire with your Christmas-loving family."

"Ouch."

"See? You're making my point for me. People in love hurt each other." She tossed the blue sweater on the discard pile. Damn, that was a nice sweater. But she didn't need it.

"Ah. So you *are* in love with me." Adam smiled.

"Knock it off. I'm . . ." Was she? *Was she?*

"That's impossible," she said. "We've only just met."

"Well, that's the best time to start falling in love, right? When you meet and you just know. Because I look at you, Brenda, and I *know*. I've never been so sure of anything."

"You *don't* know, Adam. You can't."

"It's crazy, right? But I can. Listen, after my divorce, I was an emotional wreck, and I was in complete denial about it. I lied to everyone, telling people I was doing great. I dated women like a sailor on shore leave. I hunted for relationships that made me seem happy. But eventually, I figured out how to be honest with myself. It was humbling, but I'm better off for it. I know myself now. I trust myself. I've gone head over heels for you, and I trust *that*."

"I'm happy for you," she said, "but I don't have your sense of certainty. I'm not sure of anything anymore."

"Okay," he said. "Here's another idea. I don't have Will with me for Christmas this year. It's Suzanne's turn to have him. How about we *both* skip Christmas."

"Oh, lovely. I'm sure that will endear me to your family."

"They already love you. Ivy and my mom. When you meet the others—Mason and his wife, Faith, and Simon—they'll love you, too, even if you steal me away."

"What about you? Adam, you love Christmas. I know you do. Why would you want to be with me? Remember, Dolly has a nickname for me—Scroogetta."

"Ha. And I like that."

"You like Christmas."

"I like you more. Okay, so here's my proposal. Let's have a quiet Christmas Eve together. Just the two of us. Mom will understand. It'll be like any other night. No singing. No Christmas crackers or party games. Nothing but you and me. Hanging out."

She held up her new pajamas and carefully folded them. Adam eyed them with unabashed hunger.

"I'm skeptical," Brenda said. "It sounds like a trap."

"We can get takeout food from the Thai place. As far as I know, there is nothing on the menu with mincemeat or cranberries or ginger-bread. We can watch an old movie, like *Die Hard*."

She couldn't deny that the idea appealed to her. "No carolers at the door?"

"I live in a boathouse. Nobody comes to my door." He crossed the room and lightly kissed her cheek. "It's a great plan."

"Everyone's going to be at your mom's place, doing Christmas."

"Trust me, they won't darken *my* door." Adam held her upper arms and looked deeply into her eyes. "Let's see what this can be," he urged. "Look, I won't even get you a Christmas present. That's how supportive I am of avoiding Christmas." He reached into his pocket and handed her a parcel.

"You said no presents."

"It's not a present. It's not even wrapped. And today is not Christmas."

Brenda glowered at him. "I didn't get you anything."

"You're not required to."

She opened the bag. "It's a notebook. And a pen."

"One of those fancy German ones with the nice paper. And the pen is a fountain pen. So your ideas can flow. So your feelings can flow. The big ones you're going to write about."

"Well. Thank you. It's really thoughtful. My gosh, Adam. You are so damned thoughtful." How was it that a simple gift like pen and paper felt more meaningful than all the sparkly baubles and pricey perfumes Grant used to give her?

"It's easy to think of you," he said. "I do it all the time. What do you say? Hang out with me on Christmas Eve?"

She felt a thrill of yearning, because hanging out with him for Thai takeout and a movie sounded fantastic to her. But she quickly tamped it down. "No. Thank you, Adam. But no."

"Why not?"

"Because . . . well, *Die Hard is* a Christmas movie."

He offered a sheepish grin and a shrug. "Maybe. A little."

"About a guy who's a dad."

"That's the best kind. Come on, Brenda. Why not—*really?*"

"You make me want things too much," she blurted out. "I don't dare want something too much." A life with him. A deep emotional bond she'd never felt before. "Because if it doesn't happen, the disappointment would kill me."

"And what if it *does* happen? Then will the joy kill you? You're afraid to find out, aren't you?"

"I'm not afraid," she said, resuming her packing. The cozy socks went in the discard pile. Wool socks were not needed in Houston. "Just managing my expectations."

"Come on, Brenda. It'll be fine. Trust me on this. I know about these things."

She caught her breath, hearing a strange echo of something her father had said to her long ago. On Christmas Eve. That was why she remembered the words. "Maybe," she said. "I'll let you know."

AFTER SHE PICKED up the van from the shop, Brenda went to Fairfield House to see Dolly. A girl answered the door. She was missing one front tooth and had pigtails and freckles, and a novel tucked under her arm. "I'm Tina," she said. "You're here to see Aunt Dolly?"

"That's right. It's nice to meet you. How is Aunt Dolly doing?"

"She's great," Tina said brightly. "We're reading *Wedgie and Gizmo* together." She held up the book.

"Looks really good," Brenda said. "I love to read. Always have."

"Yeah. Me, too. *Aunt Dolly!*" Tina raised her voice to a shout. "Your friend's here!"

"Pipe down, there," Dolly called from her room. "You'll disturb the other guests."

"Oops, sorry." Tina stepped into the room.

"I see you've met my favorite grandniece," Dolly said.

"I'm not your favorite. I'm your *only* grandniece," said Tina.

"Which makes you the favorite," Dolly said with a wink. "Why don't we take a break from reading. You go fix yourself a snack in the kitchen. Brenda and I can have a little chat."

"I've been working on my novel," Brenda said after Tina departed.

"How's that going, hon?" Dolly held out a dish of Christmas candy.

Brenda shook her head. "It's changed a lot. I've been getting some good feedback from Maureen, the librarian." Brenda had put more heart into the story than she'd ever dared before. She forced herself to liberate that closed-off inner child who was trying so hard not to fall apart, who was afraid she'd disintegrate if she let her emotions run wild. She wrote the story she'd been afraid to write. She wrote it for that little girl waiting for Santa Claus to come. For the kid who was broken by a loss so powerful that she'd kept her heart buried for years. Now she realized it was her heart that gave the story the kind of power that had been lacking. Maybe one day it would find an actual publisher. Maybe not. But either way, Brenda knew it was the most deeply felt piece she'd ever written, and she would always know that the story had come from a place inside her that had finally found a way to heal.

"Good news about the van," Dolly said. Then she studied Brenda's face. "Isn't it?"

"Absolutely," Brenda said, the answer sounding too swift and too bright.

"What? Come on, girlfriend. Spill."

"He wants me to spend Christmas Eve with him."

"And I should feel sorry for you because . . ."

"Because I have to go. My life is in Houston, not here." Brenda took a deep breath and finally confessed the real reason she had to leave. "I have too many feelings about Adam. It's just . . . too intense. It can't be good for me."

"Oh, honey. Everything about this experience has been good for you. I can tell. Take a chance. Let yourself fall in love with the man."

"Why would I do that? Why would I love someone if it only means a painful breakup?"

"My friend, I'm old, and I know things. I know that not letting yourself love someone isn't going to spare you any pain. It'll only cost you the joy you might have had together."

"We're not talking about a crush here," Brenda said. "This is something else. Something more powerful than I've ever felt before. If I let it happen, it would hurt too much to lose it."

"Then don't lose it. Keep it forever. It can be done. I swear."

"Only if I pull up roots and bring my whole life here. Adam can't leave because of his son." Brenda vacillated between terror and elation. With Adam, she just might find the kind of true love she'd always scoffed at and never allowed herself to feel. Yet she couldn't imagine why anyone would want a love like that, when losing it meant a hurt that would never heal.

"I've known you for a long time, Brenda Malloy," Dolly said. "You've been hedging your bets against love because you're certain it leads to pain. What you need to know is that love is the one thing that makes everything bearable. The feeling you're avoiding is not the problem. It's the solution—if you let it be."

Could she let it happen? Was she so afraid of loss that she let her fear rob her of the one thing she most wanted?

"All I see are the complications," Brenda said. "He's got an ex-wife who never got over him. And she already knows about us."

"Don't borrow other people's problems. You know better than that."

"Well, suppose I uproot myself and get involved with a man in this strange town and it doesn't work out?"

"Suppose you do that and it does work out?" Dolly countered. "Listen. You are not a chickenshit, my friend. The night of the wreck, I saw what you are made of. So I know for a fact that you have the courage to let an amazing man love you without being scared of being hurt."

Brenda's stomach churned with nerves as she went out to the van. She turned on the heater and took out her phone.

Before she lost her nerve, she sent Adam a text message:

Okay.

Okay what? he messaged back.

Okay I'll meet you on Christmas Eve at the Thai place. There. She'd said it. She was committed. *Let's see what this can be.*

Okay. You won't be sorry. The message was followed by a series of emojis—starry eyes, a heart, and a bowl of noodles.

Christmas Is Coming

Brenda decided to leave Dolly's holiday decals on the van. At least the red bulb on Rudolph's nose made the vehicle easy to find in any parking lot.

She hoped she wouldn't regret meeting Adam on Christmas Eve. He promised she wouldn't, but they were so new to each other. How could he know? She tried not to think about those other Christmases, the ones that left her grieving, fearful, disappointed, or simply empty. There had been far too many like that.

She found what seemed to be the last parking spot on the main square of town. The area was bustling with last-minute shoppers and people meeting for dinner or drinks. "We're early," she said to Tim. "Let's take a walk around town while we wait."

Adam was dropping his little boy off at Suzanne's. He wouldn't see his son until the day after Christmas. Brenda tried to imagine what that was like. After the excitement and festivities, after the joy of Christmas morning was past, Will would return to his dad. The thought of that made her wince. *Complications*, she thought.

"I suppose it feels totally normal to Will," she said to Tim, putting on his harness and leash. "I bet it still doesn't make it easier for the parents, though. God, what am I doing, Timmy? Hanging around . . . for what?"

She stepped aside as a group of carolers passed by, taking up the whole sidewalk and belting out "Deck the Halls." Some of them were in full Victorian regalia, with stovepipe hats and tails, long skirts and faux fur muffs.

"It's like a virus around here," she said through clenched teeth as she smiled and waved at the carolers. On impulse, she ducked into the outdoor store, which was still open for another hour. "Last-minute shopping?" asked the guy behind the counter.

"It's the way I roll," Brenda said. "I need a really nice pair of men's gloves."

"Ma'am, every guy needs that. I have just the thing." He sold her a pair of buttery-soft gloves lined with angora. "Want a gift bag for these?"

"No, thank you," she said with a smile. "They're not a gift." That was the rule. No gifts. If there were no gifts, there could be no Christmas. For an unguarded, perverse moment, she kind of wanted it to be Christmas.

Be careful what you wish for, she told herself. Outside, the carolers had moved on to "God Rest Ye Merry Gentlemen" in front of the library. Brenda owed Maureen Haven a debt of gratitude—as well as a proper thank-you note—for being so encouraging about Brenda's book. Maureen had even offered to introduce her to a children's book editor she knew down in Irvington. All Brenda had to do was come up with the ending of her story.

She saw a man coming toward her with a dog on a leash. Startled, she said, "Lester. It's good to see you."

Tim and the greyhound gave each other a sniff.

"How are you and Buzz getting along?" Brenda asked.

"Just dandy," he said. "I got him a nice warm coat for Christmas."

She admired the plaid dog jacket. "I bet he loves it. Greyhounds are built for speed, not for warmth."

"You got that right. Have a Merry Christmas, now."

"I will," she said, and she almost believed herself. "Same to you."

Brenda and Tim did another turn around the block, taking in the sights and sounds of the holiday. "I guess Christmas is coming whether we like it or not," she said, watching her words freeze in the cold air as she scanned the now-familiar town square.

How quickly she had woven herself into the fabric of this small town in this snowy corner of the world. She'd already made friends here; it was a community that felt light-years away from Houston. Could she do it? Brenda wondered. Could she do what Dolly said—completely fling herself into this town, into this life, with nothing but hope for a safety net?

As the minutes ticked by, she felt a twinge of nerves. What was she doing here? she wondered. She took out her phone and checked the time. He was late. Or maybe not. Maybe she'd gotten the time wrong. She sent him a quick text message, then rolled her eyes, wishing she could unsend it. She didn't want to be *that* girl, that insecure, constantly-checking-in girl.

It was snowing lightly now, and people came out to take pictures and gather in groups. The sound of sleigh bells caught her attention, and she saw an old-fashioned buckboard wagon making its way around the square. Santa Claus waved at the children, who went wild with excitement. To Brenda, it was just another dark reminder of Christmases past.

Her fingers and toes were freezing. *Cold feet*, she thought. She had told Dolly that she was having an adventure. Yes, that was what Adam Bellamy was. An adventure. And like all great adventures, it was bound to come to an end. It was ridiculous that Brenda hadn't realized that sooner. He was at Suzanne's place. He was with the mother of his child, a lovely woman who wanted him back. Maybe they were talking about it and he'd lost track of time.

As more moments ticked by, Brenda felt foolish for pursuing this mad affair, this *adventure* that could only end in heartbreak. She disappeared into the past, foraging through memories that had scarred her heart for life. She remembered little Brenda, waiting for Santa. Waiting for her father. Waiting and waiting, and he never came.

She should know by now that everything bad happened at Christmas. Life had taught her that. She was an idiot to think this would be different.

She decided that if Adam didn't show up soon, she would hit the road with Tim, leaving yet another failed Christmas behind.

"GOOD NIGHT, MY best buddy," Adam said. "You and your mom go to bed early, okay?"

"No way," Will said. He was watching Olaf and Suzanne's little dog playing tug-of-war with a knotted rope.

"The more time you sleep, the more time Santa will have to do his job."

"Well, yeah. Did you see the snacks? Mom and I left snacks." In his new fuzzy Christmas jammies, Will looked so cute it made Adam's heart ache.

"Those are some good snacks. Everybody likes chips and salsa."

"Would you like some?" Suzanne offered. "There's extra."

"Yeah!" Willy bounced up and down. "Stay for chips and salsa!"

Adam smiled through the familiar wrenching sensation. "Oh, that sounds good, but unfortunately, Olaf and I need to get going."

"Aw, Daddy. I wish you could stay."

Adam took a smelly treat from his pocket. "Over here, Olaf." The dog trotted to his side. He was getting better at minding Adam.

"You're gonna go see Brenda," Will said.

Adam tried not to flinch. There were no secrets in a small town, but that didn't make it less awkward to know Suzanne was aware that something new might be happening.

"One last kiss," he said, pulling Willy into a close hug. Over the top of the little boy's head, he caught Suzanne's look of sadness and yearning. At one time, he might have been tempted to try yet again to make their marriage work. Now, however, he couldn't picture himself with anyone but Brenda.

He looked around the house where he and Suzanne and their little boy used to live. There was the furniture they'd picked out together, the artwork on the walls from his sister's gallery, a couple of framed pictures of them, back when they'd been a family. Out in the snowy yard was the swing set he'd spent hours putting together, abandoned now. He'd tried so hard to make a happy life for all of them. Will was his greatest joy, his greatest accomplishment . . . but the marriage was his greatest failure.

Now Adam's little boy lived two separate lives, and Adam struggled to make his peace with the reality he and Suzanne had created. When Will was with Suzanne, Adam could no longer be there to protect him, to make sure the doors were locked and the windows were shut, that there were no hazards lying around the house. He took a deep breath and reminded himself that even though he couldn't be married to Suzanne, he trusted her.

Gathering strength from the love in his heart, Adam went to the door. "Merry Christmas to all," he said in a booming Santa voice.

"And to all a good night!" Will finished with him.

"I'll pick you up day after tomorrow for more fun and games, okay, buddy?"

"Okay!"

Suzanne walked with Adam out onto the porch, hugging herself against the cold.

"Are you all set with his Santa gifts?" he asked her.

"Of course. Don't worry, he's got a few years left to be a true believer."

"I hope he never gets too old to look up and search the skies on Christmas Eve. I know I haven't."

"I miss you," she said. "I miss *us*. Especially on a night like tonight."

He pictured her going back into the warm, painfully neat house, putting Will to bed, and then setting out the Santa gifts while sipping a lonely glass of wine. "I'm sorry," he said, discomfited by the mental image. "Suzanne, we tried. We did our best. Will's doing great, and one reason is that he doesn't have to live with the tension and anger we tried so hard to hide. I'm a better dad these days. Sharing custody has made me a lot more mindful when I'm not with him, and a lot more patient when I am. He's the best kid ever, so we're doing something right."

"How do you suppose he'll do when he figures out that there's a new girlfriend in the picture?" Suzanne's voice was low and tremulous.

"Having more people in his life who love him never did a kid any harm," Adam pointed out. "Suzanne, I need you to know that Brenda and I are getting serious. I can't say what's going to happen, but I think it's the start of something." Adam hoped he wasn't projecting. Maybe Brenda had bigger issues than he could handle. But he wanted her in a way he'd never wanted a woman before, with a powerful feeling that this was right, it was what he'd been looking for all his life, and it was a sweet relief that he had finally found it.

"How nice for you," she said.

"Aw, Suz. I know it's hard. I didn't think I'd ever get over us. But we can't stay stuck in limbo forever. You're a great mom and a great person, and one of these days, you're going to meet someone who makes you so happy, you'll never stop smiling. You might not see it coming, but it'll happen, I swear."

"I'm glad you've got that all figured out," she said. "It must make you feel so relieved."

He realized then there was nothing he could say to mollify her. "Okay, so, anyway, have a fantastic Christmas with Will and your family."

Suzanne lifted her hand as if to touch him, then stepped back and turned, hurrying into the house.

With Olaf in the back seat, Adam mentally shifted gear. It was true that he didn't get to have his son with him at Christmas. But now there was something new in his life, something that had awakened his heart. It wouldn't fix his loneliness for Will, but Brenda brought him a different kind of joy.

He hummed along with the radio as he drove down the mountain to town to meet her. He rounded the first hairpin curve and saw a glow of lights ahead. The lights bobbed with erratic movements that sharpened his instincts with a spike of danger. He pulled up closer to see that an avalanche had broken loose, the mass of snow and debris covering the narrow mountain road.

Adam pulled up next to the guardrail and jumped out of the truck. Olaf came bounding after him. "Olaf!" he said, but he didn't want to take time to round up the dog.

He jogged toward the vehicle, a station wagon with a few people inside. "Anyone hurt here?" he asked.

The guy in the driver's seat got out. "Naw, man. We're okay. But how are we going to get around this mess? I tried calling 911, but there's no cell signal."

"I have a radio," Adam said, taking it out of its holster.

A reduced service crew was on duty, and the dispatcher warned him that it might be a couple of hours before someone could get up to clear the road.

"Damn. We don't have a couple of hours," the guy said. "Damn. It's Christmas Eve." There were three little kids in the back seat of his car. His wife was fruitlessly looking for a signal on her phone.

At the side of the road, Olaf was engaged in his favorite pastime—

digging. Adam measured the gap between the piled snow and the guardrail. It was almost wide enough for a car to squeeze through.

"I have a couple of shovels," he said. "Want to give me a hand?"

"Oh, hell yes. Thanks, man. We got this."

The orange snow shovels they'd used to dig out the van were back in service again. Adam and the guy and his wife all pitched in. "We're on our way over from New Paltz," the woman explained. "We have family in Avalon. They're gonna be worried if we're too late."

"Then let's not be too late," Adam said.

The woman had put on Christmas music for the kids to listen to. They could hear strains of "It Came Upon a Midnight Clear" coming from the car. The woman started singing, and her husband joined in, and with a shrug, Adam added his voice to the rest. Olaf paused in his digging to sit back on his haunches, point his muzzle to the sky, and howl a few times.

Eventually, they cleared enough space for the car to inch through. Adam stood by the guardrail and called out to guide the station wagon past the slide. The guy honked his horn and rolled down his window, and the whole family shouted, "Merry Christmas!"

"Yeah, same," Adam called after them. "Damn, Olaf, we're pretty late, aren't we?" He took out his phone to see if there was enough of a signal to call Brenda and explain. At the same time, Olaf leaped at him in excitement. The phone flew from Adam's hand and landed on a snowdrift outside of the guardrail.

"Ah, shit, Olaf." Adam gritted his teeth and straddled the rail. He couldn't quite reach the phone, so he climbed over and reached out farther. The phone slid away, out of sight. Adam let loose with a string of words that would land him on the naughty list for life. At the same time, the ground beneath his boot gave way, and he was plunged headfirst into the snow, sinking down into the well under an evergreen tree.

The snow surrounding the tree collapsed onto Adam. He was engulfed in complete, cold darkness. Disoriented, gasping for air, he tried to make his way out, but his efforts caused him to sink deeper. It was getting harder to breathe. To think. He was coughing, trying to find a purchase with his hands, failing, sinking again. An image of his father flashed through his mind. Trevor Bellamy had died in an avalanche. Had he been this scared? This starved for oxygen? Had his last thoughts been of his family? Of the woman he loved? Of the regrets he had? Or had they been more prosaic, like cursing himself for making a foolish move?

Light-headed, unable to figure out which end was up, Adam was nearly spent when he felt a movement by his foot. Lots of movement. Olaf's paws, digging furiously. *Yes. Good dog.* A hole opened in the snow, and Adam glimpsed the stars overhead. The midnight clear.

It Came Upon a Midnight Clear

I give up," Brenda said to Tim as she leaned against the side of the van. Santa's wagon had left and the Christmas crowd had thinned to a few stragglers. "I give up on Adam. I give up on Christmas. On falling in love with someone who lives a million miles away. I don't know what I was thinking—that my luck was about to change?"

Somewhere in the distance, a church bell rang. Adam probably had a perfectly reasonable excuse for being ridiculously late. But the delay had given her time to clear her head and think about everything she'd battled with and failed to overcome all her life. Time to contemplate the madness of trying to start something with a guy she'd just met, a guy inexorably tied to a town where she was a stranger. Where the weather was horrific and Christmas was in your face, year after year. Who was she to think a brief, wild affair would be the remedy for a lifetime of struggle? Despite the unexpected joys of the last few days, Brenda felt utterly lost in the deepest, darkest, most fatal sense of despair.

Maybe the universe was trying to tell her something. Maybe it was time to return to her predictable, safe, nonsnowy, non-Christmassy world. Time to remember that Christmas was cheesy and manipulative and a big fat lie. Time to save herself from heartache. Right now. Right this minute, before she lost her resolve. Before Adam showed up to talk her out of it.

She didn't want to go back to the Bellamy place, where people were caroling and wassailing and whatever else people did on Christmas. She had everything she needed in the van already—Tim's gear and her work things. If she left now and drove all night, she'd be out of the snow in a matter of hours. She'd be well on her way home to Texas.

"One more quick run around the park," she said to Tim, unclipping his leash. "It's going to be a long night." While he sniffed and peed, she checked her phone one more time. Nothing. She debated with herself about whether or not to send Adam another text. No.

This was further proof of what she already knew about love. It was too hard on a heart that had suffered enough.

"Come on, Tim," she called, clapping her hands. "Load up!"

Tim trotted over to her, but he balked when she slid open the side panel of the van. "Come *on*," she insisted, gesturing at the open van. "Up!"

It wasn't like Tim to ignore a command. He took a few steps back, then cocked his head, listening. All Brenda could hear were the church bells, tolling out a song.

Exasperated, she picked Tim up to load him into the van. The dog whined and squirmed, resisting with all his might. Then Brenda heard something else. A faint barking sound.

"What the . . ." She set Tim down as she saw Olaf streaking toward her, churning up the snow, then prancing exuberantly when he reached her side.

Adam was nowhere in sight. "What's going on?" she asked Olaf. "Are you too much for Adam after all? Am *I* too much for him?" Maybe she was—too much. Too damaged. Too needy. Too—

Then she saw Adam coming toward her, disheveled, his cheeks flaming red, jacket and pants caked with snow. He held his arms spread wide, and his eyes shone in a way that made her feel weak in the knees.

"I thought you'd stood me up," she said.

"Avalanche delay," he said. "I helped some folks clear the road."

Of course he had. He was all about helping people.

She looked at him again and realized he was caked in snow, even in his hair. And despite the high color in his cheeks, there was an underlying pallor, and his lips were blue. "There's something you're not telling me," she said, her pulse speeding up, sensing danger before she knew what the danger was. "Looks like you were *in* the avalanche. What happened, Adam?"

"Remember the tree well hazard I warned you about? I kind of ended up headfirst in one. Lost my phone, too."

"*Headfirst?* You could have died, Adam." Brenda's blood seemed to freeze in her veins. The thought of losing him—before she ever really had him—caused a flash of panic.

"I got lucky. Olaf dug me out. He seemed to know just what to do."

Her knees wobbled, and she sank down and rubbed Olaf's head until he sneezed in delight. "What a good, good, *very* good boy," she said. Then she stood up and faced Adam. "See, this is exactly why I'm scared to love you. Because I couldn't survive losing you."

"You didn't lose me. I came right back to you. And I always will."

She shuddered. "New rule: no more diving headfirst into the snow."

He smiled down at her. "Noted."

She reached into her pocket and pulled out the gloves she'd bought him. "I got you these. Looks like you could use a new pair."

He put them on and closed his eyes in ecstasy. "These are really nice, Brenda. And it's not even Christmas yet. We're not going to be those people who open stuff on Christmas Eve, are we?"

He was already assuming they were "those people." That they were together.

"Adam—"

"Come here." He drew her into a hug, then kissed her long and hard. Then he drew back and gazed down at her, gently brushing the hair from her forehead. "You look worried."

"You're a mess. Are you sure you're all right? Should you go get checked out, or—"

"Nah," he said. "I'm fine now." He rested his chin on top of her head and let out a deep sigh. "Anyway, Brenda, about us."

Her heartbeat thundered in her ears. She couldn't tell if the rush she was feeling was relief or love. It was true she'd triumphed in the Christmas play, and she'd had a breakthrough in her writing. But the bigger problem was what to do about her feelings for Adam and the impossibility of loving him.

"This is happening too fast," she said.

"Brenda. What's keeping you from loving me?"

"I . . . you want so much, Adam. Do you know what kind of pressure this puts on me? I can't make up for your broken marriage. I can't make you and Will into a family."

"I'm not asking you to do that. I'm asking you to trust me. To trust *us*. To trust what you're feeling."

"What if it's not real?"

"I already know it's real. It's Christmas Eve, Brenda. That's when the magic happens."

"*What?*"

"I said—"

"That's when the magic happens. I heard you, Adam." She could almost hear her father, saying the same thing. In a deeply hidden part of herself, she imagined this was a sign from her dad, steering her toward a man he'd never get the chance to meet.

"I want to start something with you," Adam was saying. "I know you don't like things that are messy, and I can't promise you there won't be messes. And I know you don't like hard times and you worry that things can fall apart and people might get hurt. I can't promise you that won't happen either, because life is unpredictable that way. I mean, look what just happened. I almost missed you. You had one foot out the door. And I know you're scared to take a risk because of how hard it was to lose your father. But I'm not going to lie— When I was practically drowning in the snow, that scared the hell out of me. And the biggest part of that fear was that I'd never get the chance to be with you. Brenda, I can promise you this. I am falling madly in love with you."

She pressed her forehead against his shoulder, nearly reeling from his words. This was one of those moments Dolly talked about, when the world tilted and life pivoted, and Brenda wanted to take in every detail. Adam smelled of snow and pine needles, like a Christmas tree. His arms were impossibly strong, though he held her gently. She could feel the rhythm of his heart and his breath even through the layers of their clothes. The thought that she'd almost lost him terrified her. But it was also proof of how important he was to her.

She took a deep breath and let it out slowly, watching it freeze in the cold air. She finally knew what she had to do. She had to give up the life she had so carefully built for herself and leap into the unknown with a guy she barely knew. She didn't know if she could do it, could be that vulnerable, that incautious with her closely guarded heart. She only knew the decision was out of her hands. She couldn't help loving him, no matter how mad or impulsive it seemed. Dolly was right. Love didn't have to hurt. It came with the deepest sense of joy. Maybe Brenda would get her heart broken again, but a love like this was worth the risk. It was a new destination. A new life. There was danger in that, but exhilaration, too.

A sturdy sense of resolve kicked in, the way it had when she embarked on the journey with Dolly. The way it had when she'd escaped the overturned van. The way it had when she stepped onto the stage to play her part.

She was a different person from the woman who had boarded the Christmas van full of dogs. She could break through her own barriers. She could vault over her own wall. She could do this.

"I was so crushed when I didn't think you were coming tonight. That maybe you'd changed your mind. And then when you showed up, I almost keeled over with relief."

"I'm sorry you were worried, Brenda. I—"

"Let me finish," she said, wanting to get the words right as she tried to parse through the decision that was forming with hard resolve inside her. "When I was growing up," she said, "I had to move every couple of years. Once I settled in Houston, I swore I'd never move again. And now we live thousands of miles apart, and I understand perfectly well that you have to stay where Willy is."

He didn't deny it. "Brenda. I know what I'm asking of you. I know it's a lot."

"It's not a lot. It's *everything*."

He flinched a little. "Yeah, it's—"

"And I'm saying okay." The words came out on a sigh of relief. Brenda leaned into Adam with her whole body, knowing with uncanny certainty that this was right. It was a blissful feeling, knowing she'd found something she hadn't even realized she'd been looking for.

"Okay?"

Okay to everything. Suddenly it was the only answer she had, the only thing she wanted. Her truest desires and priorities pushed to the surface. She no longer had to hold back her feelings, even her fears. Yes, there would be challenges. The messiness Adam had mentioned. But she was ready now. Ready to take the biggest risk of all. Ready to fall in love. Ready to be a stepmom. Ready for the next adventure.

"I can't believe I'm saying it but yes. Yes to you. Yes to Christmas, even. I am all the way in with you, Adam. It's all a big fat *yes*."

EPILOGUE

One Year Later

Brenda sat in the children's section of the Avalon Free Library, surrounded by shelves filled with books from classics to contemporary. Outside the tall windows, the snow fell gently, softening the light and the landscape. Inside, the warm glow of lamplight brightened the reading room. A poster-size sign advertised SPECIAL HOLIDAY EVENT: BOOK LAUNCH TODAY.

The idea that she now belonged here, along with the books she'd loved as a child, filled Brenda with awe.

The past year had been a whirlwind. She had rushed back to Houston, knowing she was going to uproot herself and move yet again—but this time, it would be forever. Ryder had been gracious enough when she politely let him go. Her mom, although happy for her, also had been a bit fretful and protective—*Are you sure? It's all so sudden . . . I don't want you to get hurt again.*

Brenda was no longer afraid of getting hurt, because she wasn't afraid of loving Adam. He represented safety, not risk, and that realization had been huge for her. It had changed her life in every way that mattered. She was finally open to her emotions instead of hiding from them. These days when she wrote her books, she put her heart on paper, and it breathed life into her stories. This new love had given her a new way of looking at the world.

In a moment of conciliation, she had taken Tim to see Grant one last time before leaving Houston. Her ex had looked like a distant acquaintance to her—someone she used to know in some other context that didn't matter anymore. Her former house had seemed weirdly familiar, yet at the same time, it belonged to another person in another life.

Then she'd returned to Avalon. She had married Adam last summer in a jubilant lakeside ceremony, hosted by Alice Bellamy. Brenda's mom and Lyle attended, along with Cissy and Dilip and baby Jonathan Nicholas—named after Brenda and Cissy's dad. Dolly had sung "Thank You" by Jimmy Page and Robert Plant with such feeling that everyone cried. Marrying Adam had seemed like both a crazy impulse and a romantic inevitability. With every bit of her heart, Brenda knew it was right, and it would be right until the end of time.

A few dogs were in attendance at today's reading. Suzanne arrived with Will and their little dog, and Brenda went over to greet them.

"Can I sit in the front row?" Will asked in a loud whisper. "Can I? Huh? Huh? And Vixen with me?"

"Sure," Brenda said. "Just keep hold of her leash, okay?"

Will went over to the big braided rug in the middle of the room. Brenda turned to Suzanne. At first, they had been wary of each other, but they had developed mutual respect as Will's coparents. "Thanks for coming."

"Willy insisted. And . . . congratulations on everything. I'm happy for you. Really."

"You've been great," Brenda told her. "I appreciate how you've helped Will through all these changes."

"I'm not going to lie," Suzanne said. "Last year was pretty hard for me. It's better now." A light flush tinted her cheeks. "I think I might have met someone."

"You have?"

Suzanne smiled. "But that's another story. For another time."

More children began to arrive for the program, their faces chapped from the cold air as they hung their snowsuits and parked their boots, then assembled on the large oval rug. Brenda took her place in the reading chair and looked around at the eager faces of the kids. On the floor beside her lay Tim and Olaf. The husky dog was as calm and well-behaved as Tim these days. She and Adam had been relentless in their training.

The children whispered and giggled as Maureen Haven passed out dog-shaped cookies from the Sky River Bakery, and dog biscuits for the canine visitors. With Vixen in his lap, Willy sat cross-legged among his friends, grinning and pointing, puffed up with importance.

At the back of the room stood Adam and the publisher's rep. Daisy Bellamy had been hired to photograph the event, and she moved silently around the room, taking pictures for the local paper and the library's social media sites.

Brenda locked eyes with Adam, who looked back at her with such love and pride that it made her misty, and she had to look away. She took a deep breath, trying to figure out if there was enough room in her heart to contain all the happiness she felt in this moment. She'd found a love that felt safe despite the risk. In the most unlikely place in the world, at the most unlikely time of year, she'd found a love that felt like forever.

"I started writing this book last Christmas," she said when the program began. She held up the red notebook and fountain pen Adam had given her. "And I finished it by New Year's Day—that's how excited I was about the story. Today, you're about to be the first ones to hear me read it, and I couldn't be prouder, because it was inspired by your town."

She lifted up the book so they could see the lavish illustration on the cover. Then she settled into her chair and opened to the first page.

"*The Twelve Dogs of Christmas*," she read. "By Brenda Bellamy."

AUTHOR'S NOTE

According to the American Society for the Prevention of Cruelty to Animals (ASPCA), approximately 6.3 million companion animals enter US animal shelters nationwide every year. Rescuing a pet is one of the surest and most gratifying ways to enrich your life and help vulnerable animals.

I took a few liberties with the real-life process of pet adoption and transport. Organizations like Underdogs do exist, and pets are regularly transported long distances by expert drivers who take great care to keep the animals safe and healthy throughout the trip. Under the Animal Welfare Act, a pet transporter must be registered with the USDA.

Organizations and individuals involved should carefully check the safety records of the transport service. A list of pet transport considerations can be found on the web here: https://www.akc.org/wp-content/uploads/2020/08/Safe-pet-transport-questions_.pdf.

Please give generously to the nonprofit organizations dedicated to rescuing and caring for pets. Readers can find resources and links to donate at the ASPCA.org website. A portion of the proceeds from the sale of this book will go to support PAWS of Bainbridge Island and North Kitsap, https://pawsbink.org, my local animal rescue organization.

ACKNOWLEDGMENTS

Deepest thanks to my fellow writers, who are always the safest place to "cuss and discuss" the process of writing a novel. I'm looking at you, Anjali Banerjee, Maureen McQuerry, and Warren Read. I owe a special debt of gratitude to my dear friend, author Lois Faye Dyer, for her valuable input and encouragement.

I'm also grateful to Cindy Peters and Ashley Hayes for keeping everything fresh online. The cool posts and TikTok clips are their good work; the embarrassing ones are entirely mine.

Every book I write is enriched and informed by my literary agent, Meg Ruley, and her associate, Annelise Robey, and brought to life by the amazing publishing team at HarperCollins/William Morrow Books—Rachel Kahan, Jennifer Hart, Liate Stehlik, Tavia Kowalchuk, Deanna Bailey, Lindsey Kennedy, Laurie McGee, Lisa Glover, and their many creative associates who make publishing such a grand adventure.

Special thanks to the HarperCollins Global Publishing team, including the United Kingdom, Spain, Germany, Israel, Hungary, Italy, Scandinavia, France, Portugal, Brazil, Holland, and others. I'm so proud to be published in faraway places.

ABOUT THE AUTHOR

Susan Wiggs's life is all about family, friends . . . and fiction. She lives with her husband and two dogs at the water's edge on an island in Puget Sound. In good weather, she commutes to her writers' group in a twenty-eight-foot motorboat.

She's been featured in the national media, including NPR, PRI, and *USA Today*; has given programs for the US embassies in Argentina and Uruguay; and is a popular speaker locally, nationally, internationally, and on the high seas.

From the very start, her writings have illuminated the everyday dramas of ordinary people facing extraordinary circumstances. Her books celebrate the power of love, the timeless bonds of family, and the fascinating nuances of human nature. Today, she is an internationally bestselling, award-winning author, with millions of copies of her books in print in numerous countries and languages.

According to *Publishers Weekly*, Wiggs writes with "refreshingly honest emotion," and the *Salem Statesman Journal* adds that she is "one of our best observers of stories of the heart [who] knows how to capture emotion on virtually every page of every book." *Booklist* characterizes her books as "real and true and unforgettable."

Her books have appeared in the number one spot on the *New York Times* bestseller list and have captured readers' hearts around the globe with translations into more than twenty languages available in thirty countries. Her novel *The Apple Orchard* has been made into a film for TV, and others are in development.

The author is a former teacher, a Harvard graduate, an avid hiker, an amateur photographer, a good skier, and a terrible golfer, yet her favorite form of exercise is curling up with a good book.

Visit Susan Wiggs's Website

susanwiggs.com

Social Media

f facebook.com/susanwiggs
𝓟 pinterest.com/beachwriter1
𝕐 twitter.com/susanwiggs
g goodreads.com/SusanWiggs
◎ instagram.com/susan_wiggs_
BB bookbub.com/authors/susan-wiggs

Susan's Amazon page in the US

amazon.com/Susan-Wiggs/e/B000AQ1FJO

Susan's Amazon page in the UK

amazon.co.uk/Susan-Wiggs/e/B000AQ1FJO